PROLOGUE

From: Catherine Clark
To: All Teaching Staff

4th September 2019

Dear Staff,

As we head into a new academic year, this is an important reminder of the school's policy on relationships between teaching staff and parents.

CHILTERN HOUSE HAS A ZERO-TOLERANCE POLICY REGARDING SEXUAL RELATIONSHIPS BETWEEN PARENTS AND TEACHERS.

. . .

ANY TEACHER FOUND to be conducting a relationship of a sexual nature with a parent will face instant dismissal.

PLEASE BE REMINDED of the acceptable forms of communication with our pupil's parents:

- Face-to-face conversations and meetings on school premises
- Email using your school email address
- Telephone calls from a school landline

YOU MUST NOT GIVE **out your personal mobile number to any parent.**

THE PRINCIPAL OFF-CAMPUS parent-teacher social event this term will be the Christmas fundraiser at the Savoy Hotel in early December. I will write to remind you of this policy ahead of that event.

THANK you for your cooperation

CATHERINE CLARK
Headmistress
Chiltern House Prep School

PARENTS AND TEACHERS

SARA MADDERSON

For my sisters, Louise and Jill.
You're the best beta-readers ever!

PART I

SEPTEMBER

1

ASTRID

It was the first hockey fixture of the school year, and her carefully crafted facade shattered with a single turn of her ankle.

One minute, she was decorously cheering Tabby's goal as the Year 3s threw a summer's-worth of energy into their match against Chelsea Prep, and the next she found herself thrown to the astroturf, shouting in pain. She grabbed her ankle and grimaced. Shit, that hurt. She edged her four-inch-heeled pump off her foot.

The other mothers were beside her in a flash, some doing a better impression of genuine concern than others.

'Astrid, darling, are you ok?' asked Serena Woodhouse, schadenfreude oozing from every pore. 'What a tumble—that looked nasty.'

'Let me fetch Mr Pearce,' Natalia Beneventi said, ever-practical.

'Who's Mr Pearce?' Astrid looked around in a fog of pain.

'The head of PE! He's helping with the girls' tennis party next week, remember?'

She did not remember. Natalia had organised that element of the party; she had far more time on her hands than Astrid did. Now she was jumping up and down and waving across the pitch. 'Mr Pearce! We have a situation!'

Astrid tried to hold her ankle. It was beginning to swell already.

She raised her head to find someone standing in front of her. White trainers and socks. Tanned, tanned legs. Powerful thighs—Jesus Christ, he must be a rugby player. Navy running shorts. A white Chiltern House polo shirt. Holy shit—a seriously gorgeous face, wearing a concerned smile. Liquid brown eyes, and dark hair falling over them.

'What have we here?' he said. Mmm. Irish. She loved that accent. 'Is it ok if I take a look?'

She leant on her left hand and tried to extend her right leg around to the front gracefully. Her habitual mask—the one that portrayed assurance and self-sufficiency and concealed all of her anxious and fearful demons—fell back into place. 'I went over on it,' she explained. 'I shouldn't have been jumping about in heels.'

'Looks like it's just a sprain. I can wrap it for you. If I help you, do you think you can come into the sports centre with me?'

Astrid wasn't sure she could do that at all, at least not with the acceptable level of aplomb. However, she had no intention of exposing her inner feebleness in front of this heavenly young man or the other mothers. She nodded.

'Ok. Take my hands and pull yourself up using your left leg.'

She removed her other shoe and did so as elegantly as she could.

'Well done.'

He was speaking to her as if she were an eight-year-old

who'd scraped her knee. Bizarrely, she quite liked it. She'd felt like an eight-year-old just then, her anxiety bubbling perilously close to the surface. Her eyes had pricked with the twin injuries to ankle and pride when she'd fallen.

'Put your arm around my shoulder and let me take as much of your weight as you can.'

It was surprisingly enjoyable to have this divine creature attending to her. She slipped her arm around his neck and noted with a touch of satisfaction the daggers Serena was shooting her.

'Right. Let's do this.' He held her right hand in place over his shoulder and gripped her waist with his left. 'Miss Oliver! Back in five!' he shouted to his colleague.

It was painful to put weight on the ankle. She overrode her instincts to bear as much of the weight as she could and leant into him. He seemed to be able to handle it; his back and shoulder muscles flexed under her bare arm. His hand, on hers, was warm. He smelt of sweat, sunshine on skin, and some kind of deodorant. She was glad she'd topped up with lashings of her Sana Jardin perfume before she'd left the office. This was the closest physical contact she'd had with a fellow adult in weeks. Pathetic.

She sat on a hard plastic chair in the sports centre. He returned with a first-aid box and icepack and pulled another chair round to face her. Sitting down, he gestured towards her foot. 'May I?'

She nodded and swung her leg slowly and painfully upwards. He took it gently by the heel and rested it on his thighs.

'We haven't met before. Callum Pearce.' He held out his hand.

'Astrid Carmichael. Tabby Carmichael's mother. How come we haven't crossed paths before?'

'I only teach the middle school. Mr Kelly's in charge of PE for the lower school.'

'Ah, I see.' She winced as he probed her ankle.

He rummaged in the first-aid box and pulled out a roll of bandage. 'Before I strap you up, have a go at rotating your ankle so I can see your range of motion, please.'

She obliged gingerly, clenching her teeth at the discomfort. The hairs on his thigh were soft under her heel as she moved it.

'That looks pretty good to me.' He smiled at her. 'I'm sure you'll be right as rain in a few days.' He unwound a section of the bandage roll and started to wrap it deftly around her foot.

'I'd better be. It's London Fashion Week next week. Crutches are not a good look at Fashion Week.'

'Going to a few shows, are you?' He worked fast; the bandage was tight and the compression effect a relief. She was enjoying the sight of his slim, tanned fingers working and the sensation of their warmth against her skin.

His assumption amused her. Through his eyes, she likely resembled a lady of leisure, unnecessarily dolled up for the school gates and entertaining herself by taking in a few fashion shows here and there.

'I'll be working,' she explained. 'I have a fashion label. It's a huge week in our calendar—we'll show our Spring/Summer collection, but there's also a lot of networking to do, and events all week. So trainers and crutches won't cut it.'

'That does sound like a big week.' He pinned the

bandage above her ankle and patted it like a child admiring its handiwork. 'Well, by all means get a doctor to take a proper look at this, but it looks like a minor sprain to me. Keep it wrapped and elevated; lots of ice.'

'Thank you so much.' She squirmed. 'I'm sorry to have taken you away from the match.'

'It's my absolute pleasure.' He held her gaze with those brown eyes. 'It's a nice break for my ears. Seven-year-old girls are seriously noisy. Now, can you bear to stay here till the match is over? Twenty minutes of this icepack will do your ankle the world of good.' Gently holding her bandaged foot in place, he stood up and eased it back onto his chair.

'I believe you're helping at Tabby's party next week?' she asked, mainly to keep him there a moment longer.

He looked blank.

She clarified. 'Tabby's having a joint party with Ilaria Beneventi next weekend—at the Holland Park Lawn Tennis Club? Ilaria's mum mentioned you were going to run the tennis side of it.'

'Oh!' His face cleared. It was delightful, how close to the surface he held each tiny shift of emotion. 'Yeah, she asked me last term. Sorry—I haven't quite got all the Year 3 girls' names squared in my head yet. I'll see you next week, then, Mrs Carmichael.' He shot her a megawatt smile and raked his hand through his dark hair. Turning, he jogged back to the pitch.

She watched him go, gazing idly at that perfect backside in those snug navy shorts, his calf muscles contracting as he jogged. God, he was gorgeous. Tabby's birthday party was looking up.

2

CALLUM

The parents would never know how much time the teachers spent discussing them, dissecting and judging their appearances, their attractiveness, their wealth, their parenting styles and the pleasantness or otherwise of their interactions with their kids' teachers.

The mums and dads came in for different types of scrutiny, depending on the sex of the teachers. Generally, the mums were more interesting: they were at the school gates more often than the dads and they were a more colourful, less homogenous crowd than their husbands or partners.

It was amazing to him how endlessly the female teachers could obsess over the price tags of the school-run outfits each mother wore. They also liked to discuss over morning coffee the likely surgeries or fillers each mum had had, almost as much as they enjoyed tearing apart their parenting styles. One Year 2 girl had recently announced she received fifty pounds pocket money per week, a fact that spread around the cramped staffroom like wildfire with all the accompanying judgements a sum like that for a six-year-old inevitably prompted.

The male teachers—the straight ones, at least—fixated on which of the mums they'd shag and which of the dads made the most money. The Sunday Times Rich List usually featured a healthy sprinkling of Chiltern House parents when it came out each May. The dads wore their success casually, benevolently. They sauntered into school with their daughters at eight-thirty each morning in open-necked shirts or v-necked sweaters, high-fiving each other, the inference being that they were sufficiently senior not to have to worry about getting into work early or dressing for the job they wanted. He rarely saw them at pickup: they were far too busy doing deals and making their millions by that point in the day.

Callum took part in the lighthearted banter with his colleagues, but he didn't normally give the mums much attention. Sure, it was fun to speculate about them, but they were too old for him, and way too high-maintenance. He had no shortage of interest from girls in their twenties, and he'd rather focus on his Hinge profile and on the nubile beauties he hooked up with on Saturday nights.

But that mum today... phew. She was a ride. He said as much to Bex Oliver as they hauled the kit-bags back to the school sports cupboard after the match. Bex was gay and therefore a more gratifying bantering partner on this subject than most of the female teachers.

'Did you check out the mum I strapped up at the pitch?' he asked her, locking the cupboard. 'Astrid, she said her name was? She was fucking hot.'

Bex laughed. 'You left me reffing the match—I didn't have much time to ogle. But yeah, I know Astrid. She keeps herself to herself, though. Not a coffee-morning type, if you get my drift.'

Bex was both a teacher and a parent at the school. Her

daughter, Elsie, was in Year 3, thanks to the generous bursary the school provided for the daughters of teaching staff. Callum knew she found it difficult to balance the politics of both roles. But her position gave her the advantage of having the inside scoop on the parents.

He let his mind run back over his interaction with Astrid. She looked untouchable—like an ice-queen, almost—but there'd been some kind of undercurrent there, like fragility, or vulnerability. Understandable, given she'd just gone arse-over-tit on the astroturf. She was very blonde—so far, so on-trend for him—but her fairness was less brassy than a lot of the mothers. If he had to guess, he'd say she was Scandinavian. That hair looked natural to him. She had wide blue-green eyes and a glossy, even tan all over. She'd probably spent the summer on a yacht. She must be pushing forty, but she looked far younger. No wedding ring—he'd clocked that.

Her legs were incredible—he'd checked them out close-up when he was bandaging her ankle. The leg he'd strapped had been toned and super-smooth. She'd been wearing a little silky pink dress, and her smell! She'd smelt divine, like an exotic garden. If he turned his head, he could still catch her scent lingering on his shirt. Finally, she hadn't seemed to be a total bitch, which was a major bonus where the Chiltern House mothers were concerned.

'What's her gig? Is she single? I didn't see a ring.'

Bex exhaled. 'Bloody hell, he's got it bad. Yes, Inspector Pearce, she's divorced. Her husband ran off with some junior colleague when the girls were in... Reception, I think. He's minted, but a bit of a dick. But she's very successful in her own right. Surely you've heard of her fashion brand, Astrid Carmichael?'

'Nope.' Callum pulled out his phone and googled her,

hitting Images. Google obliged with a sea of photos of Astrid. Jesus. He thought she looked good today, but here she was standing on a red carpet outside the Royal Albert Hall, wearing some kind of glittery body-stocking. There were several similar red-carpet shots, as well as what looked like professional headshots and plenty of her at drinks events, in the studio, and some of her waving from the top of a catwalk. 'Fuck me,' he said, scrolling.

'You wish,' Bex said.

3

NATALIA

Natalia was finessing the pivot table she'd built for Ilaria's tennis party. Yes, a pivot table. She used to build financial models for EURO STOXX 50 companies, and now here she was, over-engineering a spreadsheet for a kids' birthday party, for God's sake.

Valentina was up in her room, working at her desk with the independence that came with being nine and in Year 5. Ilaria sat next to her at the kitchen island, still in her hockey kit. Her elfin face was scrunched up in concentration as she tackled her English homework. She pressed hard with the pencil, forming her cursive slowly and carefully.

'Mummy? I'm supposed to add a fronted adverbial into my sentence, and I don't know what it is.' Her little chin wobbled and her huge black eyes filled.

What the fuck was a fronted adverbial? She pulled up a browser window on her laptop and typed the phrase in. For fuck's sake. Was such technical language really necessary for seven-year-olds? She'd enjoyed a successful City career without knowingly deploying fronted adverbials in her communications.

'It's just an adverb you put at the start of the sentence,' she informed her daughter now. 'Do you know what an adverb is?'

'An adverb is a word that describes a verb,' Ilaria recited, confidence restored. 'Like quickly or slowly.'

'Perfect.' Natalia beamed at her. 'So to make it a fronted adverbial, you say 'quickly, the dog jumped up', rather than 'the dog jumped up quickly.' Does that make sense, sweetie?'

Ilaria nodded and resumed her writing.

Concentration broken, she pulled out her phone and typed a WhatsApp message to Chaucer class. It was a tradition at Chiltern House for each class to be named after a famous writer, although she doubted Chaucer was an obvious fit for children who'd be turning eight this year. God help the kids if he turned up on the Year 3 syllabus. She couldn't remember what books she'd read when she was Ilaria's age. When did children's education get so lofty, with fronted adverbials and pretentious references to literary greats? What was wrong with a bit of Roald Dahl and some spellings for homework? Of course, this was precisely what they paid exorbitant fees for, but sometimes she wished the school would pull its finger out of its arse.

Her message read: *Miss Yates confirmed at pickup that the school will issue a full schedule of school trips by the end of the week <bus emoji>*. Miss Yates was their divine class teacher, though she was unfortunately heading off on maternity leave at Christmas. It wasn't ideal. Natalia had volunteered to be class rep for both Valentina and Ilaria's classes this year, despite being one of the few mothers without a nanny. She must be insane. But if she was honest with herself, she liked the sense of purpose the role gave her.

Her phone pinged. It was Lorenzo. *Home late—forgot I*

had a client dinner. Nice. She rolled her eyes. She'd already made a shepherd's pie from scratch for their supper, but the unspoken dynamic in their relationship was that he brought home the very substantial bacon while she was essentially on some sort of retainer, there when he needed her, and expected to wait quietly in the background when he didn't.

Things had been different when they'd met. She'd been a junior analyst on the Luxury Goods equity research team at Fidelity; he'd been one of her brokers. When she'd joined Fidelity in London she'd been keen to prove her mettle and he'd helped her. Several years more senior than her, he'd advocated hard for her, spoon-feeding her stock ideas and broker reports that would make her look smarter in front of her fund managers, and getting her access to the senior management of the companies whose shares Fidelity either owned or was interested in owning. They'd first hooked up on what should have been a visit to meet LVMH management in Paris and ended up being a romantic mini-break.

Fifteen years and a few smart lateral moves later, Lorenzo ran the Equities division at Loeb AG, a bulge-bracket Swiss investment bank, while she baked and organised her children's parties. She'd forged a decent career at Fidelity while they dated, but she hadn't gone back after having Valentina. They'd discussed their options at length, and the conversation had always come back to this: what was the point of having kids if both parents worked sixty-hour weeks?

At first, she'd been so drunk with the love and terror and hormones of new motherhood that she couldn't have conceived of going back. But once she had two young girls in the house, her Cinderella syndrome kicked in. Life became about processing: puréeing organic sweet potato, tiptoeing around tantrums, breastfeeding a baby while bathing a toddler, coaxing tangled hair into pigtails and flailing limbs into nice dresses. She'd had plenty of help on the domestic front, but no formal childcare. She was adamant she would not outsource her daughters.

During those early years, she had not a moment to rest and not a thing to say for herself. She felt exhausted and frumpy. Her thought processes revolved around the kids' bowel movements; if she wasn't careful, her conversation would too. And how was she supposed to want sex with Lorenzo when she'd been grabbed and prodded and screamed at and needed all day? She just wanted some silence at bedtime. Night-time was, for Natalia, a chance not to hear her own fucking name being called for six or seven hours.

She'd come back to life as the girls started nursery and school. The guilty realisation set in that she would have up to seven hours a day of child-free time. Seven! And still, she couldn't conceive of going back to work. She had standards for how she wanted to run her home and care for her family. She made her sauces and stocks from scratch, sourced her meat, fish and vegetables in person from different neighbourhood shops. The girls worked through socks and shoes like nobody's business. Every day brought a new letter or request from school. Just keeping the family fed and clothed and where they needed to be on time was quite literally a full-time job. She'd effectively retrained as a PA.

She and Lorenzo had separate lives these days. He was under so much stress at work, and while she was pleased she could speak the language of the equity markets with him, he viewed his home as a space to decompress, not mull over the bank's risk appetite or debate its strategy. He left the house early each morning and had, in her opinion, far too many client commitments in the evenings. Finance was his domain, the house was hers.

She turned back to her pivot table. The party would be fabulous. Ilaria and Tabby had become so obsessed with Wimbledon in the summer term that they'd pleaded with their mothers for a tennis-themed party, even though the school didn't play tennis in the Autumn term. Astrid's ex-husband, Mark, had pulled some serious strings and secured permission from the Holland Park Lawn Tennis Club to host a party for eight girls on one of their back courts and under a large tree in the lawns. Natalia and Astrid weren't especially close—Astrid was so busy and impressive—but the girls were good friends and their birthdays fell several days apart. She checked her Etsy order for the personalised tennis-themed plates. The girls would eat off them at the party and take them home as part of their goodie-bags afterwards.

The plates were due to arrive tomorrow. She clapped her hands. It was all coming together perfectly.

4

JENNA

Over at St Cuthbert's prep school for boys in South Kensington, Jenna Price was working through a stack of marking with her teaching assistant and flatmate, Katie. They always spent far longer marking homework than they needed to. Katie ticked the correct answers and put a dot next to the incorrect ones (the school considered crosses too negative). She then passed the exercise books to Jenna, who let rip with her arsenal of colourful gel pens and superhero stickers—she had an abundance of both Marvel and DC characters.

Today they were marking maths, using the fairly simple exercises they'd set to provide a clearer picture of each boy's ability. The start of a new school year was always a race to get to know the boys as quickly as possible. No matter how much time they spent catching up with whoever had taught them the previous year, it always felt as though they were running blind in September. Jenna was piecing together an intricate mental puzzle of the children's natural abilities, motivation levels, personalities and possible learning difficulties, as well as trying to establish who'd been tutored the most intensively over the summer. A level playing field it was not.

Now she looked at Cosmo Langley's dot-splattered times-tables and sighed. Poor little guy. She selected a particularly fun Spiderman sticker and some firework stickers for his book. Taking a sparkly green gel pen, she wrote in clear, legible cursive: *Great effort Cosmo! Keep up the good work!* and added a smiley face. He'd be one to watch for possible dyslexia or dyscalculia issues. She must check in with his Year 2 teacher for more background on how he'd fared last year.

Jenna felt grateful that she was a Year 3 teacher. It was marginally less intense than Year 2, when the race was on to get the boys prepped for the 7 Plus exams which would grant the brightest (or the most heavily tutored) a place in the hallowed halls of Westminster or St Paul's. It was also the perfect time in a child's academic journey to spot the wide array of learning difficulties that fell under the general umbrella of dyslexia.

She'd become more and more interested in dyslexia as she'd continued to teach this age group. It was like detective work, really. By keeping an eye out for anomalies you could unearth insidious learning difficulties that presented as stupidity, laziness or lack of motivation if you weren't looking closely enough. A child who seemed middle-of-the-road could, in fact, be a wonderfully intelligent pupil making herculean efforts just to stay afloat when he or she should be soaring.

These were the children who interested Jenna the most. It was heartbreaking to think boys and girls could be academically written off at the age of seven or eight, when their marvellous brains just didn't quite fit into the largely one-size-fits-all approach to learning that the educational system was forced to adopt. She'd been incubating, for some time now, the idea of retraining as a Special Educational Needs teacher.

Their gentle rhythm was broken when Katie held out an envelope to her. 'Jen—this was in Rollo's homework. It's for you. I wonder if it's from Jackson!' She laughed.

Rollo James was one of the most talked-about kids in the school. He'd moved to St Cuthbert's just this term, having attended a pre-prep school nearby up to Year 2. He was, like most of his classmates, a fairly basic little chap, but his parents were the source of much fascination and endless speculation. Rollo's father was Jackson James, the biggest British action hero since Daniel Craig. His *Adrenalin* movie franchise was worth billions, and his piercing eyes and chiselled cheekbones were front-page tabloid fixtures. The paps had been a daily presence outside the school since term had started last week.

Rollo's mother, Honour Chapman, had been co-anchor on Britain's most popular morning TV show until she'd interviewed Jackson live on the show and he'd swept her off her feet. Millions of viewers had had a front-row seat to their instant on-screen chemistry. (Rumour had it that he'd swept off all her clothes too, right there in the dressing room afterwards.) The romance had been whirlwind and the engagement quick. Since becoming a mother, Honour had eschewed the punishing schedule of morning television in favour of launching an eponymous skincare and makeup brand. With her flawless skin and huge green eyes, she was her own best advertisement.

Little Rollo's arrival at St Cuthbert's had caused pandemonium among both staff and parents. The headmaster, Mr Hopkins, had had to fight off desperate pleas from both parties to have Rollo in their class. Everyone wanted the chance to get close to the glamorous James family.

Jenna and Katie had lucked out. Rollo was a sweet boy, seemingly oblivious to his parents' level of fame. Jackson had been at the school gates more often than Honour that first week. Presumably, he was between movies. The female staff members and parents thanked their lucky stars for the balmy September weather, which allowed him to show off his famous action-hero body in shorts and tight black or white t-shirts.

He was certainly very friendly, with a smile for everyone, and Jenna felt the heat of his gaze each morning and afternoon when he loitered at the classroom door, those eyes raking up and down her little dresses and her long legs. He'd high-five Rollo and throw her a slow grin, saying 'Thank you, Miss Price,' or 'How are you today, Miss Price?' He managed to make the most neutral pleasantries sound positively indecent. She found herself taking more time to straighten her long, caramel-coloured hair in the mornings, apply lashings of mascara and moisturise her legs. She was only human, after all.

Now, she turned over the envelope Katie had handed her, *Miss Price* written on the front. It was probably a note from the nanny about Rollo's homework. She tugged it open and pulled out a notecard and a business card. The business card was Jackson's. The notecard had *JACKSON JAMES* embossed along the top. The handwritten message was brief. In a flashy scrawl, it read:

Miss Price. You're doing a great job with Rollo. I'd love to see you outside of school sometime, get to know you better... Call me. J.

'Holy moly.' Jenna stared at the card and then held it out to Katie. 'I think Jackson James just propositioned me.'

5

ASTRID

London Fashion Week was in full swing and Astrid was out of her bandage and back in heels. Several seasons ago, her brand had dropped the predictable—and extortionate—fashion-show format in favour of a breakfast presentation at Claridges. The Astrid Carmichael presentation was now a firm fixture in the fashion editors' calendars on the Tuesday morning of Fashion Week.

The brand was at a pivotal stage in its life cycle. It had achieved that almost-mythical status of a unicorn, having secured a billion-pound valuation in its funding round the previous year. While the valuation had been a huge coup, Astrid knew her private equity investors were getting itchy, looking to offload a good chunk of their stake soon. The most obvious exits were through an IPO or a sale to a trade buyer.

She had no intention of being at the helm of a publicly traded company. Her years of marriage to Mark, who ran an enormous hedge-fund, had educated her in the vagaries of equity markets, and she was all too aware of the pressure the skittish stock markets put on companies to deliver every quarter. If they went public, Astrid would spend the majority of her time pandering to shareholders and jumping through hoops rather than running her company. It wasn't for her.

That left a trade sale. There were plenty of established and emerging conglomerates in the fashion industry, sniffing around strong brands that could provide them with the growth they so badly needed: LVMH and Kering were the major players in Europe, while Capri, Tapestry and Constellation dominated across the pond. Today's presentation was an important step in consolidating their reputation as a desirable acquisition target. They must walk a fine balance between preserving the uptown, old-money sensibility for which Astrid was known and delivering red-hot product that the millennials couldn't survive without.

Today, that conflict between the old guard and new would be played out on Claridge's version of a front row—the best-positioned tables in the Foyer with the optimal vantage-point for recording Instagram Stories or TikTok videos. The British Fashion Council's Caroline Rush and *Vogue*'s Edward Enninful would be next to the latest and hottest influencers and celebrities. These days, you had to please everybody.

Astrid tried desperately to tune out the familiar horrors of a churning stomach, light-headedness and the sensation that her limbs would fail her. As was always the case on these occasions, her anxiety threatened to spiral out of control as her brain did what it had spent years training for: playing out every possible worst-case scenario. What if the music failed, or a dress ripped or fell apart? What if one of the models face-planted? What if *she* face-planted in the finale? What if the audience hated it, or just found it samey and tired?

She focused on slowing down her breathing and told herself everything was in hand. She was surrounded by grown-ups who were in their element in this environment. She was nothing more than a figurehead on this occasion. She just had to keep her mask on and look decorative.

IT WAS SHOWTIME. The function room given over to hair and makeup buzzed with pre-show jitters and anticipation. Claridge's Foyer and Reading Room were bedecked with mountains of pale pink, white and blue hydrangeas. Each table boasted tiny English muffins, vegetarian frittatas and fruit salads on Claridge's signature green and white china. None of it would be eaten, of course. Only the coffee would be consumed.

The guests were at their tables, and the show's director was ready to send out the first girl. The format would be part show, part tableau, as the models wove between the tables in a tightly choreographed but seemingly casual manner. For the spring collection, Astrid had taken inspiration from a trip she and her creative team had made to Waddesden Manor in Buckinghamshire. The Rothschilds had built Waddesden in the style of a Loire chateau, and it looked like a fairy tale. The team had pored over the tapestries, the Gainsborough portraits, the vast selection of Sèvres porcelain, and the exquisitely wrought aviary, and emerged with a collection that was pure romance.

In homage, Saint-Saëns *Aviary* poured out of the speakers as the models meandered in a sequence of enchanting pastels: lilac, periwinkle, eau-de-nil, buttermilk, custard, palest blossom pink. Each girl was in a single colour from head to toe, and Astrid's new accessories designer, poached from Gucci at vast expense, had surpassed himself with the most lust-worthy clutches and totes in buttery, pastel leather studded with pearls, to match the girls' mary-janes. As soon as they hit social media, they'd be red hot. They needed to be. Accessories were the lifeblood of any luxury fashion brand, the only category to deliver meaningful margins.

As the last girl came out onto the floor of the Foyer, Astrid followed her. She was in a pale pink version of one of the final dresses from the collection, a gauzy silk-chiffon maxi-dress that could be unbuttoned the whole way down. The chiffon fell in thin pleats and the sleeves were voluminous, pinned with pearls at her wrists. Her blonde hair was swept back in a chignon and she wore the divine mary-janes, custom-made for her in the same shade of pink. As usual, the anxiety morphed into adrenalin and the dread into sheer joy as she stepped out.

She worked the floor, clapping the models and double-kissing the attendees while flower-petal confetti swirled around the room. The fashion industry was like an iceberg; the public only saw the glamorous tip. The rest of it was the endless slog and sheer bloodymindedness necessary to get a collection from sketch book to shop-floor. That was why it was so important to revel in moments like this, fleeting snatches when you were deliciously satiated with creative achievement.

'Darling, that was stunning. Bravo.' Cosmetics empress Honour Chapman stood to kiss her, looking resplendent in a sage silk maxi-dress from Astrid's current collection that matched those famous feline eyes. Her auburn hair fell in impeccable waves. Honour Chapman Cosmetics always did the makeup for Astrid's shows; her team had been making up the models onsite since the early hours.

'Your team is incredible, sweetie,' Astrid told her. 'I've been up since 4am; thank God for your makeup artists working their magic on me.'

Honour's husband, Jackson James, clad in a sharp navy suit, gave her a hug and a wink. 'Gorgeous, as usual, Astrid.' He smiled. The three of them posed together for a photo.

She moved on, posing for selfies with influencers and the occasional video with millenial actresses. It was always gratifying to see a roomful of beautiful women wearing her clothes—the guests in current season and the models making the guests ravenous for what would follow next spring.

Justine Picardie, long-time editor of *Harper's Bazaar*, was effusive. Justine was a big supporter of Astrid; she adored her brand's romantic sensibility and British cultural references. 'It's enchanting, my dear Astrid,' she enthused. 'I can't wait to shoot it for *Bazaar*. We simply must do it at Waddesdon!'

Hovering behind Justine was a sleek, impeccably dressed woman Astrid didn't recognise. She stepped forward and put out her hand.

'Eleanor Britten, Constellation,' she offered. 'Congratulations on a beautiful presentation, Astrid. Thanks for having me here.'

She shook her hand. 'Thank you. I'm delighted you could come.' She really was delighted. Her private equity investors, Halcyon, had started to dance tentatively around Constellation as a potential acquirer for the Astrid Carmichael business. Their portfolio already boasted several upscale European and American brands, and Eleanor's presence here today suggested it wasn't just a one-way attraction. Astrid had sent her an invitation to gauge her interest; as Constellation's VP for Europe, Eleanor was bound to make the trip over for her other brands' shows in London, Paris and Milan. And here she was.

'I'm afraid I fly on to Milan tomorrow morning,' Eleanor said. 'Here's my card. Will you call me next time you're stateside?'

'I'm in New York next month,' smiled Astrid. 'I look forward to chatting properly then. Enjoy Milan.' She accepted an espresso from a waiter and moved on, galvanised, through the colourful clusters of well-wishers, willing herself to bask in this ephemeral glow of goodwill before the moment passed and her fans ran to catch the next show.

6

JENNA

It was the last lesson of the day. Jenna sat at her desk while the boys watched a *Horrible Histories* episode about Henry VIII. She should have been taking advantage of a quiet fifteen minutes to get some marking done, but she was distracted by the presence of Jackson James' note tucked carefully inside her diary. She'd looked at it a million times over the last week, and she'd even saved his number in her phone under the initials JJ, but she hadn't worked up the nerve to contact him.

She'd been avoiding him, to be honest, leaving it to Katie to hand the boys over to their parents each afternoon. The mornings were easier. When the parents wandered into the classroom with their sons, she was already deep in one-on-one reading practice with a sequence of boys so eye-contact was more easily avoided. But this afternoon Katie was out on a training course, so Jenna was on her own.

She looked at her watch. Three-ten. 'Alright boys, it's home-time!' she called, pausing *Horrible Histories*. There was a flurry of noise. She performed the magic teacher-clap, and they clapped the sequence back to her, falling silent.

'Well done. Now, go fetch your bags and blazers from your pegs, and take a maths worksheet from my desk on your way back to your desks.'

She sighed and walked over to the door. She'd take her marking home with her tonight; she needed a glass of wine. Seven hours with twenty seven-year-old boys was utterly exhausting. Through the glass pane in the door, she saw that Jackson James was first in the queue of parents. Oh God. He was wearing the navy suit she'd seen him in on Instagram earlier, at that gorgeous Astrid Carmichael event. She was always careful not to like any of his photos, but she wasn't sure why she bothered; it wasn't like he'd notice her liking or commenting on his posts. He had thirty million followers, for God's sake. Thirty million! She couldn't begin to imagine that level of fame.

He was chatting to a couple of the mums. His body language looked neutral enough, but theirs certainly wasn't —they were practically throwing themselves at him. She opened the door and arranged her features into what she hoped was a blandly professional expression. He turned to her and his face broke into a smile. He took her breath away. She didn't know much about tailoring, but the suit skimmed his body in a way that was sheer delight. She smiled tightly at him. 'Good afternoon, Mr James. Rollo!' she called into the classroom.

'Miss Price!' Those blue eyes twinkled. 'Did you get my note about... Rollo's homework?'

She was taken off-guard. He was shameless, bringing it up in front of a queue of parents. 'I did, thank you.' She met his eyes.

'Let me know what you decide.' He gave her a wink and ruffled Rollo's curls. 'Hey, buddy! Let's rock.'

'I will,' she called after him.

'OH, GOD,' she moaned later, rubbing her eyes. She took a large gulp of the Sauvignon Blanc Katie had picked up at Tesco. It was going down pretty well for seven quid. 'I don't know what to do! Katie, tell me what to do, for the love of God.'

Katie's eyes were shining behind her glasses. 'This is by far the most exciting thing that's every happened to either of us,' she declared. 'I can't believe Jackson James fancies you. If you weren't my second favourite person in the world, this would be sickening.'

Katie's favourite person, her boyfriend Steve, was doing his teacher-training in Birmingham. They saw each other every weekend, but it meant Jenna had her friend all to herself during the week. She loved their tiny, girly flat in Fulham and their morning walks to school together, travel mugs of tea always firmly in hand.

'I've lost all perspective,' Jenna admitted now. 'I literally can't stop thinking about him, and I've spent most of the last week googling up articles about him. I must've read that *GQ* Man of the Year article ten times. I can't look him in the eye at school without worrying that I'm going to lose it. But I can't actually work out what's going on here.'

'I'll tell you what's going on. Jackson James wants to get in your pants. If you message him, you'll get to shag him, if that's what you want.'

Jenna spluttered. 'Surely that's what every woman in the world wants! But it doesn't feel real. And he's married, for Christ's sake. How could I even be considering this?'

'Oh, please. We've all heard the rumours. There's no way that marriage is anything other than a PR arrangement these days. All I can say is he must have one hell of an agreement with the press because, for all those rumours, they've never outed him.'

'Then I should stay the hell away, if he's a total tart.'

'It's pretty straightforward, as far as I can see.' Katie leant forward. 'This guy isn't going to leave his wife for you. He fancies you. A night with him is on the table. He's fair game; he's basically public property. We know he's not the faithful type, so don't feel too guilty about it. Now, do you want to shag him or not? At the very least, it'll be a great story to tell the grandkids.'

'Of course I do, but can you imagine how intimidating it would be? He's basically a god! And I'm just a school-teacher. I'm not even sure what he sees in me.'

'Seriously?' Katie refilled their glasses. 'Can you imagine the kind of groupies he has—all lip fillers and fake boobs and hair extensions? And then you come along, looking like Bambi and Alicia Vikander's love-child, and you're his son's teacher, for God's sake. You're so wholesome and caring and smart and so removed from all that Hollywood bullshit; you must seem like a breath of fresh air to him.'

'Wow, thanks! Do you want to be my agent when I publish my tell-all book?'

'Oh, there won't be a tell-all book.' Katie said sagely. 'He'll probably have a team of lawyers in the bedroom with an NDA for you to sign before anything even happens.'

'You're wasted on teaching, you know that?' Jenna shook her head. 'You should go and work for the *Daily Mail*. Ok. Let's do this. This is pretty much the most terrifying thing I've ever done in my life, so you need to help me.'

'Oh my God; try and stop me.' Katie scooted around and sat beside her on their small sofa. 'And the best thing about this whole situation is you've already left him hanging for a week! I mean, who does that to Jackson James? He'll be eating out of the palm of your hand. Ok, shoot. What are you going to write?'

Jenna picked up her phone. She had a sick feeling in her stomach, but it was an exciting, addictive kind of sick feeling. She opened WhatsApp. New Chat. She pulled up his name and started typing.

Hi Jackson. It's Jenna Price here, Rollo's teacher. Now you have my number.

'Is this ok?' she asked, anxiously.

'Sure,' Katie said. 'Don't give him too much. He started this, and he doesn't strike me as shy. Let him do the work.'

Jenna pressed the blue arrow, feeling even sicker. Then they waited. A few seconds later, the two little grey ticks turned blue.

'Ahh!' Katie shrieked. 'He's read it! Shit, this is better than Netflix. Oh fuck, he's typing!'

Jenna was laughing, from nerves and fear and anticipation. This was surreal. She was sitting in her tiny flat, as she did most weekday evenings, but she was WhatsApping Jackson James, an A-list celebrity—a man so famous and so beautiful that literally millions of women would give their right arm to be in her place right now. And here she was, with access to his private number—or whatever secret phone number he gave out to the women who weren't his wife.

A message popped up.

Hey Jenna <waving hand emoji>. It's great to hear from you finally <tears of laughter emoji>! What are you up to this evening? J x

Jenna looked at Katie in alarm. 'Is he asking what I'm up to because he wants to see me right now?'

'Surely even Jackson James isn't shameless enough to booty-call his kid's teacher like that?' Katie asked, looking doubtful. 'I think he's just making small-talk. Go with it and see. And he just kissed you. I think I'm going to need some smelling-salts.'

'I'm going to need some too,' muttered Jenna, pouring over the message. 'I'm not cut out for this; it's too nerve-wracking.' She typed a reply.

I'm hanging with my flatmate and a bottle of wine in our flat. Tiring day with the boys! How is your evening going?

She added a wine-glass emoji and a kiss at the end and pressed send. The reply came back immediately.

Lucky flatmate. I wish I was her (or him?). I have so much respect for you teachers. Toughest job in the world. I'd love to take you out one evening and spoil you. You deserve it. What do you think? x PS I'm watching Gangsta Granny *<granny emoji> with Rollo x*

'Holy shit,' Katie said. 'He is bold as brass, sitting beside his kid and asking you out when he knows damn well you know he's married. I wonder how he's planning on spoiling you? Showering you with diamonds before ravaging your body?'

Jenna had gone still. She'd been wondering the same thing, and she had a very graphic movie playing in her mind of what it would be like to be alone with him, in bed with him. Could a night with Jackson James seriously be on the cards? He said he envied Katie; he wanted to be here with her. She imagined him in her tiny, pristine bedroom, lying back on her favourite sheets she'd bought in the White Company sale. The vision was so surreal that it made her laugh, but she now knew very clearly what she wanted. She tucked her hair behind her ear and wrote back:

Flatmate is a she. Yep, teaching is tough but it's the best job ever! And that would be lovely, thank you x

He replied:

You've made my night. Next Tuesday evening any good? If so I'll get my PA Lauren to sort a venue and she will get in touch tomorrow. Sleep tight x

Wow. She had a date with Jackson James. In six days. It felt far too soon, and at the same time an eternity to wait. She'd better start up her workout regime again—and book in a bikini wax over the weekend. God, it was all too much to take in, but it was by far the most exciting thing that had ever happened to her. She looked up at Katie, an enormous beam on her face.

'Wowzers,' said Katie. 'You lucky, lucky bitch. I'm going to take you underwear shopping on Saturday. Your Primark pants won't cut it this time, my love.'

7

NATALIA

'Nice serve, Ilaria! You're up next, Grace!'

Mr Pearce was doing a great job of entertaining eight little girls at Ilaria and Tabby's birthday party. As far as Natalia was concerned, he was executing beautifully on his brief, which was to deliver just over an hour of the kind of activities you'd find at a tennis camp, keeping the girls engaged while maintaining a noise level that was vaguely acceptable to the other members of the tennis club.

The Holland Park Lawn Tennis Club was a discreet sanctuary, comprising verdant gardens and courts hidden behind, appropriately enough, a large Wimbledon-green wooden door at 1 Addison Road. The entrance was so unassuming that passers-by would be forgiven for missing it altogether.

Mark Carmichael had really pulled it out of the bag, wangling a kids' party here. Although, she couldn't believe he'd brought his girlfriend—sorry, his fiancée, Juliana—along to the party. What a twat. Juliana was as tiny and glossy and tight-bodied as only a pre-thirty-year-old could be. Her hair hung in a shiny black curtain and she was wearing little white shorts and an off-the-shoulder yellow top. Natalia had to hand it to her - she looked sensational. She was talking shop with Mark and Lorenzo and holding her own, from the looks of things. Mark and Lorenzo knew each other well from work, better than she knew Astrid. The three of them were in a little we're-in-the-City huddle. Natalia felt a jolt of jealousy, not at Juliana's youth and beauty, but at the fact that she probably knew where the FTSE 100 had closed for the week. Natalia hadn't looked at the FTSE for nearly a decade. It depressed her to think that if she sidled up to their conversation she'd have nothing of value to add, despite her years of experience in finance.

Mark had his hand on Juliana's lower back. Smug bastard. Poor Astrid—how galling for her. Although, Astrid was looking absolutely knock-out today, doing a convincing Anna Kournikova impression in a fitted white sleeveless tennis dress with a Tory Sport logo and an exceedingly short pleated skirt. Her hair was in a sleek ponytail and her perfect tan popped next to the tennis whites. She was doing a good job of hosting, moving effortlessly between the groups of parents and topping up their champagne.

Natalia realised she'd better do the same; after all, she was co-hosting this thing. She spotted Bex Oliver, the PE teacher and Elsie's mum, standing alone, watching the girls playing on the court. She was the only parent watching; the others were too busy chatting and drinking. Bex was lovely: warm, genuine and always good-natured in a way that set her apart from the other parents in the class. They'd become close friends. Unlike the rest of the mothers at the party, who were dressed up to the nines in Chloé and Isabel

Marant, Bex was in black yoga pants and a matching racer-back vest, her short, dark hair covered with a white Chiltern House baseball cap. She still managed to look better than everyone else. Her skin was flawless, except for a heart-shaped birthmark on the side of her neck.

She grabbed two glasses of champagne and approached Bex. 'Keeping away from the other parents? Very wise,' she muttered.

Bex laughed and gave her a hug. 'Hi sweetie. You look lovely.' She took a gulp of champagne. 'Yum. Yep, I'm trying to avoid getting cornered. Any conversation with that lot always ends up feeling like parents' evening. They want to know how their darlings are coming along and why I haven't picked them for the netball team.'

Natalia rolled her eyes. 'Painful. Poor you. It's much more fun to watch the girls instead—and Mr Pearce, of course. That man is divine.'

'I don't swing that way, but he's a good-looking guy, alright. And full of Dublin charm. He always has good stories on a Monday morning. But how are you doing?'

'I'm ok.' Natalia considered. 'Same as usual. I swear, Lorenzo gets more distracted every day. He's over there, drooling over Mark Carmichael's hot young fiancée. He pretends to complain when I tell him we have to go to school events—even his own daughter's birthday party, for God's sake—but he secretly loves them. They're a chance for him to one-up the other fathers and network his heart out.'

'Ugh.' Bex drained her glass. 'When will they grow up? That girl is beautiful, though. The mums won't be happy Mark's brought her along. She's a reminder that those jerks can trade them in for a younger model any time. It's about time one of you turned the tables and ran off with a hot young guy—or girl—instead.' She raised her eyebrows at Natalia. 'You up to the challenge, Nats?'

Natalia smiled. 'It's tempting. I'm not sure Lorenzo would notice I'd gone. I suspect you have the right idea, being a lesbian, to be honest. Right, they're coming off the court. Let's get these girls fed.'

8

ASTRID

She'd taken a good deal of trouble with her appearance. She knew Mark would bring Juliana to Tabby's party. It felt like an obnoxious move on his part, though her more rational side knew she'd need to get used to having this woman—girl—in Tabby's life now that they were engaged. The most galling part of the whole situation was that he'd seemed to luck out. She tried to teach Tabby that bad behaviour had consequences, and yet Mark had cheated on his wife and now looked like the cat who'd got the cream.

At least, she thought wearily, Juliana would likely want babies and Mark, already forty-five years old, would have to come up with the goods and make some effort to be a hands-on dad this time around. The heartbreak, thankfully, had faded. He was still incredible-looking, but she didn't long for him anymore. Those first few months of knowing she'd never again get to wake up next to him or feel his skin on hers had been devastating. But it had been over two years, and now all that remained was intense bitterness that he could abandon his wife, and mess up his little daughter's childhood, and walk away scot-free.

There was one welcome bonus to her efforts with her looks today, which was that Mr Pearce was here to see them. She'd thoroughly enjoyed watching him in action on the court over the past hour. He was brilliant with the girls, making them double up with laughter as he pretended to miss their serves, and finishing up the session with a singalong to *Baby Shark*. His tennis whites looked incredible on him, and she'd caught a few glimpses of his taut, tanned stomach when he'd stretched up to serve. He was easily the best-looking guy she'd seen off her TV screen recently. Now he chased the girls out of the court and over to the long trestle table they'd set up for tea, doing a Daddy Shark impression with his arms.

The table looked stunning. Green, white and purple bunting hung from the tree above it and a runner made of fake grass ran down the middle. In the centre stood an enormous cake with the Wimbledon logo iced on it. Each place-setting boasted a personalised plate, and white bomber-jackets hung over the chairs, each embroidered with a girl's name in green and purple. The straws and napkins were Wimbledon-themed.

As the little girls excitedly milled around the table, chatting, shrieking and laughing, she bent over Tabby and draped her arms around her daughter's neck, kissing her platinum plaits. Tabby looked exactly like her. It had bothered Astrid in the early years that she didn't seem to resemble her father at all; now it made her happy. She could drink in Tabby's sweet little face without any unwelcome reminders of Mark filling her head.

Tabby, like her, found life hard, as if she were in a foreign country for which she hadn't been given the guidebook. Her short life had been filled with tantrums and sensory issues and anxiety attacks and overreactions to absolutely everything. So when she was in the moment, laughing and relaxed and open and *silly* as she was now, a normal little girl without a care in the world, Astrid took it as a sweet, sweet gift.

Mr Pearce strode to the table and did that signature teacher clap—two slow claps followed by three quick ones —that seemed to hypnotise schoolchildren everywhere. As if in a trance, the girls fell silent and repeated the clap back to him.

'Right girls!' he called. 'Find your name and take your seat. It's pizza time! And don't forget to hydrate.'

Astrid caught his eye and nodded, impressed.

He grinned and winked at her. 'It works like a charm, every time.'

'Beer?' she asked. 'Or do you need to hydrate too?'

'Oh, a beer would be grand, thanks.'

She grabbed a bottle of Peroni from the ice bucket nearby and cracked it open for him. He brushed her hand as he accepted it, and took a long swig, keeping his eyes on her.

'How were they?' she asked.

'Grand. They're great little kids.' He wiped his mouth. 'Tabby's got a lovely swing. Has she been playing much over the summer?'

'A lot. We have a tennis court at our house in the country; we've had knockabouts almost every day, and she's had a few lessons.'

'It shows. Her hockey game is strong too; good hand-eye coordination.'

'I'm not sure she gets that from me.'

His brown eyes twinkled. 'Oh, don't sell yourself short.'

~

The party over, she dispatched her small guests with their parents and their personalised loot. She even managed to be civil to Mark and Juliana as they left. She, Natalia and Mr Pearce stuffed the presents into two large bags—one for each birthday girl—and packed up the bunting, cake, table decorations and leftover champagne in boxes to go back to Astrid's.

TABBY, Ilaria and Natalia's eldest, Valentina, were running around the grounds, high as kites after too much cake and tennis-themed Biscuiteers cookies. There was a shriek, and Ilaria stumbled over to them, tears pouring down her cheeks.

'Valentina shoved me in the tummy!' she roared, bending over and clutching her stomach dramatically.

Natalia rolled her eyes and went to soothe her, but she was on a roll of self-pity.

'They're knackered,' said Mr Pearce. 'You take them home, Mrs Beneventi. I'll help Mrs Carmichael finish up.'

Natalia wiped Ilaria's damp fringe off her face and sighed. 'Thanks—that would be fantastic, actually. I think we've hit a wall here.'

As she left with her girls, Mr Pearce turned to Astrid. 'How are you getting home—are you local?'

'We're just one road over, on Holland Villas Road,' she replied. 'I was planning on getting a black cab around with all this stuff.'

'I'll jump in and help you at the other end.'

She checked her instinct to refuse politely and take it all on herself. 'That would be great, thanks,' she admitted in relief.

THEY PULLED up outside her house a few minutes later. It was an enormous, square yellow-brick villa with symmetrical bay windows flanking the substantial front door and a U-shaped driveway with two gates. As they walked up the driveway, the front door opened and Teresa, their housekeeper, appeared. Tabby ran ahead and hugged her.

'Come in, please,' Astrid motioned to Mr Pearce, who was loaded up with party supplies. They walked into the blessed cool of her black-and-white tiled hallway and he gave a whistle.

'Wow. Nice place.'

'Thanks,' she said, somewhat uncomfortably. She was proud of the home she'd worked so hard for, but it was undeniably awkward showing it off to someone who'd chosen the vocation of teaching and was far less well compensated for his efforts.

'Mummy, can I FaceTime Ilaria on my iPad?' asked Tabby, tugging gifts out of the bag. 'We said we'd open our presents together.'

'Do you want to open them with me, darling?' Astrid wanted nothing more at this point than to be left alone with the divine Mr Pearce, whose proximity to her she could sense with every nerve-ending in her body, but she didn't want to neglect Tabby on her special day.

'No, it's more fun to open them with Ilaria. Sorry Mummy!' She clamped a hand adorably over her little cherry-red mouth, as if realising she may have insulted her mother.

'Shoo, then, gorgeous girl.' She swatted her playfully. 'Teresa, can you please take this bag of gifts up to Tabby's room?' She turned to Mr Pearce. 'Can I get you a drink, Mr

Pearce? It's the least I can do after you've been so kind. Unless you have somewhere you need to be?' Of course he would have somewhere to be. He was probably the right side of thirty and absolutely gorgeous, and it was Saturday evening.

He grinned at her, those chocolate eyes dancing. 'I have nowhere to be except at home with my smelly housemates. I'd love a drink, if you stop calling me Mr Pearce. That's too weird outside of school. My name is Callum.'

'I remember. And mine's Astrid.'

'I remember, Astrid.' That grin again. She could swear it was flirtatious.

She led him into the enormous white kitchen, which ran the full length of the left-hand side of the house. Grabbing a bottle of Chablis, an ice-bucket and two glasses, she handed the bucket to him and then showed him out to the garden. She and Mark had remodelled the rear of the house so the hallway ran straight through to a glass back door. You could see right through to the garden from the front threshold. They came out onto a terrace and made their way down a series of sandstone steps to the garden.

'Let's sit down at the back,' she said, 'and we'll catch the evening sun.'

They settled onto a large rattan sofa with deep cushions. She poured the wine, and they chatted. She learnt that he'd grown up in Dublin and gone to a school called Blackrock College before studying sports science at Trinity. Finding Dublin too small for his tastes, he'd moved to London to do his PGCE and hadn't looked back. He now lived in a house-share with some fellow teachers at the dodgy end of Ladbroke Grove. The wine went down quickly, and Astrid felt a glow of wellbeing as she sat and drank in his company. Not only was he gorgeous, but it was impossible to feel ill-at-ease in the face of his easy conversational skills. She fetched another bottle and some crisps from the kitchen. She took a quick look at herself in the mirror and smoothed out the eyeliner smudges under her eyes with her finger. Pulling out her ponytail, she shook out her shoulder-length blonde hair.

'This place really is incredible,' Callum said as she sat back down. 'I've never seen anything like it.'

'Thank you.' She looked appreciatively around the leafy, fragrant garden as she uncorked the new bottle. The air was still full of birdsong, and koi carp filled the rectangular pond in the centre of the large lawn. It was a verdant refuge in the middle of London. 'My ex and I spent a couple of years renovating it. It hadn't been on the market for forty years when we bought it—it was very dated.'

'I met Tabby's dad briefly today,' he admitted.

'Yes. Mark. That young Brazilian beauty with him is his fiancée.'

He whistled. 'Jesus. That must be a hell of an age gap.'

'Nearly twenty years, I believe. They work together. He came home one day and told me he was leaving me for her. I didn't see it coming.' That was a lot of personal information to impart to a stranger. She hurriedly refilled his glass and raised her own. 'Cheers. And thanks for today.'

He clinked her glass. '*Sláinte*. And your ex is a douchebag. That girl's got nothing on you.'

She laughed in surprise and took a gulp of her wine. 'That's very kind, but she's young and gorgeous. I can't compete.'

He twisted his body towards her. He said slowly, and deliberately, 'Astrid, don't be ridiculous. You're a fucking ride.'

At the tone of his voice and the look in his eyes, something snapped in her belly, and a long-forgotten heat filled her groin.

'I'm a what?' She laughed, awkwardly.

'Jesus.' He wiped his face with his hand. 'Fuck. That was completely inappropriate. I'm so sorry.'

'What's a ride?'

'Ah.' He reddened under the tan. 'It's—ah—it's just slang we use in Ireland for when someone's very... attractive. I'm sure you can work it out. I shouldn't have said it.'

'You think I'm attractive?'

'Well, I'm not blind, am I? Look at yourself; you're an absolute knockout.'

She looked at him, and the mask slipped. Her face crumpled and her eyes filled as her inner hot mess crashed without warning through her outer poise. Situations like this, where she exposed herself to the scrutiny or pity of another person, were what she spent her life trying to avoid.

'Oh my God!' He was horrified. He set down his glass and grabbed her bare shoulders. 'Are you alright? I'm such a gobshite. I'm so sorry for upsetting you.'

'No, no, it's fine.' She shook her head and avoided his eyes. How ridiculous. She needed to get a grip. She looked down at his tanned, hairy thighs, so close to her own, and felt giddy with desire. She should explain. 'No one has said anything nice like that to me for a very, very long time.' Well, no one aside from the usual sleazy gits trying it on in expensive Mayfair restaurants and bars, at any rate.

'Well, that's a fucking travesty.' His hands moved to her face. 'Why should your douchebag ex get to have all the fun?'

He kissed her, not at all politely, and that was it. It was as if someone had turned on a switch inside her. She kissed him back like a drowning person, her hands in his sleek, dark hair. She thought her brain might explode. His tongue was cold and tasted of Chablis. His hands were everywhere all at once: in her hair, on her face, running up and down her back and up the underside of her thigh. Christ; she'd been celibate for too long, and married for too long before that. She pressed her fingers against the bulk of his quads and felt delirious.

She had the fuzzy understanding that they were behaving like two teenagers in the dark corner of a night-club, not a mother and her daughter's teacher, for Christ's sake, on a tasteful garden sofa in broad daylight. He was quite literally the best-looking man she could remember having met anytime recently, he was probably ten years younger than her, and right now he was glued to her, apparently enjoying himself just as much as she was. It was a shock, after being on her own for so long, to be confronted with the physical reality of this flesh-and-blood god whom she could smell, taste and feel so vividly.

She wanted to take his clothes off very badly. She slipped her hand under his polo shirt and ran it up his smooth, muscular back. His hand was now sliding up between her legs. Thank God Tory Burch had sewn a robust set of concealed shorts, which were acting as a kind of chastity belt, into the skirt of the tennis dress. She willed herself to pull away from him before things got out of hand. As she did so, Tabby's voice shouted 'Mum!' from inside the house and Astrid shot backwards on the sofa.

Two seconds later, Tabby burst out onto the terrace, brandishing a toy. 'Mum! Amaya got me and Ilaria unicorns with our names written on them in glitter, and they're *sisters*!'

~

When Tabby had gone back inside the house, she picked up her glass and took a swig of wine. Her hands were shaking. She ventured a glance at Callum, searching for any signs of regret on his part. He was watching her, amused. He put a leisurely hand on her upper thigh and massaged it.

'Well, I reckon you're beginning to get the idea of what *you're a ride* means now,' he said. 'Actions speak louder than words, and all that.'

'Hmm.' She cocked her head. She was *flirting*. 'I'm still a little unclear. You might have to show me again. But probably not here,' she added hurriedly.

'I should get out of here before we scar Tabby for life.' He got up and gave her his hand to pull her up. *Shit*. He was leaving.

His face was serious. 'Can I see you again?' he said. 'I think we have unfinished business here.'

'Next weekend?' Her heart was pounding. She knew exactly what *unfinished business* meant—she should shut this down immediately. What on earth had got into her?

'Not soon enough.' God, he didn't mess around. 'Tuesday? Wednesday? Not here though, I assume.'

She thought. 'I can meet you after I finish work on Wednesday. Mayfair? How about Jean-Georges—it's a restaurant in the Connaught Hotel? I can book it for sevenish. It's far enough away from this neighbourhood to be discreet.'

'Never been, but I'll find it.'

They walked inside, Callum carrying the empty bottles and bucket.

He put them down carefully on the kitchen island and slid his hands around her waist.

'It feels highly inappropriate to be paying you, given what's just transpired,' she said, handing him an envelope of cash, 'but thanks for helping at the party. You were brilliant with the girls; I don't know how you hold their attention like that. Tabby had a great day.'

'It was my pleasure,' he said, kissing her again as he ran a hand over her backside. 'This is a fairly decent bonus, I have to say.'

9

NATALIA

She let herself into the house, sweating from her Monday lunchtime spin class. It was insanely warm for September. She'd come second on the leader-board today; her twice-weekly sessions and her sheer bloody-mindedness were paying dividends. Her body, always voluptuous but neglected since she'd had kids, was responding. She'd kept her curves in the right places, but her waist had reappeared and her arms and legs were growing sculpted.

She walked through to the kitchen and dropped her Ottolenghi paper carrier bag on the island in surprise. The doors to the garden were open and Lorenzo was sitting outside. His head was in his hands, his shoes and socks were off, and a glass of whiskey stood on the table beside him.

'Hi darling,' she said as she stepped outside. 'What are you doing home at this hour?'

He looked up and spoke gruffly. 'Let's talk inside.' Back in the kitchen, he sat at the island and took a swig of his whiskey.

Alarmed, she sat down next to him. 'What on earth is going on?'

'Jochen told me to make myself scarce for the rest of the day.'

Jochen Koenig ran the investment bank. 'Why?'

Lorenzo pinched the skin at the top of his nose. 'There's been an allegation made against me.'

She froze. There was so much red tape these days; it felt like the regulators were constantly trying to get bankers to slip up. 'What sort of allegation? Compliance?'

'HR. Some stupid girl on the sales desk has submitted a complaint that I've behaved inappropriately.'

'What? As in, sexually inappropriately?'

'Yep.' He raised his head and put a hand on hers, in a rare gesture of affection. 'I don't need to tell you, *cara*, that nothing happened. She came onto me. I'm a sitting duck for this kind of MeToo bullshit; there are so many girls out there who think they can sleep their way up the ladder, that if they fuck the Head of Equities, it'll further their career, and of course when I turn them down they decide to preempt any damage to said career by accusing me. *Porca puttana*!'

She hadn't realised this was one of the worries she was supposed to carry around with her on a daily basis. Her head was constantly full of obsessions with the girls' nutritional intake, the conundrum of how to pick them both up from different sports fixtures at the same time, the reality of climate change, and the low-lying but constant fear of whether she would get breast cancer or Lorenzo prostate cancer. They were both getting to that age, after all. There were so many things to worry about already, but all this time she should have been focusing more on what sounded like the endless swarm of young, hot, ambitious girls around her husband on the trading floor.

'God, darling, I'm so sorry.' That was the right response, surely? He sounded as if he was saying the interest only ran one way, that he never engaged with these women. Right? She swallowed. 'What's she accusing you of, exactly?'

'She is accusing me,' he intoned wearily, 'of groping her when we were on a trip to Edinburgh last week. She said I felt her up and tried to kiss her in the hotel bar after the clients had left, that I gave her a key to my room and told her if she came up we could discuss her career prospects. Seriously—it's like a line from a bad movie. As if. Lying little bitch.'

She flinched at his tone. 'So... sorry, darling. Let me get this straight. You're saying it was the other way around? She came onto you?'

He pulled his hand away and picked up his scotch. 'This feels like an interrogation, Natalia.'

'I'm sorry,' she said again. 'It's a lot to take in. I'm on your side; I'm just trying to understand what happened, that's all.'

'She gave me her room key; slid it across the bar to me as she was saying goodnight.'

'And you didn't go up?'

'Jesus Christ!' He pushed his stool back and stood up. 'For fuck's sake, Natalia. No, I did not fucking go up. I would never do that.'

'Ok, ok.' She put her hands up in a gesture of surrender. 'What are the next steps—did they tell you?'

He sighed. 'There's a process. They're going to start looking into her allegations. They won't suspend me yet. I'll go back in tomorrow and I'll know more then. Hopefully, they'll clear my name soon and give her the boot. Jesus. I hope she never works again.'

'What's her name?'

'Come on,' he said. 'It's an internal investigation; it's confidential. I can't tell you that.'

She studied her husband. Handsome—very. Successful, yes. Powerful, yes. Charming—incredibly so, when he wanted to be. Cut-throat—much more so as he'd risen up through the ranks of the industry. Misogynistic? Although he thought the sun shone out of his daughters' arses, she didn't hear him speak much about his female colleagues: about their talents or successes or potential. Trustworthy? She didn't know. She stared at his face, the face she'd seen most days for the last decade, and she didn't bloody well know.

10

JENNA

She stood at the threshold of the Corinthia Hotel's Hamilton Penthouse. A car had picked her up from her flat and brought her here. Jackson's PA, Lauren, had WhatsApped her while she was en route to give her the details of Jackson's room. After lengthy discussions, she and Katie had rejected her wardrobe of kooky high-street dresses and granny-chic cardigans and sought the help of Jenna's friend Mimi from university. Mimi was a trust-fund babe with immaculate taste and a job in fashion PR. She'd lent Jenna the most stunning little black silk dress from Stella McCartney—it was simple, beautifully cut and showed off her tan, which was still going strong thanks to lashings of moisturiser.

She was really, really nervous. Her stomach wouldn't stop doing flip-flops. She'd seen Jackson a couple of times at school over the past week. This morning, she'd looked up from her reading session with Miles as he was dropping Rollo off. He'd given her a huge grin, and it had been all she could do to make her face and her body behave.

She rang the penthouse's doorbell. She wasn't sure what

to expect—Lauren, in the flesh? A butler of some sort? A bodyguard, even? But it opened almost immediately, and there stood Jackson. He looked breathtaking in a white open-necked shirt and jeans. He smiled.

'Hi. Wow—you look beautiful.' He leant forward and kissed her on both cheeks. He smelt amazing, of something clean and herbal. Then he stood back and gestured for her to come inside.

'Oh my God,' she murmured. 'Look at this place.'

She'd walked into a square lobby. The entire space was luminescent. The floor was marble, the walls white, and in the centre, below a crystal chandelier designed to look like the branches of a tree, stood a round, mirrored table bearing endless vases of soaring, pale pink orchids. Several sets of glass doors led off the lobby. It had the instantly calming effect of a spa.

Jackson picked two flutes of champagne up off the table and handed her one. 'Cheers. Would you like a tour?'

She beamed at him. 'I'd love one.'

Off the lobby lay a an elegant curved drawing room with a grand piano, a small, formal dining room and a little butler's kitchen.

'I thought we could eat out on the terrace upstairs,' he said. 'It's still so warm, and it has a superb view of London.'

She followed him up a shallow, gently spiralling marble staircase, each step illuminated below its overhang. White plaster blossom branches covered the curved walls of the staircase. They came into the most beautiful bedroom she'd ever seen, a dazzling mix of mirrors and artwork and marble, all its furnishings in white and ivory. A vast bed dominated the room, and she tensed at the reminder of why she might be here. Then they emerged through the French doors onto the terrace, and she gasped.

'No way! This is incredible!'

They were facing north, and beyond the nearest rooftops they had an unobstructed view to Nelson's Column, standing in pride of place in Trafalgar Square. To their left, the sky was a painterly daub of apricot and rose.

'Do you like it?' Jackson asked softly.

'I've never seen anything like it—it's absolutely enchanting. Everything—the suite, this terrace, this insane view—even the sunset! Did you arrange this too?' She gestured west.

He looked sheepish. 'I may have looked up what time sunset was and hoped for a clear night.'

'Wow.' She laughed. 'You're seriously smooth.'

He shrugged smilingly. 'Less smooth, more obsessively detail-oriented—and wanting to make it as perfect as possible for you. I told you I wanted to spoil you this evening.'

'Well, I'm overwhelmed. Thank you. This feels like a different universe to the London down there.' She took in the vista of her beloved city, twinkling at dusk, its sounds indistinct in this rarified setting. The terrace itself was small but charming. A round table was set for dinner with starched white linen, and a bottle of champagne stood chilling in a freestanding ice-bucket. A curved marble bench ran around the side of the terrace, and from it rose a glass-fronted gas fire, which was already lit. The space was made even cosier by a tall, pyramid-shaped outdoor heater, and up some steps, on a timber deck, a hot tub bubbled away. The flames of creamy church candles danced in the hurricane lanterns dotted around the perimeter.

'Shall we sit?' He gestured to the table. 'They've already delivered the food. I didn't want us to be disturbed.'

They sat at the table, where an array of sushi lay. Jenna

gazed around her, at the view, the candlelit terrace, and the stunning bedroom beyond the French doors. This was her Cinderella moment. She was here, in this suite that must cost thousands of pounds a night, with a breathtakingly handsome, world-famous movie-star. It was insane. It was also a lot of pressure. This guy had invited her to what must be one of the most expensive hotel suites in London. That was fairly intimidating. She took a deep breath, and a long drink of her champagne. Jackson was watching her.

'Are you ok?' he asked. 'I realise this whole situation is quite... full-on.'

'It's a lot to take in,' she admitted. 'But it's incredible.'

'Tuck in. I hope you like sushi? If not, we can get something else sent up.'

'I love it, and this looks a lot better than Itsu.' She selected a piece of sashimi with her chopsticks.

He laughed. 'Let's hope so. Here, try some of this yellowtail with jalapeño—it's my favourite.' He set a piece down on her plate. 'I want to get to know all about you, Jenna. I have lots of questions. But first, I should probably address the elephants in the room.' He averted his gaze to the champagne bottle and refilled their glasses. It was, she noticed, Dom Perignon. Wow. No wonder it tasted so sublime.

'I'm really glad you came, and I know I'm putting you in a tricky position because you teach my son and you're familiar with my wife. First, I asked you here for some food and good conversation. This place affords us the privacy I just can't get otherwise. I have no expectations; there's no pressure. Ok?'

She nodded nervously, unsure of whether he was being disingenuous. It was reassuring to hear him say those words, but unsettling that he'd read her mind so easily. Perhaps she was just too predictable. Or perhaps seducing young women in penthouse suites was a well-trodden path for him.

'Good. Second, my wife and I have a funny old marriage. She certainly doesn't know I'm here with you, but she knows I hang out with other women, and she gives a lot less of a shit than you might think. I won't bore you with the details of our relationship, but you shouldn't feel guilty or awkward about being here.'

'Got it.' She cleared her throat nervously. 'But why me? I mean, why ask your son's teacher out? Surely you've got supermodels hanging off you everywhere you go?'

He grinned. 'That gets boring very quickly. Believe it or not, I actually have a brain, and I enjoy decent conversation.' He put his hand over hers and squeezed it. 'I asked you here because I haven't been able to stop thinking about you since I walked into your classroom on the first day of term and watched you with Rollo. You were so sweet and patient with him. It didn't help that you had a particularly tiny dress on that day—I might have to write to Mr Hopkins and complain. It's pretty pathetic when you realise you're jealous of your seven-year-old son.'

He was stroking her hand! And the look in his eyes spoke volumes. But his joke had diffused some of the tension. She felt herself relax a little. 'I can give you a super-hero sticker too, if you're a good boy.'

'Tempting,' he said, 'but my chances of being a good boy around you are zero.'

He was nothing like she thought he would be, and nothing like his testosterone-fuelled on-screen persona. He was smart, witty, well-read and interested in her. She suspected the media underestimated him, writing him off as an action hero. She told him about her growing interest in dyslexia, and he admitted he was severely dyslexic.

'Audible's my salvation,' he told her over *petits fours*. 'Otherwise it'd take me a year to read one book. I'm listening to Michelle Obama read *Becoming* at the moment, and I swear having her read it makes it far more meaningful than if I read it myself.'

'I didn't know you were dyslexic—do you talk about it much?'

'It's not a secret, but perhaps I should open up about it more.'

'You should!' she urged. 'So many kids and teenagers adore you. You're so successful—it can make the world of difference to these kids to know that learning difficulties aren't impediments to going far in the world.'

'You're right.' He kissed her hand. 'I hadn't thought about it that way. You're an angel, do you know that? Those little lads are lucky to have you in their corner.'

'So,' she said. 'My turn to ask a question. Are you really going to be the next James Bond?'

He laughed. 'If I told you, I'd have to kill you. No, it's not beyond the realm of possibility, but between us I'm leaning in a different direction. I've been typecast for most of my career, and it's served me well, but I want to flex my acting muscles and I'm also keen to have a shot at directing. I'm looking at a script right now; it's about a US vet with PTSD. It's really powerful and I'm probably going to do it. I just need to get my American accent straight.'

'If Damian Lewis and Hugh Laurie can do it, so can you.' She polished off her macaron. 'Mmm. That was delicious.'

He was still stroking her hand. He held her gaze. 'Do you —' he jerked his head towards the hot tub. 'Do you fancy a dip? I took the liberty of getting some swimwear sent over for you. It's in the bathroom. There are robes too.'

She felt the atmosphere shift, and her stomach convulsed. *Come on,* she told herself, *live a little. Just let go and enjoy this.* He was watching her, and she saw a flicker of uncertainty cross his face. He was beautiful, and caring, and considerate. She wanted nothing more than to be in the warm water with him as the London skyline danced on the horizon. 'Ok,' she said. 'Let's do it.'

11

JENNA

The bathroom was as glorious as the rest of the penthouse, with a huge, oval tub. She found a black string bikini and a black one-piece hanging on the door. Both were size 8, and the tags said Erès. He was good. Well-practised, more like. She selected the bikini—may as well do this properly—and put a robe on over it.

He was already in the hot tub, his body immersed and his arms resting along the sides, those world-famous biceps in full view. She swallowed and walked up the wooden steps. As he watched her, she took off her robe and stepped into the swirling water. Wonderful, life-affirming heat enveloped her. Heart pounding, she made her way over to him and settled in beside him, in the crook of his arm. He draped it around her.

'That bikini fits you like a glove,' he murmured.

'But you already knew it would,' she said. 'Like I said, you're smooth.'

She looked up at him and he bent his head and kissed her, pulling her tightly towards him. Her head spun. *Jackson James is kissing me in a hot tub*, she thought. *I swear, I'm going to wake up in a minute*. But he didn't feel like Jackson James, public property. Tonight, right here, in this rooftop cocoon, he was just Jackson, a heavenly man who'd chosen to spend the evening alone with her.

His kisses were languid to start with: slow, exploratory. He smoothed her hair away from her face and down her back. She had the impression he was holding himself back, waiting to let her set the pace. She went with it and then started to kiss him with a greater intensity. It was uncomfortable, kissing him sideways. She threw her leg over and straddled him, taking his face in both her hands. He ran his hands up and down her back and drew her towards him. She rubbed her pelvis into his groin and could feel him hardening beneath her. He moaned into her mouth.

She was so turned on, it was ridiculous. She couldn't see much of his body, but it felt incredible, his muscular bulk rippling beneath her hands.

He fondled the tie at the back of her bikini top with his fingers and said, 'Can I—?'

In response, she reached around and yanked the tie herself, tugging the top over her head and throwing it onto the deck. She lowered herself onto him and resumed kissing him.

'I want to see you,' he whispered. He grabbed her upper arms and held her away slightly. 'Jesus Christ, you are so beautiful.' He lowered his mouth onto her nipple and she ground down deeper onto him, furiously pulling at the ties on her bikini bottoms. They came loose and floated to the top of the water.

She needed very badly to get his trunks off, too. She fumbled around under the water, but they didn't feel elasticated.

'Here, let me,' he said, and, arching his back, tugged them off.

'Mmm,' she sighed, and wrapped herself around him. He was delicious. He was so extraordinarily delicious that she was losing all sense of everything; she was only aware of him beneath her, his arms around her, his tongue in her mouth.

He pulled away. 'Jenna. We should go in.'

'I'm happy here,' she managed. She was struggling to string a sentence together. 'I need you inside me.'

He laughed. 'Believe me, that's exactly what you're going to get, but my condoms are in the bedroom. I'm afraid I wasn't quite smooth enough to have them sitting by the side of the hot tub, despite what you think of me.'

She giggled. 'Major fail.' God, she'd forgotten they'd need a condom. What the hell was wrong with her? Here she was, throwing caution to the wind because this guy had turned off all of her brain functionality aside from her pleasure centres.

He eased her off him and stood up. 'Wait here.'

She swivelled and watched him get out of the tub and walk into the bedroom. Good lord. His body was ridiculous. He came back out a minute later, one towel wrapped around his waist and another in his hand. He was perfectly V-shaped; his torso disappeared into his towel while his upper half was broad. He had a smattering of hair on his chest. She didn't remember that from his movies—they must wax him.

He held out the towel. 'Come on. I'll dry you off. I don't want you getting cold. You won't be putting clothes on for quite some time yet.' He gave her a dirty grin. Her groin ached. She hauled herself out of the water and walked down the steps towards him, wringing out her hair. His eyes didn't leave her. He flung the towel over her shoulders and softly rubbed her arms dry while he kissed her. Then he lifted a corner and gently wiped her face, before moving down to her breasts, lightly chafing her nipples with the towel. He pulled it off her and, kneeling down, dried her legs one by one, while he covered her stomach in feathery kisses. She held his head in her hands and thought her legs might buckle. Then he threw down the towel, got to his feet, and picked her up. She wrapped her legs and arms around him. He carried her inside, kicking the doors shut one by one, and laid her on the bed, crouching over her.

Her legs were still around his waist; her arms encircled his neck. He was kissing her again, but more slowly this time. She felt herself shift into a dreamlike state: not sleepy, but perfectly at peace, knowing that, in time, she would get everything she wanted.

'Jenna,' he said.

She opened her eyes.

'God, you're perfect.' He shook his head. 'You're even more perfect than I imagined, and believe me, I've been doing plenty of imagining.'

Even though she was already naked, lying there with her limbs wrapped around him, she felt the blood rise to her face. She reached down between his legs, but he took hold of her wrists and pinned them above her head with one hand, the other tracing a line down her stomach.

'Not yet,' he said. 'I'm not in any hurry.' He dropped his head and ran his tongue downwards, between her breasts, over her stomach, and then settling between her legs, his fingers circling her nipples.

A small part of her, somewhere, was mortified by how quickly and violently she came, moaning and bucking against him. The rest of her was far too far gone to care.

'You're so beautiful,' he told her, kissing her as he lay

back down beside her and she clung to him. He leant over and opened the top drawer, unwrapping a condom and deftly sliding it on. She climbed on top of him and eased him inside her, sinking onto his hips and catching her breath at the intense sensation of fullness. He sat up and pulled her legs around his waist.

'Christ, we're a good fit,' he growled, his hands gliding all over her skin.

'You can say that again.' She lowered her mouth to his neck and her hair fell over his shoulders as they moved together. *This isn't normal*, she thought. *First-time sex with anyone is never this good. This is bliss, heaven, ecstasy*, she considered incoherently, as he shuddered and came inside her.

12

JENNA

She awoke to the sound of her iPhone alarm at six the next morning, alone in the enormous bed. The night before, Jackson had peeled himself off her.

'I have to go shortly, for obvious reasons,' he'd warned her, 'but you should stay here, enjoy this place for a few more hours.'

'I couldn't!' she protested. 'I'm not doing a walk of shame through the Corinthia lobby tomorrow morning in my cocktail dress.'

He'd jerked his head towards the wardrobe bashfully. 'I already thought of that. Control freak, remember? I had Lululemon send over some stuff to get you through the lobby, and the car will take you home, or straight to school. I figured you were too much of a nice girl to turn up with an overnight bag.'

She'd shoved him playfully. 'Not sure I've been much of a nice girl tonight.'

'No, on the contrary, you've been very, very bad. Now, I need to have a shower before I can show my face at home. Come and help me soap up, you little minx.'

Afterwards, she'd sat on the bed, robed and turbaned, and watched him dress.

'Don't worry about a thing with checkout,' he'd told her. 'You can just walk out of here. Get what you want for breakfast—just pick up that phone and you'll get straight through to the dedicated butler. And pick up the same phone when you want the car.' He bent over and kissed her. 'Jesus, I wish I was waking up here with you tomorrow morning. But I'll see you in'—he looked at his watch—'about nine hours.'

'You're doing drop-off?' she gasped.

'Oh, try and stop me, gorgeous. I wouldn't miss it for the world.'

Now she was exhausted but giddy with the memory of the night before. His hands still felt imprinted on her body. She'd set the alarm for six so she could take her time and enjoy the penthouse before she was due at school. School! It felt like it existed in a parallel universe of stultifying normality. She padded over to the French doors and threw open the curtains to see a grey dawn breaking over the London skyline.

Turning the shower on full-blast, she stepped in and was transported back to the previous night. The second time, in the shower, had been just as spectacular; they'd soaped each other up maddeningly slowly before making love up against the marble wall of the shower cubicle. Her body had surprised her with the depth of its need for him. As she turned her head this way and that and the shampoo ran down her back, she considered her feelings. The sex had been ridiculous; their chemistry was, from where she was standing, insane, and sexually the evening had been a huge high-point in her life.

Of course, all the threads of his carefully planned seduction had added to the extraordinary nature of the experience. It had been a real treat to be in the hands of a true professional. She thought back to the candlelit rooftop, the hot tub, and the swimwear and morning-after outfit delivered in advance. He'd been very generous, very thoughtful —but he was a smooth operator, no doubt about it, and having an unlimited budget definitely helped his seduction abilities. That said, the magic had happened when flesh met flesh. The way his skin had felt and smelt and tasted, the way he'd fit inside her and the look in his eyes when he'd made love to her had triggered a series of emotions whose intensity surprised, and even scared, her.

The most surprising part of it all was how much she liked him. Beyond the inevitable crush she, like most people, had had on his public persona, she'd had a great date with him: warm, witty conversation and mind-blowing sex. If he wasn't married, world famous and terrifyingly wealthy and successful, she might be in with a chance of a second date.

EATING GRANOLA and sipping a delicious cup of fragrant breakfast tea on the terrace, she stretched languorously in her new Lululemon gear and WhatsApped Katie.

Date was AMAZING. Need clothes for school! Pretty please can you bring my pink wrap dress, underwear, flat pumps + makeup bag? Can't wait to tell you about it + thx xxx

Katie replied immediately:

You lucky fucking cow. CAN'T WAIT. Need all details. See you 7.50? X

The air felt different up here. She walked up the steps to the hot tub deck, cup of tea in hand. Nelson's column rose from the rooftops like, appropriately enough, a giant phallus, the Neoclassical splendour of the National Gallery lying just beyond it. It was the ultimate luxury, in a city of nine million people, to remove oneself from the noise and craziness sufficiently to feel only the inspiration that London provided.

That was how she felt this morning—inspired. Before last night, she hadn't even known that places like this existed. Her vocation as a teacher would never, ever yield this kind of wealth, but Jackson had opened the door, however briefly, to show her what was possible in life. She could live here very happily indeed. It was a shame one night here probably cost the equivalent of six months' rent. Closing the door of the Hamilton penthouse behind her a few minutes later, she was painfully aware that she was likely closing the door on a bitterly brief slice of heaven.

WHEN THE HOTEL'S SLEEK, black Mercedes dropped her at the school gates, she ran inside and went straight to 3P's classroom, where Katie was waiting, squirming with excitement. She hugged Jenna and pushed a bag at her.

'You've got five minutes to get yourself sorted and then I want all the details. Every. Last. One. Go.'

Jenna squeezed her hand gratefully and ran off to the ladies' loos, where she changed her clothes and put on her makeup. She'd already blow-dried her hair at the penthouse's beautiful dressing-table. She kept the makeup fresh and dewy, adding coral blush to her cheeks and lashings of mascara.

By the time she got back to the classroom, Katie had fetched them both a mug of tea from the staffroom.

'Tell me.' She demanded. 'I was going demented last night, wondering what you were up to. I had to put on *Love Island* to distract myself.'

Jenna told her about the penthouse, the sushi on the candlelit terrace, the hot tub, the bed and the shower sex. She told her how hard Jackson had worked to make her feel at ease, how smart and funny he was, and how intense the chemistry had been.

'God,' groaned Katie, 'I can't believe you've shagged Jackson James! It's like Cinderella, or *Pretty Woman*, or something—this is just the most exciting thing ever. How did you leave things?'

'He had to get home last night,' Jenna admitted, 'but he persuaded me to stay and enjoy the suite. He's doing drop-off this morning, though.'

'Hence the sexy pink dress. I hope I can control my facial features when he rocks up with Rollo.'

'Seriously, I'm going to have the same problem,' Jenna said, going red at the thought.

THIRTY MINUTES LATER, she was reading with Nitin when she became aware of the vague stir among the other parents in the room that usually signalled Jackson's arrival. She looked up and swallowed. He was in his running gear and looked *hot*. He let go of Rollo's hand and strode over to her desk, stony-faced.

Brandishing an exercise book, he barked, 'Miss Price.

Can I have a word about your comments on Rollo's creative writing homework? Privately.'

His tone caught the attention of one of the mums in the room, who looked at her in alarm.

She wasn't sure what to think. Was he messing with her? 'Um, sure.' She pushed her chair back and peeled an *I am a Super Reader* sticker off the sheet on her desk. 'Nitin, sweetie, go and work on your journal, please. I'll be back in a few minutes.'

She led Jackson out of the classroom and into an empty music room a couple of doors down. He followed her in and locked the door behind him. His face broke into a sexy grin.

'Morning, gorgeous,' he said softly, pulling her into his arms.

She swatted him, laughing with relief. 'You're such a dick. I thought I was in trouble there for a minute.'

'Oh, you are in trouble. You're locked in a room with me. And despite what you and the general public may think, I'm actually a pretty decent actor when I want to be. God, I wish I was still in that bed with you.'

Her stomach convulsed. 'Me too.'

He kissed her, his hands moving over her breasts. 'Fuck me, this dress should be illegal. What are you trying to do to those poor little boys? Did you sleep ok?'

'I slept brilliantly, thank you.' She cupped his face, her thumbs running over his stubble. 'It was an amazing evening. Thank you for spoiling me.'

'The pleasure was all mine, believe me. Mmm, I wish I was my son so I could just sit at a little desk and stare at you all day.'

She giggled, and he put his hand up the skirt of her dress, his other arm wrapped around her waist in a vice-like grip. He kissed her on and on, and she abandoned herself to the deliciousness of his mouth and his tongue and his body under her hands. Finally, reluctantly, she broke free. What sacrilege, to pull away from Jackson James. What an absolute bloody waste, especially as she didn't know if it would happen again. He held all the cards. She could weep right now. But she had to rescue poor Katie before lessons started.

She stroked his cheek one last time and looked him in the eyes. 'I need to get back to class.'

He sighed and leant his forehead against hers. 'What are you doing Friday night?' he whispered, running his hands up her bare arms. 'I have a flat in Knightsbridge. Fancy a proper sleepover this time? Spoiler alert: you won't need your PJs.'

13

NATALIA

Her name was Isabella Whitney.

Lorenzo was working from home today. He hadn't been suspended, not yet anyway, but he was trying to lie low at work, it would seem. She watched him like a lioness stalking her prey. Her best chance of finding out his accuser's identity was getting into his Loeb email account, no mean feat given the layers of encryption that the firm's remote-access technology employed on both desktop and mobile devices.

The only times he left his home office without logging out were when he took or made a call. Lorenzo was a pacer when on the phone. He'd been one of the earliest adopters of the bluetooth headset on the trading floor, years and years ago, back before he'd had a corner office. She imagined the pacing helped him to approach all his calls with suitable vigour and machismo, from a dominant position, as it were.

His office was on the return one flight of stairs up from the kitchen. She drank coffee at the island and waited. She needed to leave for school pickup in, like, ten minutes. Then came his footsteps. She heard him bark '*Si,*' and then '*Ciao, David.*' He clattered down the stairs and strode past her, into the garden. She grabbed her phone, shot upstairs and pulled up his Outlook on one of this three monitors, while Bloomberg flickered its colourful, split-second price adjustments of stocks, currencies and commodities on the others.

She took a deep breath. Nothing suspicious, or auspicious, among the first few emails in the reading pane. She hit the search bar and typed 'human'. Bingo. Outlook served up an email from Human Capital Management, entitled *CONFIDENTIAL: Lorenzo Beneventi: Internal Investigation.* She swallowed and clicked to pull the contents up in the preview pane. It was a short email, but there was an attachment—she opened it up and took a quick snap with her phone. His voice and footsteps grew louder again. Shit. She hastily closed the attachment, cleared the search field and scrolled back up to the most recently received email. Scurrying out of the room and up another flight of stairs, she fled into their ensuite bathroom and locked the door.

Opening up her Photos application, she zoomed in and scanned the attachment. *A member of staff has made a very serious accusation of unwanted sexual advances against you... Loeb AG treats any occurrence of sexual impropriety with colleagues with the utmost severity... The initial step in the firm's investigatory process is to conduct a full interview with the alleged victim...* She kept scanning. *Isabella Whitney, Managing Director.* There it was. A Managing Director? So this 'girl', as Lorenzo had referred to her, wasn't some stupid, foolhardy graduate but a senior member of the sales desk. Shit.

Double shit. She needed to pick Ilaria up from hockey. They didn't have a fixture this week; instead it was a regular Wednesday practice session. She grabbed her bag and car-keys and headed for the school's hockey pitches up near the A40.

THEY'D JUST WRAPPED up the session when she arrived. Mr Pearce was packing the bibs into a large duffle bag as Bex shooed the girls over to find their book-bags and blazers from the chaotic pile at the side of the pitch. Ilaria spotted her and ran at her, a wide, unguarded beam on her face. For how much longer would she be so unequivocally happy to see her? Valentina was already getting funny about public displays of affection with her parents.

'Mummy!' she shouted. 'I was the goalkeeper and I saved two goals!' She threw herself against Natalia, who enveloped her in a bear-hug, kissing the top of her damp head.

'Well done, my darling,' she cooed. 'I'm so proud of you! Now, go and get your bag from Miss Oliver.'

Bex spotted her and sauntered over. She took off her baseball cap, tousling her hair, and touched the sleeve of Natalia's Burberry trench.

'How's it going, sweetie?' she asked.

It was a casual enquiry, but it came from a place of affection, and Natalia felt her eyes prick.

'Not great,' she said. 'I'm having a bit of a shocker, actually.'

Bex steered her a few steps further away from the pitch. 'Why? What's up?'

'Um.' She looked at her feet. 'It's Lorenzo. He's been accused of something at work—some woman says he propositioned her and groped her.'

'Fuck!' Bex stared at her. 'Holy shit, Nats. That is not good. What's going to happen?'

'He may get suspended; we don't know yet.'

'Do you think he did it?' Bex was up to speed on Lorenzo's shortcomings as a husband.

'He says not, but it's hard to talk to him about it. He snaps at me whenever I bring it up. He must be so worried about it; I wish he'd talk to me.'

'Do you know the woman who's accusing him?'

'That's the thing. I hacked into his email right before I came here and found her name. I don't know her, but I'm going to go home and have a drink and get stuck into Google.'

'Hey, don't do that,' Bex chided, 'at least, not alone. Do you guys want to come to ours and we can feed the girls together? I'll drink with you, and we can stalk away to our hearts' content.'

She considered. Valentina was doing a joint tutoring session at her friend's house and would stay for tea. Bex and Elsie lived near the pitches. She'd love some moral support. 'Count us in, thanks,' she said decisively. 'I'll drive you guys back.'

Bex and Elsie lived in a small ex-council flat in a low-rise complex. While the area and the building were dingy, the flat itself was warm and welcoming. She'd had been there once before, briefly, to pick Ilaria up from a play-date with Elsie last academic year, and it looked like they'd redecorated over the summer. The kitchen, dining and lounge areas were all in one room, and the furniture was basic, but there was no mistaking that Bex had an eye for interiors. Natalia tried to pinpoint what it was that made the space so vibrant. Plants, that was it. There were plants everywhere—

palms, cheese-plants and ferns. Bex had picked out the green accents in some of her vases and cushions too.

'It looks lovely,' she said, looking around. 'Did you guys repaint?'

'Yep. And we did a big Ikea trip.' Bex squatted down and pulled open the under-counter fridge. 'Are new potatoes and chicken escalopes alright for Ilaria?'

'Perfect, thanks. What can I do to help?'

'Open this.' Bex handed over a bottle of screw cap white wine. It's just from Sainsbury's, so I hope it's ok. I'll put the potatoes on to boil and then I'm going to take a super-quick shower. Don't google that woman till I'm back!'

While she was gone, Natalia hunted down a couple of glasses and cracked open the bottle of wine. She checked in on the girls, already absorbed in a game in Elsie's room, and settled at the table, wine in hand. Bex was as good as her word. She was back within five minutes, wet hair slicked off her forehead, wearing some low-slung jogging bottoms and a white vest. She pulled up the chair next to Natalia and sat down.

'God, your figure's amazing,' sighed Natalia. 'You look depressingly good.'

'I spend the whole day running around; it's an unfair advantage.' Bex took a sip of her wine. 'And you're looking fantastic—that spinning's definitely working. I'd kill for your boobs. The grass is always greener, right?'

'Indeed,' reflected Natalia, reaching for her phone. 'Right. She's called Isabella Whitney. Let's see what Google has on her.'

She typed in *Isabella Whitney Loeb*. The first entry was a link to her LinkedIn profile. She clicked through and they peered at it. Her full name was Isabella Brooke Whitney. The image was a corporate headshot that couldn't disguise the woman's beauty. *She's a WASP,* thought Natalia. *I bet she's American, East Coast.* She'd worked with plenty of them at Fidelity. She had dark blonde hair in a perfect blow-out, strong, shapely eyebrows and exquisite bone-structure. She wore a pale blue shirt under a dark suit—all very Brooks Brothers. On the basis of a single photo, she didn't look like a sleep-your-way-to-the-top kind of girl.

'She's beautiful,' she commented to Bex.

'Yep.' Bex grimaced apologetically.

She kept scrolling. Predictably enough, Isabella was American. She'd gone to Duke for undergrad, and had an MBA from Harvard Business School. Between Duke and HBS she'd done a few years at McKinsey, moving into banking after her MBA. So far, so blue-chip. Her current role at Loeb was, apparently, head of UK Institutional Equity Sales. Again, not quite 'some girl', as Lorenzo had claimed. According to LinkedIn, she'd been made Managing Director in the previous year's promotions round.

She seemed hot on affinity networks; clicking into her Interests tab yielded plenty of women's and diversity networks, as well as several charities related to neurological injuries. Natalia wondered what had happened there. She hit Activity. Isabella's posts were fairly dry, sharing Loeb's macro forecasts, cheerleading her fellow females within the industry when they posted about promotions or achievements, and posting the odd photo of a women's event. Natalia checked out the photos. In all of them Isabella looked immaculate and consummately professional. She sat back.

'What do you think?' Bex asked.

'I think,' she said slowly, 'there's nothing here to suggest this woman tried to screw my husband, or that she's the type to falsely accuse someone. I mean, she's already senior, she's attractive, she seems successful...' Her voice trailed off.

'Maybe go back to Google?' Bex suggested. 'See if you can find anything else on her?'

She hit the Back key and changed the search term to *Isabella Brooke Whitney*. There was a wealth of results. The first was a Wikipedia entry containing a Whitney family tree dating back to the seventeenth century. How blue-blooded. The second was a *New York Times* announcement from two years ago, announcing the engagement of Isabella Brooke Whitney to John Fitzgerald Markham III. The accompanying photo looked to have been taken at a black-tie function. Isabella was radiant in a sleek, one-shouldered black dress. She leant into a dark-haired, square-jawed adonis with a gleaming white smile who was surely every WASPy mother's fantasy son-in-law. Natalia bet she could guess this guy's entire biography from that one photo.

'They look pretty loved-up,' Bex observed.

'Hmm,' she said. 'And the *New York Times* says the wedding was last July. I'm not sure why she'd be trying to seduce Lorenzo; it doesn't fit.'

She fixed her gaze on Isabella's megawatt smile. From what she could glean, she was a beautiful, well-bred, well-educated woman with a successful career and a hot new husband. There was no way in hell she'd jeopardise all that for Lorenzo. So his version of events didn't stack up. That meant this woman was either lying to sabotage him for another reason, or she was telling the truth and he'd tried it on with her. Ugh. She drained her glass.

'Want another one?' Bex proffered the bottle.

'Better not, thanks, if I have to drive. Believe me, I'll get stuck in back at home.'

'What are you thinking?'

'I'm thinking Occam's razor—the simplest solution's the best one. She accused him of groping her and propositioning her—most likely, that's what happened.'

'Shit,' Bex said. 'I'm so sorry, sweetie. What are you going to do?'

'I don't have a bloody clue. Obviously, I need to wait and see how this investigation at work plays out. They'll be able to get to the truth more easily than I can. But if he did it, I have no idea what this means for us as a family. He has two daughters, for fuck's sake! How would they feel if they grew up knowing their dad's a slimy bastard who assaults women and abuses his position to try to get laid? I mean, *seriously*.'

She closed her eyes and pinched the bridge of her nose. It was too painful to imagine the girls having a potential sexual predator for a father. She hadn't yet let herself consider what it meant for her if Lorenzo was guilty of attempting to cheat on her. Her inner saboteur was rearing her head, galvanised by the sting of potential rejection, reminding her that if she'd lost more weight more quickly or had more interesting things to talk about than tutoring and hockey practice, her husband might have stayed more captivated by her. His dull, stay-at-home wife or dazzling women like Isabella? It wasn't even a contest.

Bex put an arm around her and Natalia relaxed into her friend, her head on Bex' shoulder.

'Hey.' Bex kissed her hair. 'You and your girls are all strong, amazing women. Whatever he's done, it won't fuck them up because I know you won't let it. But don't get ahead of yourself. Try to sit tight, I guess, and see what his company says. It's going to be alright, I promise. We'll get you through this. You're not alone, sweetie.'

Bex smelt of some kind of citrusy shower gel, and the hand on Natalia's shoulder was soft and warm. A jolt of recognition flashed sweetly, somewhere deep in her gut, the revelation of some obvious truth, but it was gone before she could grab onto it.

Right on cue, the oven pinged. She raised her head. Let's get those girls fed,' she said, springing up from the table.

14

CALLUM

When he came out of Bond Street tube station, he had to consult Google Maps. The area south of Selfridges was new to him. He strolled down Davies Street, admiring the charming red-brick buildings that seemed to house mainly art galleries and wine merchants.

He'd taken the hockey kit back to school on his own after practice. Bex had seemed in a hurry to run off with Mrs Beneventi. He wondered if Bex had a thing for her. Maybe they were just friends; they'd probably got to know each other pretty well over the last few years.

His phone informed him he was passing Grosvenor Square, and a minute later he emerged into a pretty triangular junction and found the Connaught Hotel on his right.

He shrugged off a flicker in his belly, unsure whether it was nerves or anticipation. This wasn't his usual type of date, in a noisy bar or a cosy tapas restaurant, if he was making an effort. However, Astrid wasn't his usual type of conquest. He had a well-honed radar for interested females, and he'd picked up on a vague frisson when he'd bandaged her ankle and a stronger undercurrent at the girls' party. Still, lunging at a parent in broad daylight in her own home had been risky. He'd surprised himself, but he'd been acting on some sort of primal instinct rather than making a soundly judged move. And it had been worth it; she was fucking delicious.

It was beautiful around here. He took in the jewellers masquerading as townhouses and the imposing, old-world shop fronts. It wasn't much of a surprise that Astrid had chosen this area. Polished and expensive, he suspected it was her natural habitat. He was glad he'd brought his smart blazer. Shrugging it on, he ran lightly up the hotel steps.

'Jean-Georges restaurant, please?' he asked the doorman.

'To your left, sir.' He gestured with a gloved hand, holding open the door. 'Have a wonderful evening.'

He walked into the elegant, curved space with its wall of stained-glass windows. It felt more like a posh bar than a formal restaurant, which was a relief. He saw her halfway down the busy room, a picture of stillness amidst the bustle. Her wineglass was in her hand, and she was staring out of the window, looking like some kind of madonna. He felt a pull of desire as he took her in. Her gorgeous hair was swept back in a bun, and she had some kind of pale blue, very long, floaty dress on, with tiny buttons all down the front. He saw that a decent number of these buttons had been left undone at the top, and a large number at the bottom. The result was that the skirt fell away at the sides, generously exposing her glossy, tanned legs up to mid-thigh.

He approached the table, unseen by her. 'Hey, you,' he said softly.

She looked up, startled, and her face brightened.

'Hi.' She matched his tone. Uncrossing her legs, she

stood up to greet him, and he saw a flicker of uncertainty as she evaluated the right way to do so. He'd save her the bother and save them an hour or two of dancing around the reason they were here. He put his hands carefully on her gauzy shoulders and drew her to him, bending his head to kiss her slowly and fully on the lips.

He felt her start—presumably, she wasn't expecting him to come on quite so strongly at the outset—before she softened into him. When she drew back, she blushed and sat, avoiding his eyes. She was adorable. He felt a pleasurable rush from having disconcerted her.

'What are you drinking?' she asked him.

'I'll have what you're having.' He took off his jacket and laid it next to him on the sofa.

'It's Chablis. I ordered a bottle,' she said, leaning over to the ice bucket.

'Well, Chablis seemed to do the trick for us on Saturday, didn't it?' He raised his eyebrows suggestively and she laughed, breaking the tension.

'It certainly did. Why do you think I ordered it again?' She looked up at him through her eyelashes as she poured him a glass

'I like your style.' He held up his glass. '*Sláinte*. You look incredible, by the way.'

'Thank you.' She looked embarrassed. 'I stole it from my new collection, hot off the runway.'

'Nice steal. Even I can tell it's a stunning dress. You're obviously very talented. But you must have come here in a hurry tonight.'

'Why?'

'Because you forgot to do up most of the buttons. But that's alright, because it'll make my job of unbuttoning them all later a lot easier.' He swallowed a mouthful of wine and settled back, watching for her reaction.

She twisted her mouth and briefly shut her eyes. God, she was exquisite. He leant over and put a hand on her smooth, golden knee.

'Astrid. Are you ok?'

She reached for her glass and took a hurried gulp. 'I'm fine. Just—um—you don't beat about the bush, do you?'

'Not with you sitting there, looking like that. Come here, will you? Don't worry, I don't bite.' He patted the sofa next to him.

Eyeing him, she picked up her glass and moved to the sofa, nestling in beside him. He put his arm around her.

'That's better. Now it feels more like a date and less like a job interview. You seem tense, though. What's wrong?'

She shook herself. 'Sorry. Nothing's wrong. I'm just—I don't date much. I'm a bit rusty, and I've come straight from work. It's been a long day. I just need to unwind a bit and I'll be fine.' She brandished her glass. 'I'll get drinking.'

He twisted his body to face her. 'Look at me. You don't need to apologise. I'm delighted to be here, with you, in this place. It's not exactly an average Wednesday night for me, ok? You're gorgeous, and I'm fucking thrilled with myself.'

She laughed, nodding. 'Ok.' When she laughed, she seemed to shed the weight of the world.

He kept talking to warm her up. It was one advantage of having the gift of the gab; he was never stuck for words. 'I googled you,' he said.

She flashed a smile. 'Did you?'

'Yep, and you're fucking amazing. I also now follow you on Instagram. You're literally the only women's fashion designer I follow, so I hope you're suitably grateful.'

'I'm honoured,' she giggled.

'So,' he said, pulling out his phone. 'Talk me through... *this*. I'm very, very interested to hear more about it.' He showed her the photo he'd found of her in that glittery body-stocking on the steps of the Royal Albert Hall.

'Ah.' She raised an eyebrow. 'That was one hell of an evening. I didn't make that—it's by Julien MacDonald. I was his plus-one for the British Fashion Awards. Usually I'd wear my own stuff to that kind of thing, but he was being honoured that night, and it was very sweet of him to have asked me.' She gestured at the photo. 'I don't think I ate for a week before I put that on; I was terrified of how revealing it was.'

'Well,' he said, 'it gets my vote, alright. It's very Kim Kardashian—but somehow, you managed to look very classy while virtually naked, unlike our friend Kim.' He ran his hand up her bare thigh and over the light, filmy fabric of her dress, brushing his lips against hers.

They were interrupted by the arrival of some food.

'I ordered this; you can't come here without trying it,' Astrid said. 'It's black truffle pizza.'

He picked up a piece and took a bite, the dense muskiness of the truffles assaulting him. Jesus, it was delicious. Truffles always reminded him of sex—they must contain pheromones. He balanced the thin wedge on his fingers and presented it to Astrid, who took a bite, her eyelids flickering closed in bliss. He watched as she chewed it and licked the crumbs from her lips.

'This is insane,' he said.

'Isn't it? It's the food of gods.'

'Are you a regular here?'

'Sort of. It's near my office, and good for drinks after work—and pizza, of course.'

'It suits you.' He looked around at the tasteful furnishings and well-heeled men and women surrounding them. It was the perfect habitat for her. She was so refined, so flawless, draped in her pale blue silk. The memory of kissing her on her garden sofa flashed into his mind, his hands grasping at her white-blonde hair, the girlishness of her little tennis dress. She hadn't been refined then; he knew she'd wanted him as badly as he'd wanted her. He put a hand on the back of her neck and pulled her to him, kissing her deeply. She tasted of truffles. He was fairly sure he shouldn't be doing this in such a swanky place, but he didn't care. Christ, she was so delicious. He kissed her harder.

She pulled away from him, her breathing ragged, and stood up, grabbing her handbag.

'Excuse me a minute?' she asked, and made her way quickly through the now-thronged bar.

Shite. He hoped he hadn't scared her off. He was confident she'd come tonight for the same reason he had. But where could they go, at any rate? Not to hers, with poor little Tabby around. Could he persuade her back to his? It wasn't a particularly appealing prospect for her, he realised, though he could call ahead and warn his housemates to behave themselves. He wasn't used to being presented with the logistical problem of a lack of location to have sex; he usually went back to the flat of whichever girl he was hooking up with. He felt like a teenager again. He dug into another slice of the excellent pizza.

She was back five minutes later. She sat down next to him.

'Callum.' She held something up and smiled at him tentatively. It was a Connaught key-card.

15

ASTRID

His reaction was priceless. He stared at her, his mouth forming an O. 'Is that a room key? For here?'

'It is.' She was having an out-of-body experience again, but she was inordinately pleased with herself, both for being brave enough to make such a bold move and for pulling off one hell of a surprise for him.

He beamed at her and pulled her towards him, kissing her. 'You little beauty. Let's get out of here.' He jumped up, draining his glass. He was as enthusiastic and guileless as a child. 'Oh. We need to pay.' He looked around for a waiter.

'It's ok,' she said, standing. 'I've transferred it to the room.'

As they walked towards the lift, he grinned at her and squeezed her hand. 'You're full of surprises, d'you know that? I thought you'd done a runner on me.'

'Not quite.' She gave him a shy smile. 'I thought there was a good chance of you getting us kicked out of there for inappropriate behaviour, so a room seemed like a wise move.'

They got into the lift and the doors slid closed. Her heart was hammering against her chest. To say this move was out of character was an understatement. She couldn't quite believe she'd had the nerve to march over to the reception desk and request a room for the night. But there was something so straightforward about him. With Callum, there was no game-playing—he was quite simply a young, ridiculously attractive guy who wanted her. His forthrightness, so different from her own anxiety-ridden artifice, had a calming effect on her; his carefree attitude was infectious. Really, he was a tonic.

She looked up at the beautiful curve of his mouth, his classical nose, the tendrils of dark hair falling over those eyes. She hadn't stopped thinking about him since he'd kissed her in her garden; he'd got under her skin. She was sick of being sensible and ricocheting between the worries of mothering a child and running a company. It was exhausting, frankly. This evening was for her.

'It's very extravagant,' he said.

'It's my treat,' she said hastily, and then more playfully added, 'I'm sure it'll prove a worthwhile investment.'

His grin was back, and he shook his head at her. 'Oh, you have no idea. I told you we had unfinished business.' He ran a finger over her breastbone and down the tiny, covered buttons on her dress.

The lift doors opened and Astrid looked for room 322. She slid the card into the lock and pushed the door. Inside lay a small but luxurious room, dominated by a large darkwood bed. Oh, thank God—they'd already delivered the wine she'd requested downstairs. She was going to need it. Hotel-room trysts with wildly unsuitable younger men required serious dutch courage—she was still far too sober for this. She grabbed the bottle and poured two glasses, handing one to Callum. She took a swig.

He stepped towards her. 'You look nervous. Are you?'

She nodded. 'Do you want to know something pathetic?' she asked in a small voice. 'I haven't slept with anyone since my husband left me.'

She hadn't planned on telling him that, but it was proving increasingly obvious she couldn't keep her mask on in this instance. When she held others at arms-length her performance was flawless. But she couldn't get naked with this straight-talking guy and keep her poise; she simply wasn't that good an actress.

He gasped. 'You're shitting me. How long ago was that?'

'Just over two years.' She studied her wine glass.

'Fuck. You poor baby. I don't understand—you must have had plenty of opportunities. There's no way men don't crawl all over you.'

'I've been on a few dates, but most of them were older—successful businessmen who are very charming and urbane in a boardroom or a bar, but then the idea of actually seeing them naked...' She screwed up her face in distaste.

He laughed. 'Jesus. Poor guys. You're a hard woman. I hope you're feeling differently tonight?'

She rolled her eyes. 'You could say that.'

'Ok then.' He took her glass off her gently and put both of them down on the console table. His dark eyes gleamed. 'Tonight, we're going to have some fun. I told you last time, your ex is a douchebag. It's time for you to move on. I'm going to show you what you've been missing. Are you with me?'

She nodded, eyes fixed on his, mesmerised by his face and his mouth and his proximity to her. Right now, she was alone in a beautiful hotel room with this man who appeared more divine than mortal, and who she suspected knew exactly what he was doing. She was in his hands, and everything else could fade away for a few hours.

He kissed her, his tongue twisting against hers. He drew back and began unbuttoning his shirt, tugging it off.

'I've been thinking about you all week,' he whispered, 'thinking about what I was going to do to you when I saw you tonight—though the location is an upgrade on what I had in mind.'

She giggled, and ran her fingertips over the taut flesh of his stomach, recalling the flashes she'd seen of it when he'd been playing tennis with Tabby and the girls. It was better than she'd imagined. As it had in her garden, the sheer reality of his physical presence overwhelmed her. Over the past few days he'd felt like a distant fantasy, and yet here he was in flesh and blood, standing close to her. Soft brown hair covered his chest, and his skin was indescribably soft. Youth, that's what it was. She nuzzled his shoulder and inhaled his skin. She had an ache between her legs, the same ache she'd had in the garden, but more intense.

'Let's get this off you.' He slowly unbuttoned each tiny button, starting at the top, and his fingers lazily grazed the flesh beneath as he liberated it. Squatting down to release the last few buttons, he parted the fabric and dropped soft kisses on her stomach.

He stood again, lightly pulling the unbuttoned dress off her shoulders. His face contorted and her belly mirrored the movement, sensation spiralling deep inside her as he studied her body. She wore a new underwear set of ice-blue lace. She stepped out of her stilettos and draped her arms around his bare shoulders. She recalled them straining when he'd taken her weight at the hockey pitch. They were even better without a shirt on.

'Jesus,' he groaned. 'Look at you. You're so beautiful. God, I can't wait to have you. Ok. Hang on a sec.'

Hopping on alternate legs, he pulled off his shoes and socks and dropped his chinos, standing in a pair of snug black boxers. She drank in his tanned, muscular body and swallowed. He had an erection; he came closer to her.

'Can you feel what you're doing to me already?' he asked hoarsely.

She nodded, overwhelmed, willing herself to stay still.

'I need to feel your nipples,' he said, and moved his hands downwards, palming her breasts through her bra. 'Jesus, they're gorgeous.' His thumbs circled her nipples, the seam of the lace bra chafing at them. She gasped and involuntarily pushed her pelvis towards him.

'I'm glad you're wearing lace,' he breathed. 'It'll give you more friction. I'm not going to take your underwear off yet. Ok?'

'Ok,' she managed. Holy shit.

'Good girl.' As one hand thumbed her nipple, the other moved down, and he started to massage her backside through the lace. Then he brought his hand back around to the front and stroked between her legs, again through her knickers, kissing her all the time.

She clung to his arms and heard herself moan into his mouth.

'Do you like this? Can you feel my fingers through your panties? I'm going to take them off in a minute; would you like that?'

'Yes.' Her mouth was filling with saliva; she swallowed. Jesus Christ; who was this guy? She couldn't believe what his words were doing to her. She'd previously been of the opinion that the less said in bed, the better. With Mark, she'd relied on the odd moan, as well as a dash of telepathy, to let him know what she wanted. If anyone had told her she'd find a guy narrating what he was doing to her a turn-on then she would have cringed, and probably run for the hills. But this was insanely hot.

'Yes, what, Astrid?'

'Yes, I want you to take off my underwear, please.' Mortified that he'd made her say it, she pushed her face into his neck.

'Well, because you asked nicely...' He reached around and snapped open her bra, dragging the lace over her swollen nipples as he removed it. 'Can you lie down for me?'

She lay back on the bedcovers in just her knickers and kept her eyes on him, feeling wanton and trying to anticipate his next move.

He pulled off his boxers, watching her, and climbed naked onto the bed next to her. She raised her hips as he approached, but he tutted.

'Not yet.' He held up his hand. 'Look what I found for you.'

It was an ice cube. Holding it between his thumb and forefinger, he ran it over her right nipple. She bucked. *Shit.* The cold ignited what felt like every nerve-ending in her body. She moaned loudly. He drew a lazy line with the ice cube to her left breast. The sensation was just as violent, just as shocking.

He chucked the ice cube over his shoulder. Running his icy finger down over her stomach, he stroked the lace and then slipped it inside her knickers. She moaned again. *Holy fuck.* She wasn't going to last very long at all; she tilted her pelvis up desperately to meet him.

He peeled her knickers down and off, and knelt between her legs, almost reverently, balanced on one hand, leaning over to kiss her. She reciprocated greedily. Slipping a couple of fingers inside her, he rubbed her clitoris with his thumb. 'How does that feel? Tell me how it feels, Astrid.'

His breathing was getting deeper and those hypnotic brown eyes were glazing over. Thank God she wasn't the only one affected by what he was doing. She was melting, pushing into his hand.

'It feels like *heaven*,' she panted. 'I can't hold on much longer...'

'I know, baby, I know. Hang on a second.'

He pulled away and bounded off the bed. She threw her arm over her eyes and exhaled, trying to get a grip. She heard the rip of foil, and he was back on the bed, rolling on a condom.

'Ok.' He knelt between her legs again and took hold of her hands. 'Come and sit on me.' She wrapped her legs and arms around him and he eased inside her, holding onto her hips as she rotated them gently to accommodate him fully. God, she'd forgotten how sublime this fullness was, how complete it made her feel.

'Fuck, you're wet,' he groaned, and she saw delicious anguish in his face. 'We're going to come together, baby; are you with me? Hold on with your arms.'

She nodded and held him tighter. He kissed her, his tongue probing hers. Holding her in place with one arm clamped firmly around her lower back, he eased his other hand down between them and began to rub at her again. He slammed into her rhythmically, increasing his pace, his breathing growing more ragged. Her eyes closed, she was aware only of the exquisite liquid heat swelling inside of her, and then she exploded, bursts of red and orange and purple cascading behind her eyelids as her consciousness fractured and she became molten flesh.

He cried out, his face buried in her neck, his hands

clenching and grasping at her hair, which had become unpinned and now fell over him. He lowered her onto the bed while still inside her and rained kisses down across her face, her neck, her breastbone. 'Fuck me,' he panted as she, too, tried to catch her breath. This was what she'd been missing—how could she have forgotten *this*? This made the world go round. Right now, it felt as though nothing else mattered.

He pulled out of her gently and raised himself up onto his elbow, grinning down at her.

'Did you like that?' he asked innocently.

A laugh rose up from deep in her belly, and she drew her fingertips down his beautiful torso. 'Oh, yes, I liked it. You definitely know what you're doing, don't you?'

'Thank you.' He smirked immodestly. 'Did you like it when I told you what I was going to do to you?'

She squirmed, grinning despite herself. 'I did.'

He splayed his fingers lightly across her stomach, and she shivered. 'You're beautiful, I find you incredibly sexy, and it was a massive turn-on for me to be the one to break your drought.'

'You were worth waiting for,' she admitted drily.

'I'm glad. Now we've broken the ice, we can have a lot more fun. You have a lot of lost time to make up for and I'm delighted to be of service.' He looked at his watch, which was still on his wrist. 'The night is young, we have this beautiful room and this very accommodating bed.' He patted it and she giggled. 'Let's have a glass of wine and then we'll go again, ok? This time I'm going to make you tell me exactly what you want, and to make it fair I'll tell you exactly what I want. Deal?'

She drank in his naked form as he hopped off the bed to shed his condom and refill their glasses. He was right; they'd broken the ice and now she felt relaxed and desirable. Gone was the toxic mix of stage-fright and desperate need that had curdled in her stomach over the past few days, and in its place sat pure, sweet anticipation. She stretched out languidly, knowing his eyes were on her, and accepted a glass of wine. 'It's a deal,' she said.

16

JENNA

She was thoroughly enjoying the pretence of being a proper grown up. It was Friday night, and rather than suffering some loud bar in Balham with her uni friends, she was sipping Bollinger and listening to dinner jazz. She sat at the breakfast bar of Jackson James' charming flat in Hans Place, a picturesque oval-shaped garden square nestled right behind Harrods, watching him expertly construct a lasagne. She'd figured him more as a floor-to-ceiling-windows type of guy, expecting a sleek, chrome-filled bachelor pad. Instead, the flat was classically elegant, with lofty, ornate ceilings and two pairs of French doors off the main living area that overlooked the leafy square. It looked to her untrained eye as if it had been decorated by an interior designer—the neutral palette was flawlessly coordinated, and the overall effect was sumptuous and serene.

The past couple of days had dragged as she waited impatiently for their sleepover. Oh, the promise of that word! It suggested mischief, indulgence, and the sheer delight of spending an entire night wrapped around him.

She'd been gratified and relieved by his amorous stunt in St Cuthbert's music room the morning after she'd slept with him—she'd told herself in no uncertain terms as she'd left the penthouse that that may have been a single night to cherish, a memory to entomb in a glass box and pour over reverently when she allowed herself. She could so easily have been consigned to the presumably ample dust-heap of his former indiscretions. But his pleasure at seeing her, mere hours after he'd left her in that bed, spoke to the power of their connection that night. He'd felt it, too.

He hadn't allowed her much time to pine in the last couple of days. He'd done every pickup and drop-off except for today, though he hadn't dragged her off to the music room on any subsequent occasion. Each time he'd left the classroom he'd followed up almost immediately with WhatsApps ranging from sweet to downright dirty, telling her how beautiful she looked that day and what he was planning to do to her when he had her to himself. Each evening, he'd called her to bid her goodnight. On Wednesday, a breathtaking bouquet of white flowers delivered to her at school from Wild at Heart had had the staffroom buzzing with speculation.

She sipped her champagne and watched him painstakingly cover the top of the lasagne with béchamel sauce and grated parmesan.

'The ragù smells divine,' she told him. 'Has it been cooking all day?'

He smiled at her. 'Five hours. I had some paperwork to do, so I did it here while it this thing simmered away. I like being here... it's peaceful and private.'

'I can see that.' She looked about her appreciatively. It was warm enough to have the French doors open, and the small space felt secluded and restorative, which must be prized attributes when you were a major celebrity. 'Does your... family come here?'

'Nope.' Carefully, he loaded the lasagne into the oven. 'This is my bolt-hole, for when it all gets too much, or I need privacy. The kids would find it weird to see Daddy in a different home, and Honour has no interest; this place is too cramped for her. She needs her vast dressing room and her three million pots and tubes of makeup to function.'

She shifted uncomfortably at his tone, and he came around the breakfast bar and put his arms around her.

'Sorry. I'm becoming one of those sleazy bastards who slags off his wife to his other woman—not cool.' He kissed her softly on the lips. 'Come on. The lasagne needs about forty-five minutes. Let's chill on the sofa for a bit and then I'll make a salad.'

Taking her hand, he led her to the sofa. Lamps dotted about the room emitted a soft glow through their pleated silk shades. She folded her legs underneath her and studied him. He'd called her his other woman. That was interesting. He hadn't said he criticised his wife to his other women. And the phrase *other woman* wore a flavour of permanency, suggesting a status that possibly warranted capital letters. Did he intend her to be his Other Woman?

She herself was besotted, out of her depth, entranced by his beauty and mesmerised by his energetic pull. *You and the rest of the world*, she told herself. He operated in an arena that bore no resemblance to her world of scratched knees and head lice, of column addition and instant coffee. He played with the big boys: he had Hollywood directors and broadsheet editors in his phone contacts, he was a UNICEF ambassador and he'd just admitted to her that Jamie Oliver had personally shown him how to make the lasagne that currently bubbled away in his oven. Jamie Oliver, for pete's sake!

Her night with him, inconceivable a few short days ago, was now recalibrated in her mind as fact, but the idea that their relationship could settle into any semblance of permanence was laughable. Wasn't it? On the other hand, this evening already felt special in an entirely different way from the hedonism of the Corinthia penthouse. That had been a performance, a grand seduction; this was easy and intimate. Presumably, if he'd just fancied screwing her again he would have booked another hotel room and breezily bid her farewell when he'd got what he wanted.

Instead, she was in his personal bolt-hole, he'd cooked for her from scratch, and he hadn't even tried to get in her pants yet. She didn't know what to think. She would go with the flow, she decided. Whoever he wanted her to be, whatever void he was trying to fill in his life, she'd be it, fill it. Not the most progressively feminist of approaches, but she was in unchartered territory.

He gazed at her and touched her arm. 'Penny for them.'

'What? Oh, sorry.' She started and smiled. 'Nothing.'

'I'm sorry I brought up Honour. It must be awkward for you.'

'It's ok. You have a family and I respect that. This is all new for me; I haven't been with a married man before.'

'I know this must be strange for you, not just the fact that I'm married and I'm Rollo's dad, but my... profile. I'm sorry I can't stroll down the street with you like normal people do; instead we have to hide out here.'

'This is perfect. There's nowhere I'd rather be,' she said shyly.

'Glad to hear that.' His grin was broad. 'The upside is I

get you all to myself.' He took her hand and the grin faltered. 'There's something I wanted to discuss with you.'

'What is it?' She felt her mouth go dry and hastily sipped her champagne.

'I told you the other night that I see other women. That's not strictly accurate. I have sex with other women. My wife knows that and, to be honest, it works for both of us. I have needs, and she's happy not to bear the brunt of those needs all the time—she's a busy, ambitious woman and she has a lot going on.'

She nodded, unsure where this was going. Was he telling her it was just sex? It sounded like he and Honour had a weird marriage; she couldn't imagine a wife accepting that her husband played away.

'Most of these hook-ups are onetime things; I don't want to complicate my life any more than I need to. But you may have noticed you haven't been able to shake me off this week.' He turned her hand over and massaged her palm with his thumb in rhythmical, circular motions. She stared at his hand on hers, transfixed.

'You've got under my skin, sweetheart. God, you're so... sweet and refreshing. When I see you with those kids, I just melt. I check Rollo's homework and you've written such beautiful words of praise and encouragement—you're like an angel. Everyone else in my life, including my dear wife, is a political animal, and you're not. I can tell you're a good person, and I feel better when I'm near you.

'I'm not trying to freak you out; I know it's only been one night. But if you're enjoying this, then do me a favour and stick around, sweetheart. I realise I'm offering you a bizarre set-up, when you probably just want a nice, normal boyfriend, but I'll do my best to make up for it in other ways. What do you think?'

Her mind was reeling. She hadn't expected any kind of declaration of intent from Jackson and here he was, offering her the chance to be his... His what? His mistress? She drank in his beautiful, anxious face and put her free hand up to stroke his stubble. That jaw... those eyes... they were searching hers intently for answers. The thought of a nice, normal boyfriend who'd take her out to the cinema was turgid beyond belief. She wanted *him*; she found him mesmerising. And he seemed to be offering himself to her. Not all of him—she'd have to share him with his wife, his kids, his fans, the press; everyone wanted a piece of him. But a piece was more than enough. A piece of him was worth more than the entirety of anyone else she could think of.

'I think,' she whispered, 'nice, normal boyfriends are over-rated.'

'I've heard they're very dull,' he said. 'And usually pretty crap in bed. Best to stay away.'

'Yep.' She kissed him. 'Especially after I've been seduced by *you*. You've ruined me.'

'Thrilled to hear it. Is that a yes? To giving it a shot?'

'It is indeed.'

He bowed his forehead to hers. 'Thank you, sweetheart. I can't wait for later. Anticipation is my favourite aphrodisiac—apart from you. Now, get off me before I throw anticipation out the window and ravish you, right here on the sofa.' He slapped her on the backside. 'We've got a salad to chop.'

PART II

OCTOBER

17

NATALIA

'I wouldn't ask you if it wasn't important.' Natalia rubbed her eyes. 'I know it stinks, but I'm desperate.'

'Nats, it's more than my job's worth. If I give you her phone number, I'm breaking the law. The firm's super-anal about this kind of stuff.'

Natalia had concluded that she had to speak to Isabella Whitney in person to understand whether Lorenzo was guilty of the charges. The investigation was dragging on and he hadn't been suspended, which was encouraging. She was worried on so many levels: he might lose his job, he'd potentially tried to cheat on her, and most importantly he could be a sexual predator. She was on the phone with his assistant at Loeb, Lottie, who'd taken on more of his personal admin over the years and to whom she'd grown close.

'I get it,' she said now. 'I just need to look her in the eye, Lotts—I truly believe that if I do, I'll get my answer. I'm at my wits' end here, and I can't talk to Lorenzo about any of it. You know what he's like.'

'Look.' Lottie's tone was softer. 'Why don't I speak to

Kyung—that's her assistant. I'll see if she thinks it's safe for me to approach Isabella. Maybe I can pass your number onto her and explain that you just want a chat? Then the ball's in her court as to whether she contacts you or not.'

'Yes, that would be amazing, thanks,' sighed Natalia. 'I don't want to pick a fight with her; I just want to talk to her, woman to woman. Hopefully she can empathise with that, at least.'

LOTTIE WAS as good as her word. Three days later, Natalia headed into the City to meet Isabella for coffee. Emerging from the Central Line at Bank, she crossed over Poultry and entered The Ned through its weighty double doors. The former bank bustled with well-heeled financiers who were doubtless sounding out deals and conducting clandestine meetings with recruiters over mid-morning coffee.

She made her way to Millie's Lounge, as Isabella had directed in their brief WhatsApp conversation. She spotted her immediately, sitting alone, head lowered over her phone, her hair falling over her face like a glossy shield. Suppressing a wave of nausea, she approached.

'Excuse me—Isabella?'

The other woman looked up and stood, extending her hand in a formal but not unfriendly manner. 'Mrs Beneventi. Isabella Whitney.'

'Please, call me Natalia.' Natalia sat down and the words tumbled out of her mouth. 'I'm so grateful you agreed to meet me. This must be really awkward for you—as it is for me. I promise you, I'm not here to make trouble.'

A waitress appeared to take their drinks order. While Isabella consulted the waitress on the tea selection, Natalia studied her. She had commendable posture, holding herself erect on the highly stuffed sofa, and far more poise than Natalia felt she herself possessed. She was beautiful, too, in a natural way, with luminous skin and fine features. She dressed older than her age, wearing a navy pantsuit that Hilary Clinton would surely approve of, though that may have been for Natalia's benefit. When she handed the menu back to the waitress, a substantial pavé-ringed solitaire flashed on her hand.

The waitress departed, Isabella fixed her with a steady look. 'I shouldn't be meeting you, but if I were in your shoes, I'd have done the same thing. So—how can I help?'

'I'm going crazy at home, not knowing what's going on with this investigation.' Natalia threw her hands up. 'I just had the idea that if I could see you, meet you, I'd get a bit of clarity.'

'What would you like to know?'

I'd like to know if you're telling the truth about my husband. 'Are you—can you bear to tell me what happened in Edinburgh? I'm sorry to have to ask you to relive it.'

'I can tell you, if you're sure you want to hear it,' Isabella said. 'Let me be clear; I'm not traumatised by what your husband did; I'm just freaking mad.

'So, we were staying at the Balmoral and we'd had drinks there with the senior fund managers from Standard Life Aberdeen. After they'd left, Lorenzo and I stayed at the bar to talk through how the day had gone, and he had another drink.'

'Was anyone else from Loeb on the trip with you?'

'No, it was just the two of us. I'd taken him up to show some love to the Scottish clients—we saw most of the big accounts and we'd put Aberdeen last on the schedule so we could take them for drinks after.'

'I'm sorry to ask—were you drinking much?'

'I'm pregnant.' Isabella's hand flew to her stomach. 'Your husband doesn't know, but I told HCM as part of my statement. I'm only ten weeks so I'm not going public with it yet.'

'Oh, God—congratulations.' Natalia hadn't realised how badly she'd wanted Isabella to have been lying until that moment. A pregnant, sober, newly-wed accuser: Lorenzo's defence was toast. Why hadn't they suspended him yet?

'Thank you. And so—no, I wasn't drinking. I made sure I ordered all the drinks that night; I was drinking soda out of tumblers so they looked like G&Ts. But the others got pretty wasted. The clients had Lorenzo trying a lot of different scotches.

'They left around nine. I was exhausted; you know how tough the first trimester is, and I'd been up at four-thirty to catch the flight up. I just wanted to go to bed, but Lorenzo insisted; he said we should have another drink and chat through the meetings before we went up.'

The waitress appeared with Isabella's herbal tea and Natalia's espresso. Once she'd deposited the drinks, Isabella continued.

'But then he started asking me about myself, about how I was enjoying married life, how I felt my promotion was going—they made me MD in last year's promotions round and, to be fair, Lorenzo had a big part in making that happen. He said he was always looking out for me and wasn't I lucky to get him to myself for the evening? He asked what was I going to do with that opportunity—are you sure you want to hear all this?'

Natalia's horror was mounting, both on her own behalf and on Isabella's, but she had to know what had happened. She took a sip of her espresso. 'If you can face telling me, then I can handle hearing it.'

'He told me he'd always been a supporter of mine but that he also found me very attractive and he thought we'd make a great team. I'm sorry—he was so vulgar. He was like, 'If you start fucking me, baby, I'll give you the world. You can have any job you want in this place'.' Isabella's mouth made a little moue.

'Then he stood up and came right up to me, and put his hand on my thigh and just—*lunged*—at me. He tried to kiss me and I—I didn't want to make a scene. We were right at the bar, you know? So I just pushed him away and said, '*No*, Lorenzo, what the hell are you doing?' and he said, 'Come up to my room and I'll fuck you into oblivion.' He was begging me, 'please, please'. He was like, 'You're so uptight. I can help you to chill the fuck out'.'

Natalia's hands were clamped over her mouth. She was appalled by how easily she could insert the image of Lorenzo in the scene that Isabella was conjuring up. 'I'm so, so sorry,' she said. How pitifully inadequate, but she'd had no training for this. 'Did he scare you?'

Isabella considered. 'He completely freaked me out, and it was horrifying, but he didn't scare me, no. I mean, we were in a public place and also, I know him pretty well so I knew I could stand up to him. But still, I didn't want to antagonise him because of some sort of respect for his seniority, I guess? I feel stupid about that now—that's how these men get what they want time and time again.

'So I just told him, 'You're wasted. This is never going to happen. I love my husband. Touch me again and I'll start screaming. Go to bed.' And I just got out of that bar as quickly as I could and called the elevator.' She rubbed her forehead and poured herself a cup of herbal tea.

'And did you report him the next day?'

'It took a couple of days. I changed my flight back. We

were supposed to fly back to City and head straight into work, so I switched to a Heathrow flight and I called my husband from Edinburgh airport and asked him to stay at home. I knew if I'd called him when I'd gone up to bed, he would have freaked out. Then when I got home on the Friday, I called in sick and Fitz—that's my husband—helped me write out an account of what had happened. Then I went in the following Monday and filed the complaint with HCM.'

'Jesus.' Natalia stared at her. There was no doubt in her mind that Isabella was telling the truth. 'Why haven't they suspended him yet?'

'I have no freaking idea.' Isabella shrugged. 'I guess because he's so senior, they don't want to take such a public step until they've investigated thoroughly. But they're running out of time. If I don't hear back from them this week, I'm going to escalate it.' She leant forward. 'Here's the thing. I've had my fair share of drunken guys come onto me; I can handle myself. But it's the abuse of power. I mean, what if it had been one of my graduates in that position? What if he'd offered them a promotion or threatened them if they wouldn't sleep with him? I'm pretty sure they wouldn't have felt as comfortable as I did telling him where to get off. He's so senior, for chrissakes; he runs the goddamn division. And using that position to trade sex for career moves—seriously? It's completely unacceptable. I'm sorry, but he has to go.'

'I'm as appalled as you are,' Natalia said, 'but can I ask you something: do you think it was the booze talking?'

'Oh, for sure,' Isabella said. 'But that doesn't make it ok.'

'No, no, of course it doesn't. But had you had—vibes—from him before that night?'

'Vibes, yes.' Isabella hesitated. 'But nothing that's

crossed the line. I mean, we get on well. He's been flirtatious in the past, but I've chosen to overlook it. I've never, ever given him any signals but I do suck it up and I have, until now, always made an effort to engage with him and to be on his radar. There's still such an old-boys' club going on at Loeb. So I was actually looking forward to getting some quality time with him in Edinburgh—I just got a lot more than I bargained for. I can overlook drunken indiscretions. But sexual abuse of power is a whole other ball-game.'

Natalia studied the woman who was seemingly the object of her husband's desire. It was odd to side with a stranger over the man she slept next to most nights. She quashed a faint, patronising urge to tell her she was proud of her. Isabella was how she hoped Valentina and Ilaria would turn out; assured and self-sufficient. That was the best defence against men like Lorenzo: to be self-confident enough to reject out of hand whatever twisted quid pro quo they offered. But they shouldn't have to defend themselves, for Christ's sake. It wasn't okay to have a culture where master's degrees and handmade suits provided a sufficient veneer of respectability to allow men to prey on those professionally beholden to them.

She was looking forward to it. She would sit in the front row and cheer while her husband was stripped of the trappings that had facilitated his predatory behaviour. She'd watch as he was forced to learn that his own desire did not guarantee his targets' reciprocal feelings, nor did it deem their feelings irrelevant to the situation. She'd cheer as if it wasn't her marriage, and her daughters' innocence, unravelling right alongside Lorenzo's career.

18

ASTRID

'Seriously, you have to let me drive this beauty. Please, baby!'

Astrid and Callum were in her driveway in Holland Park, bags stashed in the boot of her silver DB10. It was four-thirty on a Friday afternoon and they were taking advantage of Tabby's weekend with her father to get out of London. Callum had turned up straight from school, still wearing his Chiltern House hoodie and those ridiculous, snug navy shorts. He looked positively edible. He was hopping around the driveway like a small boy, enchanting her with his wide grin as he drooled over her Aston Martin.

She laughed. 'You think I'd trust you with my newest toy?'

He drew her into his arms and kissed her neck. 'You trust me with your daughter, five days a week. Are you saying the car's more important to you than Tabby? Fuck me, you smell good. Mmm.'

He must think she was being a control-freak over the car. She was, but not because she cared about denting it. Since she and Mark had divorced her anxiety over keeping herself safe had grown. She was now her daughter's primary carer; she was one cancer diagnosis or car crash away from ruining Tabby's life. Some of her most noxious, intrusive thoughts pertained to driving. It was Friday afternoon; the M40 was likely to be full of jackasses in a rush to get out of London.

When she was behind the wheel, she could control her own reactions, even if she couldn't control how anyone else drove. She could stick to the speed limit and avoid other cars as much as possible. Letting an overexcited thirty-year-old behind the wheel of a fast car would mean ceding a level of control that she wasn't used to granting to any third party.

He was kissing her properly now, his tongue moving urgently in her mouth as he pressed her to him. She grabbed onto his hair and melted into him, savouring the sensation of his body against hers, his smell, his taste. They'd had several more evenings together at the Connaught, each one more carefree and familiar than the last—especially since she'd had her coil reinstalled. Now, they just met up in the room, had great, uninhibited sex, and then ordered room-service. They ate black-truffle pizza in the bath or while watching crappy TV.

The delight of their trysts was spilling over into other areas of her life, too. His mantra for life seemed to be *fuck it*. He didn't overthink, or stress over what-ifs. He gave the girls at school the benefit of his boundless energy and positivity, and seemed to have plenty of both left over for himself. This was in contrast to Astrid, who regularly felt like a vessel whom work and parenting had poured dry. She found herself attempting to emulate his breezy nature when she wasn't with him. Perhaps if she could fake it enough, she'd trick her psyche into chilling out.

The car would be a sound way to test out her capacity to unwind a little. After all, it was insured for anyone to drive. She reluctantly pulled away from him, alarmingly aroused.

'Ok.' She held out the keys. 'I'm not sure I'm in a fit state to drive after that kiss. You can drive as long as you have your driver's licence with you.'

'Yesss.' He grabbed the keys and kissed her on the lips. 'Excellent decision, baby. I won't be a dick; I promise. I know I have precious cargo. You're in safe hands.'

THEY ROLLED up Marstrand's sweeping, up-lit driveway two hours later. There was something about the crunch of tyres on gravel that always signalled home. An elegant manor house just outside Chipping Norton, it had long Georgian windows that cast a golden glow onto the gravel. Its honeyed Cotswolds stone was home to ancient, gnarled wisteria whose feathery clusters were turning amber.

This was Astrid's refuge, named for the beautiful Swedish coastal town of Marstrand where she'd spent every summer as a girl. She and Tabby came here as much as they could to escape from London's incessant demands. It was the first time she'd come here alone with another adult, let alone a thirty-year-old adonis. She watched Callum's mouth open in appreciation as he took in the view. He slid the car smoothly to a halt.

'Jeez. This place is stunning. Fair play—you have a good set of homes. And this car... I think I just died and went to heaven. She's almost as good a ride as you.'

'You're a true gentleman. But you did a nice job of driving; got us here in one piece.' He was an excellent driver, but she wouldn't tell him that. It had been surprisingly fun to sit back and enjoy the journey, as well as his obvious delight at being behind the wheel. Traffic had been on their side, and they'd chased the sunset through the Chilterns.

'Come on.' She brushed his forearm. 'If you can bear to drag yourself away from the car, supper awaits.'

'Is someone here?' he asked, leaping out of the car and stretching. She loved how unselfconsciously he did that. He'd shed his hoodie, and his stomach flashed below his school polo.

'I have a housekeeper who lives locally—Sheila.' She popped open the boot. 'When we come down here, she gets the house ready ahead of time and pops something nice in the Aga.'

'Yum,' he said. 'I'm starving. But I could do with a shower first.'

'That I can help with.'

She opened the front door and he followed with their bags. The entrance hall was a large square; paintings clustered the walls and fresh flowers adorned the central table. The scent of Boeuf bourguignon wafted tantalisingly through from the kitchen at the rear of the house. She led him up the shallow staircase that snaked around the sides of the hallway, and into the master bedroom. In the morning, Callum could admire the view out to the pool and beyond; for now, the curtains were drawn, the bed turned back, and a fire crackled merrily in the grate. Not for the first time, she gave silent thanks for Sheila's diligence.

She gestured, slightly awkwardly, to the bathroom door. 'The shower's through there,' she told him. It was one thing to hook up with him in hotel rooms, but bringing him here, to her and Tabby's precious bolt-hole, was akin to peeling off another layer of her armour.

He strolled over and put his arms around her, kissing

her head. 'I'm a lucky bastard, to be here with you,' he said. 'I know that. Will you shower with me?'

Of course she'd shower with him—anything to feel his skin on hers after three days apart. In the bathroom, she cranked down the weighty shower handle and water gushed from the oversized shower head. He'd already torn off his top, shoes and socks and stood before her in his shorts.

'I have a thing about these shorts.' She ran her finger along the inside of his waistband. 'May I?'

He grinned at her. 'What kind of thing do you have for them, pray tell?'

'That day when you bandaged my ankle.' She squirmed under his amused gaze. 'I was quite distracted by your shorts. They're very snug—quite unsuitable for a teacher, in my opinion.'

He pulled her towards him and whispered, 'Well, Mrs Carmichael, in my opinion I should feel safe to do my job without being objectified by predatory parents. I've a good mind to report you to Miss Clark.'

'You'll be out on your ear if you do.' She reached around and slid the shorts, and his boxers, down over his thighs. 'And I wasn't responsible for my actions. Not with this bum in those shorts.'

'Don't joke. She did send around a memo at the start of term, reminding us that if we shagged the parents we'd get fired. It was a scream. I'd say there's plenty of it going on, wouldn't you?'

'Definitely.' Astrid was desperately tugging off her jeans. 'She needs to reconsider her hiring policy if she thinks I'm going to stay away from you. Look at you.' She sighed.

'I'm all yours, beautiful.'

He lifted her and she wrapped her legs around his waist as he stepped into the shower. A blast of boiling water hit them and she tipped her head back in pleasure. Callum bent his head and kissed her neck and breasts. She squeezed out some shower gel and massaged it slowly into his back, across his shoulders and down his arms, luxuriating in the sensation of his supple body under her fingers.

Wriggling out of his arms, she stood and ran her soaped-up hand under his balls and up the length of his erection. He groaned, kissing her hungrily, his hands clamped over her ears and jaw. No matter how inappropriate or short-lived this relationship might be, right now he was, as he'd said, all hers. The reassurance was powerful, but at the back of her mind sat the kernel of certainty that she was even more deeply in his thrall than he was in hers. She pushed the thought further back and revelled in the knowledge that right now, being inside her was the only thing on his mind.

'You're so beautiful,' he groaned. 'Turn around for me.' She turned, spreading out her hands against the marble, arching her back and grinding her backside against him. Her senses were overwhelmed: the steam intensified the botanical scent of the shower-gel, water roared past her ears and pelted her body, and everywhere her skin touched his felt molten.

'I want to try something with you. Hang on, baby.' He picked the smaller hand-shower attachment off the wall. 'Can I get both these showers to work at the same time?'

'Mm-hm.' She yanked a lever and the second shower burst into life.

He eased into her and started to move, slowly, behind her. One hand, splayed across her stomach, held her to him, and with the other, he aimed the handheld shower and flicked the spray over her nipples.

She convulsed. 'Oh my God!'

'Ok?' he asked. 'Not too much pressure?'

She shook her head, and he aimed the shower-head at her breasts again, lingering on each nipple until she thought she would cry out. Then, moving it lower, he aimed the jet of water directly at her clitoris.

'Ah!' Sensation consumed her, and she writhed against him.

'It's not sore, is it?' He took the nozzle away and thrust against her.

'No, no! Keep doing it!' She leant further into him. Her legs were shaking like crazy; she tried to focus on keeping herself upright and her hands on the wall.

'Stay still, baby,' he panted. 'You're doing grand—I'm as close as you are.' He held her tightly in place while he aimed the flow of water directly, mercilessly, at her clitoris. Her feeling of pure bliss escalated swiftly until the pressure of the water and of him inside her sent her over the edge and she exploded around him, crying out. He dropped the shower attachment and wrapped both arms around her to hold her up as he came.

After he'd withdrawn, she sank to the floor and sat on the shower tray, letting the torrent of water cascade over her. 'Oh my God,' she said. 'Oh my God! What the hell was that?! Jesus.' She wiped her hands over her face.

He crouched down and sat next to her, pulling her into his arms. 'That was you, baby' he said. 'You're amazing. Fuck, I love coming inside you.'

She grabbed his face with both hands and kissed him deeply. 'I had no idea that was a thing—I'll never be able to look at a shower the same way again. Especially not *this* shower.'

He laughed. 'Happy to help. Maybe I should start a blog. *Callum's Handy Household Hints*, like.'

'Well, if Mrs Clark fires you for having your wicked way

with the mothers, it could be a good alternative career for you.'

'Not mothers. Just you.' He smoothed her hair away from her face and rubbed her nose with his.

DOWNSTAIRS, the kitchen was wonderfully cosy, thanks to the Aga. They sat at the table in bathrobes and devoured the boeuf bourguignon with fluffy baked potatoes and sauteed greens. Sheila had decanted a bottle of claret at Astrid's request, and it flowed silkily through her mouth. She felt like a rag-doll—floppy with relaxation, happiness and post-coital sleepiness.

Callum was shovelling up his food. It was lovely having him here; his breezy manner precluded any awkwardness that might have arisen at their first weekend away together —in fact, their first overnight stay—and his childish enthusiasm, at everything from the house and car to the food and her, was infectious. While she loved being here with Tabby, she was always in her role of Mummy. With Callum, she felt like a carefree teenager.

When they'd stuffed themselves to the brim, they moved into the drawing room with the remains of the wine and a large bar of dark chocolate, and sat on the floor before the enormous fireplace, backs against the sofa. Callum had his arm around her, and her damp head was on his shoulder.

She snapped a piece of chocolate off the slab. 'Can I ask you a question?'

'Sure,' he murmured.

'How did you get to be so good in bed?'

'Seriously?' He sat up straighter and she raised her head and looked at his grinning face.

'Seriously. You're bloody fantastic. Is it just instinct, or... I mean, how do you know all those tricks you do to me?'

'Well, I watch a lot of porn in the staffroom between lessons.'

Her face must have been a picture, for he laughed and planted a kiss on her forehead. 'Of course I don't. Not in the staffroom, anyway. I don't know... I guess practice makes perfect.'

She shoved him and pulled the chocolate bar away from him.

'You must get a lot of girls—looking like that.'

'I like sex.' He shrugged. 'A lot. But most of the women I date are in their twenties, and I think you'd be surprised how knowledgeable they are around sex. I can't get by on my looks. They know exactly what they want and they'll tell me straight up what I need to do to get them off, or how they want me to talk to them to turn them on... I'm telling you, it's an education! But if it's given me a few tricks that light you up in bed, then I'm glad I've been paying attention in class.'

It felt strange to be talking to this man, sleeping with him, in the knowledge that his sexual landscape was so different from hers. He operated in an arena with gloriously empowered millennial and Gen Z women who probably brought their vibrators along to dates, and she'd been celibate for two years and monogamous before that. It was intimidating to know she was just one stroke on the vivid canvas of his sex life, while he already dominated hers.

'It's amazing,' she said. 'We thought we were liberated compared to our mothers, but women my age still have so many hang-ups about sex. Can I ask you something?' She picked at an imaginary speck of fluff on the carpet.

'Shoot, baby.'

'Why are you with me then—instead of these empowered twenty-something sexual animals?' It was what she'd been wanting to ask him since he'd first kissed her in her garden. It didn't make sense.

'Surely that's obvious,' he said. 'They don't have DBios. Come here.'

He pulled her onto his lap and wrapped his arms around her. 'Baby, you're more beautiful than most of those girls will ever be. Seriously, you're fucking stunning. I asked Bex Oliver about you as soon as I'd finished strapping that gorgeous ankle of yours. You can check with her; she teased me about it.

'Also, those girls are so fucking predictable. Honestly. All they care about is posing for Instagram or making a TikTok video—you have no idea how many TikTok videos I've had to record. It's all about their image; nothing's ever real. Even in the gym; they're always looking over their shoulders in the mirror, snapping their fucking silicone arses. I've literally never seen you pull your phone out when you're with me.'

It was true—when she was with him she was completely immersed; she couldn't wait to turn her phone off and be unreachable to everyone but him.

'I guess your age is part of the attraction for me,' he went on. 'Well, not your age exactly, but where you are in life. You've built a massive company, and you're a mother, you've raised a gorgeous little kid, and you're always in the press. You make it look so effortless, Astrid. You're like Grace fucking Kelly, all glossy and expensive and successful, with your silky dresses and high heels and I... I get to go past all that. Do you have any idea how turned on I get from seeing you at school or on Instagram, all glammed up and looking like an ice-queen, and knowing I'm allowed to shatter that disguise, and rip off those gorgeous dresses, and see the real you? It's fucking unbelievable watching you come apart in my hands.'

He saw the mask for what it was, and he'd seen what was behind it, and he hadn't run. He liked it—more than liked it. She hadn't had him down as a particularly profound guy, but it was incredibly moving that he saw her true self.

He slipped a hand inside her robe and stroked her stomach unbearably softly. His eyes bored into hers. 'Because you are not an ice-queen, baby; you are as hot-blooded as they fucking come. And I get to be the one to enjoy that.'

19

JENNA

The axe fell swiftly and devastatingly.

One minute, she was wrapping up the maths lesson and waving her small charges outside for fifteen minutes of horseplay. The next, a call from the secretary informed her that the headmaster, Mike Hopkins, would like to see her. She headed down, wondering if he'd perhaps had a chance to consider her recent request for time off to train as a SENCO, or Special Educational Needs Coordinator.

When she walked into the office, he was stony faced.

'Sit down, please, Jenna.' He gestured to a chair in front of his desk. As soon as she was sitting, he said, 'I'm afraid I have a serious matter to discuss with you. It's come to my attention that you are conducting a sexual relationship with one of our parents, Mr James.'

It was extraordinary how quickly her body betrayed her. Her mouth was instantly dry; her cheeks and temples throbbed with an onslaught of blood. She didn't know what to say. Deny it? No point. Who the hell had told him? Apologise? Seek forgiveness? Yes. It was much better to hold her hands up in this situation.

'It's true,' she said. 'I am. I'm sorry, Mike—'

He held up a hand, cutting her off. 'You're aware, I'm sure, that any kind of sexual relations with a parent is grounds for dismissal?'

The bile rose in her throat as her head swam with the implications of what he was saying. 'I'm aware of the policy, yes, but I've been careful to keep the relationship separate from my role here.'

Could Jackson protect her, if it came down to it? He seemed even more smitten than she was; he'd taken the lead at every step. Surely, if he put his foot down, the school would back off from threatening her job? He was their highest profile parent, after all, and most likely their most generous donor.

Mike grimaced as he made a fist and pounded the table. She flinched.

'For God's sake, Jenna. You've put me in an impossible position. You're one of the most promising teachers here and I have no choice but to let you go, effective immediately.'

'Mike, seriously—please, please reconsider,' she blurted. 'I know I've messed up; I'm so sorry. I can—maybe I can change classes, so I'm not teaching Rollo any more? I adore this place; it's my whole life.'

'Jenna. My hands are tied here. I don't want to lose you but the James family have put their foot down and they want you gone immediately, or they pull Rollo out.'

The James family? 'What do you mean, the family? You mean this is coming from Jackson?' She was crying now, trying to stem the tears with her hands, black trails of mascara crawling down her forefinger.

'It's Mrs James.' Mike's voice was softer, and he handed her a box of tissues. 'I don't want to get too involved in the sordid details of their personal lives, but it seems she's found out about you both and hit the roof. I had a rather unpleasant conversation with her on the phone first thing this morning. She's made it clear you're to go, and I have no defence against that argument, Jenna. What you've done amounts to gross professional misconduct. It's an abuse of your position.'

'An abuse of my—' Jenna gasped. 'It was all Jackson! He pursued me. He told me she didn't care, that they had an open relationship... Can't you speak to him about this, see if he can overrule her? At the end of the day, we're both consenting adults.'

'I can't. I'm afraid their lawyer is sitting outside right now, waiting to speak to you. He has a proposal for you, I believe. And as far as I understand, he represents both Mr and Mrs James.'

It was like a blow to the stomach. Only two nights ago, Jackson had been wrapped around her in their Hans Place refuge, making love to her, whispering to her and never breaking eye contact as he moved inside her.

'What happens now?' she said. She took another tissue from the box and tucked the sodden one up her sleeve.

'I must formally notify you that your employment here has been terminated.' Mike steepled his fingers. 'You'll need to leave the premises as soon as you're finished with the James' lawyer. You can use this room. I'll have someone fetch your things from 3P and the staffroom, and leave them at reception for you.'

'What about a reference—will I be able to work again? There's nothing else I want to do, Mike.'

'They can't stop me giving you a reference,' he said.

'You're a wonderful teacher—passionate and instinctive—and you would have made a great SENCO here. I will, of course, reflect all that in any reference I'm asked for. But I'm still furious, Jenna. I'm livid with you for jeopardising everything for that bloody man, and I'm deeply unhappy with the way they've forced my hand here. I really hope you can salvage something from this mess.'

He stood and held out his hand. 'Keep me posted on your next chapter.'

THE MAN who now sat across from her was large, blonde, with an expensive-looking suit. He may have had a law degree, but his role was most likely nearer to that of a fixer. So, this was how the rich and famous handled their dirty work. Since she'd met Jackson, she'd felt as though she was in a parallel universe; it had quickly turned dystopian. She couldn't equate the caring, attentive man who'd swept her up in his passion with someone who'd use a lawyer to get rid of her—and ruin her career into the bargain. This made the ex who'd once dumped her on WhatsApp look positively gallant.

The lawyer's name was Alex Draycott, and he mansplained to her, slowly enough that her seven-year-old pupils could have understood, that the NDA he slid in front of her should have been signed right at the beginning of her 'dealings' with Jackson.

'This was an oversight on the part of Mr James,' he assured her, smoothly. 'It's very standard for people with the James family's profile.'

She had no intention of publicly sharing any of the

details of her and Jackson's relationship, but his presumption that she would galled her.

She crossed her arms. She'd just been sacked; he was picking a fight with the wrong woman. 'Then that's an unfortunate oversight, isn't it?' she shot back.

A ghost of a smirk. 'The family very much regrets that your career has been any way inconvenienced by your dealings with them, and they've furnished me with the authority to compensate you on their behalf.'

He slid a cheque across the table, and she picked it up. Fifty grand! That was two years' salary. Her eyebrows shot up as she looked at him. His smirk widened.

'It's a very generous offer.'

She examined the cheque. It was in the name of, and signed by, Ms Honour Chapman.

She waved it at him. 'What's Jackson's role in this? Is he even aware of what's going on?' A shot of hope, futile or not, flew through her. Perhaps Jackson had been left out of the loop; perhaps this move was Honour's alone.

'Don't read any significance into the signatory,' he snapped. 'I can assure you this offer comes from both Mr *and* Mrs James. I sat down with them both in person this morning.'

God. The pain was intolerable. Jackson had WhatsApped her when he woke up this morning at 6am. His usual—*Good morning gorgeous. I miss you xx*. They had their standing plan for a quiet evening in Hans Place this coming Friday. It would have been their sixth night together. He had to have been blindsided by Honour on this. And yet, if this guy was to be believed, he'd stood by and watched while his wife handed their lawyer an NDA and a cheque in Jenna's name. He'd chosen Honour, and his reputation as an all-round, decent family guy, over her. It shouldn't have come as a surprise. It wasn't a surprise. She felt like a grubby, foolish, star-struck little girl. She'd been seduced with style and speed, and then spat out equally stylishly and speedily, by a master.

She blew her nose again. 'Give me the pen,' she muttered.

As she walked down a damp, slippery Kings Road, she couldn't resist one last attempt to contact him. She hit the call button by his name and was informed by a robot lady that the number she'd dialled had not been recognised. Wow. His henchmen didn't mess around when they cleaned up his dirty work. He was everywhere, on every newsstand, and yet in the real world he'd vanished. He was a mirage.

The next morning, she sat in her flat alone. Cups of cold tea surrounded her, the milk curdling grimly on their surfaces. The doorbell rang. It was a Harrods deliveryman with a box that contained an enormous, plush teddy bear and a postcard of Nelson's column. She recognised his scrawl from that first note he'd sent her in Rollo's homework. It said:

I am more sorry than you will ever know.

You are perfect.

The bear is a lucky bastard.

Jx

She climbed wearily back onto the sofa and pulled the dratted bear down next to her. Wrapping her arms around it, she bawled into its velvety neck.

20

NATALIA

Three days after her eye-opening conversation with Isabella, Lorenzo was suspended.

The following week, two more women came forward.

Two more women.

One was the long-standing assistant on the futures desk. The other was a twenty-six-year-old associate.

She was sick to her stomach.

Lottie called her to fill her in on the details. As soon as he'd been suspended, the Equities trading floor had lit up with speculation on the nature of his disgrace. Isabella had apparently maintained a dignified silence in public, but Lottie'd heard from Kyung that Isabella had rounded up all the women on the institutional sales desk and had a private word with them, emphasising that if anyone had suffered at the hands of Lorenzo or other colleagues, they should have no qualms about coming forward.

'What are the others accusing him of?' Natalia asked her wearily. She trudged up to Valentina's attic bedroom to ensure she was out of earshot from Lorenzo.

'It sounds similar to Isabella—unwanted attention, propositioning, offering career opportunities in exchange for putting out, and groping.'

God. Lorenzo seemed to spend his days walking around the trading floor, grabbing people's arses, leering at them over mentoring coffees and trying to lure them into bed with offers of promotions.

'Jesus, Lotts. And who are the women who've come forward? Do you know them?'

'Emily's a friend of mine—she's the assistant on the futures desk. She's a very attractive blonde; comes from Bromley; she's been here since she was eighteen. She always looks immaculate; puts the rest of us to shame. She's made the odd passing comment to me about Lorenzo being a bit pervy, but I didn't know the full extent of it. Apparently he's pressed himself up against her at the coffee machine before, and she said once when she was getting him to sign some paperwork in his office, he put his hand up her skirt.'

'Good God!' Who was this brute she'd married, and why the fuck did he feel he needed to get his kicks from unwilling participants at work? 'And the other woman?'

'She's an associate on the cash trading desk. We hired her from Credit Suisse last year. The word is—'

'The word is what? You can tell me.' She wasn't sure Lottie could shock her anymore.

'The word is she did actually sleep with him. I'm so sorry, my dear.'

Natalia inhaled sharply. Part of her wasn't surprised. A small, twisted fragment of her brain had been wondering why all these women seemed to have rejected Lorenzo. He was classically good-looking, debonair, with a killer smile. He was also very senior, and in the corporate world, power was still a potent aphrodisiac. It was a currency men like

Lorenzo had always traded in. Perhaps the women who'd come forward were the tip of the iceberg: perhaps scores of them had said yes, and were quite happy with the bargain they'd struck.

'What do I need to know about her?' she asked now.

Lottie sighed down the phone. Her attempts at discretion were less valiant now that Lorenzo's suspension was public news.

'She's called Lara. Lara Sugarman. She trades the telecoms sector. The word is she's slept with him a couple of times, and she's claiming he told her he could make a promotion to VP happen more quickly.'

The machinations of her brain were exhausting her. She thanked Lottie, hung up, and lay down on Valentina's neatly made single bed. The pillow was crisply comforting, and smelt of her daughter. Lara Sugarman. The little slut. She tried to imagine her: perky, firm-bodied, a swingy ponytail, trading and making markets with aplomb. Was she a slut—was that fair? She'd screwed a married man. But a lot of these women considered men like Lorenzo fair game, and, at the end of the day, he was the one who was married; he was the one breaking his vows (as well as firm policy).

Since he'd been suspended, she and Lorenzo had upheld an uneasy truce. He was in a foul mood and seemed intent on playing the victim. He was either delusional or trying to wrong-foot her. Well, there'd be no more of that, buddy.

She trudged downstairs to the basement where he was working out in their home gym. He must have an excess of energy to expend in lieu of having a trading-floor-full of women to screw. He was giving the rowing machine a pummelling; he looked up questioningly when she got to the foot of the stairs.

'Does the name Lara Sugarman ring a bell?' she spat out. 'Or Emily, the futures desk assistant? I hear they've both slapped you with formal complaints too.'

He scowled at her and slid to a halt. 'Fucking Lottie,' he said. 'I'll have her fired when I get back; that women's lack of discretion is a disgrace.'

'I'd put good money on Lottie being at Loeb long after you,' she said. 'Stop lying to yourself. And stop fucking lying to me. I'm your wife. *Talk to me.* Just... tell me your side of things. You can't make my opinion of you any worse than it is right now, believe me.'

She dropped onto the sofa and folded her arms. 'Well?'

He sighed, and picking up a towel, came to sit heavily beside her. He was drenched in sweat; she passed him his water-bottle.

'Thanks, *cara*,' he said, still panting, his expression softening from outright hostility to uneasy affection. 'Ok.' He held his hands out in surrender. 'Let's talk. What do you want to know?'

'Tell me the truth. I know you slept with Lara. I know you assaulted Emily, and you came onto Isabella and offered her a promotion.'

His eyebrows shot up at her mention of Isabella's name, and she jerked her chin defensively away. 'I have my sources.'

He seemed to be weighing something up. 'I'll tell you, but I need you not to overreact, Nats. I have enough on my plate at the moment.'

The cheek of the man. God forbid she should feel a need to rage or grieve because, through no fault of her own, her husband was a cheat and a predator. Her hands fisted in her lap and she noticed she still had her apron on. She felt like his skivvy, not his wife. She yanked at the ties and pulled it over her head.

'Just tell me,' she said in a small voice.

He put down the water bottle and started to count on his fingers. *He ran Equities, and he needed his fingers to help him keep track of his victims at work? Jesus.*

'Lara pursued me from the start, as soon as we hired her. It was all her. I'm not a saint, Nats; I wasn't going to turn that down. She made it very clear she was interested. So, yes, I fucked her a few times.'

She flinched. Never had she expected to be sitting down with her husband, discussing women he'd casually 'fucked' during their marriage. For some reason, she imagined Lara to look like Mark Carmichael's fiancée Juliana: dark and glossy and lithe. 'Did you offer her a promotion?' she asked.

He shrugged, dismissively. 'That was just to keep her onside. She was getting a bit unhinged.'

'And Emily? She said you molested her in your office.'

He threw back his head and laughed. 'Oh, for fuck's sake. She's always all over me. So I made a move and she flipped out. It would seem I misread her very mixed signals.'

'What about Isabella?' she asked.

He shifted uneasily. 'She's attractive and we have a good spark. I thought we could have some fun together, even if she is way too uptight about work. But again... apparently not.'

She'd been concerned about what impact Lorenzo's actions would have on their daughters, but now she was struck by a wave of relief that they didn't have a son. Imagine trying to overcompensate for the twisted model of manhood his father provided.

'You do understand, don't you,' she said, 'why what you've done is so wrong? It doesn't matter how much someone flirts with you, or how attractive you find them; you don't get to grope them or... inflict yourself on them. And you're their boss! At the end of the day, they're under your care. They need to know their career is safe to flourish without you pressurising them into sex!'

It was uncomfortably like talking to an adolescent boy who couldn't see beyond the end of his dick.

'Look,' he said. 'You're overreacting. 'They're big girls. They're free to say yes or no. There are lots of people in the city getting it on without bloody Human Capital Management breathing down their necks. We're all grown-ups. I don't play God with anyone's careers; I just take advantage of opportunities when they present themselves.'

'So, while I've been bringing up the girls and keeping house for you, you've been screwing your way around the city over the last decade?'

'Nobody's forced you to stay at home, Natalia. And obviously I didn't want these two worlds to collide. I love you and the girls very much. What I get up to at work really should have no impact on you—that was the theory, anyway.'

She stared at him, and he met her eyes defiantly.

'How can you say it should have no impact on me? You sleep with other women! I haven't even looked at another man since we started dating!'

It was as if they were operating in two different relationships with opposing rules—somehow, people like him and Mark got the memo that work was a fertile hunting-ground as long as their wives remained oblivious.

He sighed, as if she were a small child with whom Daddy was bored of having an irrational, circular conversation.

'Natalia. I know this must all be a lot to process, and I'm

sorry. I'm sorry if I've hurt you, and I'm sorry you've had to find out this way. But you have a good life and this is a pretty happy marriage, I'd say. So before you get on your moral high horse and say something you'll regret, I'd think carefully about what concessions you're willing to make for this lifestyle. Every marriage has its compromises. And meanwhile, I'll focus on making this mess at work go away so your Amex can still get magically paid off every month. Now, if you'll excuse me, I'm going to finish my workout.'

She watched, stunned into silence, as he strolled back over to the rowing machine and straddled it. Its rhythmic whirring filled the room as she stumbled upstairs, eyes pricking with humiliated tears. She had a real, live monster in her basement. She just needed to find a way to evict him.

21

NATALIA

She spent the rest of the school-day obsessively cleaning out the kitchen cupboards. It was that or collapse on her bed with a bottle of wine while weeping over their family photo albums. She rearranged mugs, threw out a bottle of red wine vinegar that was two years out of date—how? She was a militant housekeeper—and ruthlessly erased every trace of ground cumin or nutmeg from the shelves. Her blood boiled. Anger was far more welcome than heartbreak. She wondered if he was an actual, clinical sociopath. He seemed so unmoved by the pain he'd caused her or these other women that it was genuinely freaky.

And tonight were the fucking Year 3 mums' drinks. Of all the nights to have to socialise. She had zero interest in going, but as the class rep and organiser of the event, she had no choice. It would be a comfort to talk to Astrid, at least. Their situations were different—Astrid had been cast aside by Mark, while Lorenzo had apparently been happy to have his cake and eat it—but she knew Astrid would understand in a way few others could. They could drink away the memory of their sleazy, philandering husbands together.

Besides, she wanted the name of Astrid's divorce lawyer. She couldn't bear to have Lorenzo in her bed or fathering their daughters full time. Her heart hurt at the pain this would cause them, even if she'd withhold the details from them for as many years as she could. But there was no coming back from this; she couldn't expose them to his disposable attitude towards women, and even more importantly, she couldn't model wifely behaviour that involved standing by your man when he betrayed you and your fellow females.

SHE GOT to Chucs on Westbourne Grove at exactly seven-thirty. They'd taken over the lower-ground area of this Notting Hill stalwart, a chic, nautically themed restaurant and wine bar. She'd WhatsApped Astrid to fill her in on the bare bones of her situation and ask her to come early. She was already there, bless her. And she looked incredible. Tight jeans under grey suede thigh-high boots made her legs look endless. Her sweater was pale grey cashmere, with a snug fit and a huge cowl-neck. She seemed softer, more relaxed than usual—it must be her hair. She had it down, for a change, and it framed her face in pale golden waves.

Natalia sketched an outline of Lorenzo's misdeeds while they got stuck into the Sancerre. Other women arrived, but the resolute commas of their bodies as they sat huddled on a leather banquette bought them some privacy.

'Shit,' Astrid said when she'd paused. 'I'm so sorry, Nats. Ugh, you must be sick to your stomach.'

She shuddered. 'I am. I haven't even had time to process

the fact that he's been cheating on me; it's the idea of him prevailing on these women who've had to suck it up because they were scared of what would happen if they made a fuss… I can't believe the father of my daughters would inflict himself on women like that.'

'It makes me wonder about Mark,' Astrid said slowly. 'I mean, I always thought it was sleazy of him to hook up with Juliana—she's so much younger than him. And obviously I was devastated; for me it was about being cast aside for a younger model—that old cliché. But I didn't really consider how inappropriate it was of him to date a subordinate in his own company. It doesn't make him that different from Lorenzo, except that obviously it was consensual.'

'Well, Mark's legitimised the whole thing with a big fat diamond, so now their relationship's acceptable in whatever circles they choose to move in.' Natalia sloshed more wine into their glasses. 'But, you know, one of the girls did sleep with Lorenzo—the trader. Was that really consensual, even if she put out at the time?'

'Just because she said yes—or even if she pursued him—it doesn't make it ok,'said Astrid. 'He's still her ultimate boss; he still calls the shots on her career. So it's a gross abuse of power on his part—he can't be allowed to go around screwing young women and then having the authority to play God.'

'Do you think Mark knew?'

'Probably. They probably bragged about it to each other. God, how the hell did we make such terrible errors of judgement with our husbands?'

'They're both hot, and very charming, when they want to be,' Natalia said. 'We got sucked in. But never again. I might join a convent.'

'I heard a new phrase the other day,' Astrid said. 'Heteropessimism. I thought it was priceless.'

'Heteropessimism.' Natalia tried it out. 'That's brilliant. I feel very bloody heteropessimistic right now, because men are just so bloody disappointing.' She was really guzzling her wine. She needed to be careful. But the anger was shifting in her belly into something heady and galvanising. It would dissolve when she got home, but for now she'd take it.

'They're not all bad,' Astrid said. She gave Natalia a knowing smile.

Natalia sat up straighter. 'Astrid. Do you have some gossip for me? Are you seeing someone?'

'Kind of,' Astrid said. 'Well, I think it's just sex, but it's sex that makes me feel pretty hetero-optimistic right now.'

Natalia stared at her. 'Who the hell is he?'

'I can't tell you. Sorry. He's completely inappropriate, and much younger than me. But it's a lot of fun. I'm seeing him later this evening.'

'Booty call, eh? You lucky cow! Is that why you're so disgustingly glowy tonight?'

'It must be. Maybe they should prescribe him on the NHS. Honestly, he's perfection.' She glanced at her phone and covered her giggles with her hand.

Natalia was open-mouthed. 'Is that him? Is he sexting you?'

'Kind of.' Astrid wouldn't meet her eyes, but continued to chuckle away as she typed on her phone. This was fascinating. Two years on, and Astrid was glowing and giggling—she looked like a different person from the tense, sedate woman who usually showed up at the school gates. Natalia felt a stab of envy, before realising that this was a good thing for her, too—it meant there was light at the end of the tunnel that was a marriage break-down. Even if it was likely to be a long and painful tunnel.

'Good for you,' she said. She meant it. 'Honestly, have one for me tonight. You look pretty loved-up, Astrid. Are you sure it's just sex?'

Astrid's lovely face twisted. 'No,' she said. 'Not for me, anyway. He just—he lights me up. But I can't see a future in it, and I think what we have right now is quite enough for him. I don't want to frighten him off. So we'll have to see. Anyway,'—she slipped her phone into her bag and turned to Natalia—'let's not talk about my illicit affair anymore. Let's talk about you. Have you considered getting a job?'

'A job?' She was taken aback. 'Why? If I want out of this marriage, I'll need to be there even more for the girls.'

'Nats, you're an amazing mother. You're always there for the girls, far more than I am for Tabby. But let me tell you something. When Mark walked out, I thought the pressure of running the company too would be crazy, but actually, it saved me. It was my little empire, nothing to do with him, and there I was in complete control. It was a constant while everything else was up in the air, and I can't tell you how much I loved walking into that office every morning. Also, I felt much better having my own income stream.'

'Well, your income stream's a lot fatter than anything I'd be able to pull out of the bag. I haven't worked in over a decade. But I take your point, especially as I have no idea if any bank will touch Lorenzo with a barge-pole after this.'

'What did you do before?' Astrid asked. 'Finance, wasn't it?'

'I was a luxury goods analyst at Fidelity,' Natalia said. The room was filling up. She caught the eye of a hovering mother and gave her a tight smile and quick wave, before turning back to Astrid. 'I covered the big European names—

Hermes, LVMH, Kering, back when it was PPR, and Burberry.'

Astrid sat forward. 'I had no idea! Did you enjoy it?'

'I loved it. I don't miss the hours or the politics of the City, but I loved the sector. It was so much fun, going off to the Basel watch fair and visiting the companies.'

'And do you still follow the sector?'

'I do—not the stock-prices, or the financials, but I follow the shows and the news flow; I still get excited by it. And, of course, I love the product.' She smoothed down the skirt of her Gucci dress. She was always glad she'd made an effort when she was with Astrid, who radiated effortless style. 'And I love following what you do. Your brand is very special, Astrid. You've created something really beautiful. I take my hat off to you—it's a tough industry.'

'It is.' Astrid sighed. 'And thanks for those kind words. I love every second of it.'

'What's your next move? You must be looking to move on from Halcyon soon?'

'You're spot-on. Well, they're looking to move on from me; they want to cash in on their investment.'

'You wouldn't go public, surely?'

'No, it's not for me. We're looking at a trade sale.' Astrid paused. 'Ok, here's a test for you. Who would you pair us with, if you were me?'

'Ooh, goodie. I like a challenge.' Natalia steepled her fingers, that old rush of intellectual challenge flooding her blood stream. 'Let's see. Kering could be an option, given they haven't got Stella McCartney anymore. But I'm guessing the US is a more important market for you than Europe, am I right?'

'You're exactly right. American women love our timeless British thing.'

'Ok.' she frowned. 'Capri Holdings are too... jet-set for you. I don't see you with Kors and Versace. Tapestry's portfolio's too US-centric. I know! What about Constellation? Their portfolio has a very old-money vibe.'

'Bingo.' Astrid rewarded her with a blinding smile. 'Wow, you're good. We're talking to them, or beginning to dance around each other at least. I'm in New York in a fortnight to do some trunk shows, and I'm hoping to meet them. It's all very early stage, so I don't think there's any problem telling you this.'

'That's fantastic. Who are you meeting there?'

'Well, Eleanor Britten came to my show last month, and she's setting up a dinner.'

Natalia shook her head. 'I don't know her.'

'She's their VP for Europe,' Astrid said. 'But I'm hoping their CEO will come along—Grayson Landau?'

'Oh, he's amazing. His background is watches. He's American, but I knew of him when he was at Jaeger Le Coultre. I'm sure he'll be interested in whether you can expand your brand into more hard luxury and bags—the bulk of your revenue is still apparel, I assume?'

'It is.' Astrid's eyes widened. 'And you're right, again. The opportunity is indeed in bags and accessories.' She leant in towards Natalia. 'I'll tell you what. I need to run in a sec, but why don't you come in and have a look around the office next week? Then we can go for lunch.

'This isn't charity, I promise. You have a feel for this stuff. I need a killer pitch for Constellation, and my Finance Director is great, but she's pretty dry. I need someone who can help me sell the dream and pitch the investment opportunity perfectly. I could do with some fresh eyes on it. Come and do some consulting for me, Nats. It's a win-win for both of us.'

22

JENNA

The fog of grief was so thick she couldn't see through it, let alone navigate a path out of it. In the space of five minutes, she'd lost everything she cared about: Jackson and her vocation. That was two weeks ago now, and the fog wasn't lifting. She should have got straight out of London and hidden at her parents' place in Suffolk, but she was too mortified to face them. She'd told them she'd clashed with the headmaster and had to leave, but not about Jackson. They'd have been horrified to hear she'd got involved with a married man, a father. They'd be ashamed of her.

She'd tried to regain some kind of perspective over the relationship. She'd known it was wrong, and she'd also known it had no future. Despite the words he'd said to her, despite the magic when they were together, she'd always known it could amount to nothing in the long term. They'd both been in a bubble; Hans Place had been a fairytale refuge for them to cook and goof around and make love and be normal. In hindsight, it had been a false cocoon; it couldn't have protected her from the heartache that would inevitably engulf her.

In the long days and nights following her dismissal, the most confounding part of the situation had been Jackson's involvement. She still couldn't believe she might have been mistaken in his feelings for her. If she'd been a neutral third party, the whole thing would have sounded highly suspect, but she'd been there, in their cosy little nest, with him. She'd sensed his need for her; each morning she'd found his body wrapped around her, his arms clinging to her desperately. She'd read the message in his eyes every time he'd woken up to find her next to him. That was another thing—he'd started openly spending entire nights with her, even mid-week. If anything, he'd been in deeper than her.

The last evening they'd spent together had been perfectly, wonderfully normal. They'd cooked a Thai stir-fry and caught up on the latest episode of Graham Norton on BBC iPlayer. Jackson had been full of fascinating gossip into the workings of the show and the intensive preparation its researchers did for each guest. He'd been on it a few times.

That night, they'd brushed their teeth together like an old, married couple and climbed into bed. Lying in his bed with her legs and arms wrapped around him, his forearms flanking her head and his mouth on hers as he moved inside her, had been an almost spiritual experience. She'd felt surrounded by him, consumed by him. Afterwards, she could have sworn his eyes had been wet as he'd stroked her face and whispered her name over and over again.

Fast-forward two weeks, and the closest she could get to him was watching his movies and cuddling her bear. The bear had quickly become her most treasured possession. She watched all five movies in the *Adrenalin* series, even though she usually hated action movies. This way she got to binge on him, and when each storyline hit the inevitable sex scene, she tormented herself by watching him seduce whichever leading woman was starring opposite him this time. She'd seen that look in his eyes; she knew that position. From her perspective, those sex scenes were pretty damn authentic.

While she wallowed, it seemed to be business as usual for him. He was active on Instagram, so she had the peculiar torture that was watching him go about his golden, rarified life. He'd been to an awards ceremony, all stubble and cheekbones in a Tom Ford suit, with Honour looking luminous on his arm. There were Instagram stories of Rollo's dribbling skills on the football pitch, and some of Jackson's culinary endeavours in what must be his kitchen at home. She wondered if he was being a good boy, keeping his head down, plying his wife and kids with attention and biding his time until he could get away with his next indiscretion. His note was still under her pillow. *I am more sorry than you will ever know.* Did *sorry* mean that he felt bad for messing her around, or that he hadn't wanted to break it off? She had no way of knowing, but she hoped he was suffering too.

Meanwhile, her chosen career lay in tatters. Thanks to that fifty grand in her bank account, she didn't have to worry about rent for now, but she hadn't touched it. It felt like dirty money; it had tainted the deeds she'd done with Jackson. She didn't want to be here, lying on the sofa, watching her favourite person in the world pretend to shag Marion Cotillard or Jessica Chastain. She wanted to be back at school, surrounded by her beautiful, innocent seven-year-old boys with their boundless energy and incessant questions.

It frightened her how alone and purposeless she was outside the confines of school. Katie had been great: attentive, furious on her behalf, and encouraging. She'd even suggested Jenna put Jackson's pay-off to good use and train to be a SENCO. When she'd said it, a reassuring warmth had bloomed in Jenna's belly. There was something pleasingly circular about using the funds for such a cause, especially as Jackson was dyslexic. She suspected he'd approve. But she didn't have the energy to look into additional training or the confidence to apply for temporary teaching positions—she dreaded having to explain why she'd found herself out of a full-time post a mere six weeks into the school year.

It was the start of half-term, and Katie had gone up to Birmingham to spend time with Steve. It was horrible being in the flat on her own. She'd looked forward to Katie coming home every afternoon with news from the boys. There was a temporary teacher in place in 3P who apparently was fine, but didn't hold Jenna's view that the teacher and teaching assistant should share the marking burden equally. Katie came home most nights laden with homework books. Jenna pounced on them eagerly, pouring over them to see how her little menfolk were doing and thrilling when they mastered a new maths technique or wrote something particularly hilarious in their creative writing. One of her few outings had been to Paperchase on the Kings Road to stock up on stickers, and her most quietly fulfilling moments were sticking them into the boys' books as she helped Katie mark them.

It was particularly poignant to see Rollo's work. He was such a likeable little guy, with his dad's innate charm and an enormous smile. She flicked through his English book. There were definite signs of dyslexia there. It wouldn't surprise her; the neurobiological issues that caused it were genetic in origin. Katie would have to prompt the supply teacher to keep an eye on it. Rollo was at the right age to get his first educational psychologist assessment.

Her phone rang. It was a London number she didn't recognise. Probably ambulance-chasers.

She answered. 'Hello, Jenna speaking?'

'Jenna.' The voice on the other end was crisp. 'My name is Catherine Clark. Mike Hopkins passed on your number to me. Is now a good time to speak?'

She sat up straighter on the sofa, scrambling to get the tangled throw off her legs. 'Sure—of course.'

'I'm the headmistress of Chiltern House. It's a girls' prep school in Notting Hill. Do you know it?'

'I—I do, yes.' Where was this going?

'I'm afraid to say we have an emergency. Our Year 3 teacher for Chaucer class, Rebecca Yates, was due to go on maternity leave at Christmas. Unfortunately, she's suffered some complications with her pregnancy and has been put on bed-rest for the duration of her third trimester. This leaves us one Year 3 teacher short from next week onwards. I wondered if you'd be interested in providing maternity cover.'

Her mind reeled; she was stunned Mike had suggested her, despite his kind words at the end of their awful meeting.

'Can I just check—did Mike recommend me? Did he explain my situation?'

'He did.' A softer note crept into the older woman's clipped delivery. 'I'm aware of your unfortunate situation—prep school headteachers are a small community here in west London. Mike assured me you are a passionate and gifted teacher, and that I would have no regrets if you came on board. In fact, he said we'd be lucky to have you.'

Jenna's eyes pricked at the unexpected kindness. 'Thank

you for being so understanding. And yes—I'm available—I'm in London. Would this just be cover for the next term, or—'

'We certainly need cover for the rest of Michaelmas term, from next Monday. But we hadn't finalised any of Miss Yates' planned maternity cover, so if this term goes well then we have a position open for at least a year from January. We'd love you to join us, Jenna. You'd be welcome to come in this week and get acquainted with the school.'

It was a gift from heaven. The timing was serendipitous beyond belief. But girls! What would girls be like to teach? Boys were so straightforward; she imagined that seven-and-eight-year-old girls would be full of tantrums and cliques—like mini *Mean Girls*. But the stationery aspect would be a lot more fun. She'd better hot-foot it down to Paperchase again and stock up on unicorn stickers.

23

ASTRID

The third floor of Bergdorf Goodman tinkled with the sound of decorous laughter and champagne flutes. Astrid floated between her colourful, glossy clients, women who'd either popped over from their Classic Six on the Upper East Side or travelled in from Greenwich, Connecticut, to rub shoulders with her. Saks and Bloomingdales were also putting on shopping events for her while she was here.

She always dreaded these soirees, but found she enjoyed them when they happened. The stores did most of the heavy lifting around them; she merely had to show up and sell the Astrid Carmichael dream so that the women who met her would be compelled to shop tonight, and so that whenever they pulled out one of her pieces over the course of the winter, they'd feel one degree closer to her and to the brand.

These trunk shows were vital, especially for the Autumn/Winter collection. It was such a short selling season: in London and New York, it had only just got cold enough to prompt customers to invest in new-season pieces, and they had less than a month until Thanksgiving, when Black Friday Cyber Monday would signal a frenzy of discounting that was hell for the brands. The full-price selling never recovered before Christmas, so this was her window to sell, to inspire, and to tantalise women into making an emotional purchase, however steep the price.

Tonight she wore a dove-grey pencil skirt that hit at mid-calf, with a matching satin pussy-bow blouse. She had some oversized pearls from Dior in her ears—costume jewellery, but they gave the outfit a kick. It was simple: what she wore at these events was what would sell. People didn't have much imagination, and she never failed to be amazed by women's lack of confidence in putting an outfit together. By modelling these clothes tonight, she would bring them to life for the customers and illustrate how perfect the same pieces would be for their upcoming fundraising lunch or Thanksgiving dinner. It was hand-holding, and it was what clients wanted.

Her mask was firmly on this evening; she was the Astrid her clients knew from social media and wanted to meet. She'd landed yesterday and had a restorative night's sleep at the Pierre, enjoying a coffee early this morning in the hotel's enchanting rotunda before slipping out to the nearest *Le Pain Quotidien* for a chance to drink hot chocolate from a bowl and watch the pre-work crowd queuing at the counter and milling in the street outside. She'd paid homage to some of her favourite paintings at the Frick—she'd do the Met tomorrow—before settling down to do get some work done in her hotel.

She was appalled by how desperately she missed Callum, and how yawning the distance between them felt. They'd kept up a steady stream of WhatsApp chat that veered from the hilarious to the downright filthy. A large part of her had been tempted to invite him out here, but this trip needed to be about work. If he'd been here, she wouldn't have left her huge marshmallow of a bed at the Pierre. Nevertheless, she missed how carefree and animated she was when he was by her side.

Now here she was, freshly blow-dried, and holding court at Bergdorf's. She recognised a familiar face: Caroline Prescott, a long-standing client who'd generously held a trunk show for Astrid at her Westchester home years ago, when the company was in its infancy. Caroline was a former attorney who now channelled her fearsome mix of energy, ambition and humour into running the lives of her husband and children. She was fabulously fun, and a wonderful ambassador for the brand.

Having exchanged pleasantries, Caroline got straight to the point.

'Astrid, honey,' she said, gesturing around the area of Bergdorf's where they were gathered, 'you deserve an upgrade from here. This is lovely, but it's time for some decent real estate! What percentage of your online sales come from the US?'

Her ideas were always worth listening to. 'Just under thirty percent. You're our biggest market after the UK.'

Caroline clapped her hands. 'I knew it! What does that tell you? You know we all adore you. The clothes are great, but we're all desperate for the full Astrid Carmichael experience! Last time I was in London I popped into your store on Bruton Street and it was just to die for. You need stores here, to give us a bit of England.'

She was right; Astrid had known it for years. She just hadn't had the capital, the bandwidth, or the personnel needed to take on such a big project.

Caroline was still talking, gesticulating theatrically as

she warmed to her argument. 'You need a little boutique around here, that's for sure. Maybe Madison. And you definitely need one in Greenwich. I tell you, honey, it would be so popular. Fill them with antiques and flowers; work your magic. They'll love it.'

~

THE NEXT EVENING found Astrid sitting opposite Constellation Holdings CEO, Gray Landau, in an intimate bistro off Madison in the seventies. The clientele looked as though they'd been coming here for years; immaculate Carolina Herrera clones dined with dapper gentlemen across small tables with starched white cloths. There was more starched linen in the bread baskets, and decades of stiletto-heel dents studded the polished ebony floorboards.

She was glad she'd gone for uptown glamour, in a scarlet silk dress and matching lipstick, her hair in a chignon. The splash of colour was unlike her, but New York always made her feel like a more fearless, energised version of herself, and the vivid palette was an appropriate way to reflect that. Besides, she needed to make a lasting impression on Landau. She'd dropped into Constellation's offices earlier that day for a chat with Eleanor Britten; he hadn't appeared.

'He wants to chat to you alone tonight,' Eleanor had laughed. 'I'm not invited.'

He was younger than she'd expected; likely late forties. His black-grey hair had receded at the temples, and his hazel eyes were hooded. He was tall and lean, with broad shoulders, and he was very good-looking in a craggy, professorial sort of way. Wire-rimmed glasses added to his intellectual air, and he removed them and pinched the bridge of his nose.

'Excuse me,' he said, folding them carefully and putting them on the tablecloth. 'Long day. But this is a fine way to end it—chatting with you about the beautiful brand you've created.'

They sat back as the sommelier opened and poured an exquisite bottle of white Burgundy.

'Cheers,' he said. 'I have to say, we've been watching you with interest for some time. You're one of Eleanor's most-worn labels, and she has impeccable taste.' He grinned and looked years younger. He had lovely teeth.

'I wasn't aware of that—she didn't mention it,' Astrid said, taking an appreciative sip of her wine. Gray was right; this was a fine way to round out a day in New York. If only she could conduct all her business in such gentile surroundings.

'Well, I'm glad we could meet up in person. Thanks for coming up here. This is one of my favourite neighbourhood places; I'm two blocks away. Besides, there's something I'd like to show you after dinner, around the corner.'

'I'm glad we could make time too,' Astrid said. 'I'm here doing trunk shows, manically trying to sell before Black Friday's upon us.'

'How have the trunks gone?' Gray broke a bread roll in two.

'Well. One of my longest-standing clients was berating me for not having standalone shops here. The concessions are great for discoverability, but the big department stores as painful to deal with as ever.'

'I agree with her,' he said. 'You're a magic-maker, Astrid. What you do is enchanting. I haven't seen anyone who can world-build like you since Ralph Lauren. You don't need me to tell you that having stores this side of the pond is a critical part of that magic.'

He leant forward. 'I haven't brought you here tonight to talk numbers. If we're both in agreement about moving forward, the next stage is to get a look at your books. I have the utmost respect for Halcyon, but I suspect they've pumped the margins up as much as they can.'

'You're right,' she admitted. 'I hate seeing them do it, but I know they have to make their profits. We're under-invested, though. Hence the lack of physical US footprint.'

'Don't worry about that,' he said. 'That's where a partner like us would come in. We'd want to help you invest in your dreams. I can tell you're a dreamer, or you couldn't have conjured up such an immersive brand. Tell me your dreams, Astrid. Where do you want to take this company? We have good wine, good food on its way, and I have all evening. So forget margins and capex limitations. Tell me what's in your mind's eye.'

OVER *COQ AU VIN*, a house speciality, the conversation took a more personal turn. Gray, she discovered, had got into watches because his love of skiing had prompted him to find an industry that would allow him to base himself in Switzerland.

'It was watches or chocolate, I guess,' he said.

'Or private banking,' she said.

'Nope.' He forked some *dauphinoise* potatoes into his mouth. 'I had a useless English degree from Princeton. I knew I wanted to get into industry, build things. And ski. Do you ski?'

'I do.' Skiing was one of the many things that terrified

her: driving up narrow Alpine passes, heights, the constant threat of avalanches or incompetent skiers taking you out. She hated skiing; her anxiety never left her until she was safely back on the flat streets of London. Unfortunately, it was something her public persona demanded she do, and so she dressed the part, booked up stunning chalets every February half-term and posted the obligatory après-ski shots on Instagram.

To change the subject, she said, 'So, were you a nerd or a jock at Princeton?'

He laughed. 'A bit of both, I guess. I rowed, so that earned me my place in a frat house. But honestly, I was happiest in the library; I never wanted to leave it. And you?'

She thought back to that distant time at Edinburgh. 'I suppose I was a nerd too. At least, I didn't lack motivation. I wasn't one of those students who never went to lectures. It stood me in good stead for running my business.'

'It seems to have,' he said. 'You're incredibly productive. And a single mother too, these days, if my research proves correct?'

She shouldn't have been surprised that he'd thoroughly vetted her. 'I am,' she said. 'I've been divorced for over two years now. I have an eight-year-old daughter, Tabby. Her dad's taken her to Oman this week, for half term.'

'I'm divorced too. The entire process is so much fun, isn't it?'

She chuckled at his warmth and rolled her eyes. 'It is. So much fun that I'm not sure I'll ever recover. Do you have kids?'

'Twin girls. They're both freshmen at Harvard and Princeton.'

'Wow. Smart girls. The one who didn't follow in Daddy's footsteps is more of a character, I bet.' She speared some chicken and thought how much she was enjoying his company and gentle banter. There was none of the sexually charged back-and-forth there was with Callum. The pressure was off here, in a romantic sense, at least. She still had to prove herself a worthwhile business investment.

'Oh, she is.' He shook his head. 'She's a real firecracker. And are you seeing anyone now, or are you still licking your wounds?'

'I was licking my wounds for a long time and hoping work would help them heal. But I've been seeing someone for a few weeks.' Her face broke out in a ridiculous smile at the mere mention of him.

'Let me guess,' he said, cocking his head to one side. 'Successful, establishment, debonair?'

'You've just described my ex-husband,' she said drily. 'Or, possibly, yourself. Try ten years younger than me and deeply inappropriate.'

'*Really*? Well, aren't you something, Ms Carmichael. Nothing in my research suggested you'd say that. Is he an employee?'

'No!' She nearly spat out her food. 'I'd never do that. And if I did, I'm hardly likely to admit it to you, am I? I suspect it would be a deal-breaker, in the most literal sense of the word.'

He sat back in his seat and smoothed his napkin over his lap, hazel eyes dancing. He was laughing at her. '*Touché*. So are you going to tell me why he's inappropriate, then?'

'I am not. I have a reputation to preserve.'

'So you do. Well, good for you. I mean it. Life is short; divorce is brutal; parenthood is hard. Enjoy this relationship, whatever it is. Anyone who can put a smile that dazzling on your face is obviously doing something right.'

You have no idea, she thought.

THE MEAL HAD BEEN excellent and Gray's company delightful. He was disarmingly straightforward, and his slightly nerdy brand of humour had put her at ease. He'd listened while she shared her wildest dreams and ambitions for the Astrid Carmichael brand, shooting none of them down but asking probing questions and, once or twice, embellishing her suggestions with ones that were even more far flung. He certainly got the brand, and she could see her baby being in capable hands with Constellation.

As they left the restaurant, he helped her on with her coat. It was a cold, clear New York night, and she was glad she'd packed her bulky faux-fur number. She was shattered. It was three in the morning London time, Callum would be fast asleep, and the shivery misery of jet lag assaulted her as they hit the chilly air. He must have sensed her energy plummeting.

'I'll walk you back to the Pierre,' he said. 'You must be exhausted. Do you mind if we walk down Madison? The thing I'd like to show you is just a few blocks.'

They strolled down the quiet avenue, its chic boutiques shuttered up for the night. Just north of Seventieth Street, he stopped her with a hand on her arm.

'What do you think of this?' he asked.

It was an art gallery with a stunning, spacious facade and an enormous picture window, white pillars and bay trees flanking the black front door.

'Gorgeous place,' she said. She peered through the window. 'Um—I'm not sure about the art though.'

He laughed. 'Me neither. It's doing very badly; they're desperate to get out of their lease. I know the landlord. I thought it would work better as the Astrid Carmichael New York flagship.' He raised his eyebrows in query.

'Really?' She beamed at him. 'Oh my God, it's fabulous!' She looked back through the window at the dimly lit gallery. It was a great space, with high ceilings and classical details. She saw it decked out like an English townhouse. It would be the most perfect showcase for her brand.

She felt a rush of appreciation for his thoughtfulness.

'I'm blown away that you pin-pointed this for me, Gray. Do you really think it's an option?'

'Why not?' he said. 'They'll be able to muddle on for a few more months.' He smiled. 'I'm not playing strictly fair. I had a feeling you'd fall for it, and I thought it might twist your arm. Think of it as a kind of dowry. I buy into your vision for your brand, Astrid. I'm as excited about the size of your opportunity as you are. I just want you to understand what we could achieve together. I think we'd make superb partners.'

There was something in the gravity of his eyes, and in the intensity of his voice, that she didn't want to examine too closely. But it looked, for now, as if they'd found their buyer.

PART III

NOVEMBER

24

CALLUM

On the first day back after half-term, Callum had Chaucer class for PE. Their teaching assistant, Sofia, brought them down to the netball courts. She was a sweet, painfully shy Spanish girl prone to making puppy eyes at him. He was unmoved. He'd had a phenomenal, and highly energetic, reunion with Astrid on Friday night after her return from New York, and last night he'd even slept in the *Irishman in New York* t-shirt she'd brought him back as a joke. She was a babe, there was no doubt about it, and she was a hell of a lot more fun now she'd chilled the fuck out with him. She was a different woman.

He busied himself with getting the girls sorted into teams and their bibs on. Elsie helped him hand out various coloured bibs. She was a great little lass; Bex did a fantastic job with her. They warmed up with dribbling and shooting practice for the first ten minutes and then switched to playing some actual matches. Callum ran back and forth along the court, whistling, critiquing and praising.

As they wound down, Tabby stepped up to sort the bibs

back into their colours. She was glowing from her holiday and made some of the others look like little winter ghosts.

'Cracking tan, Tabs,' Callum said to her. 'Where's Ilaria today?'

'She has a tummy-ache,' Tabby told him. That figured. An email had gone around this morning from Miss Clark; Mrs Beneventi had apparently asked her to share the news that Mr Beneventi had moved out over half-term, and both girls were taking it badly. She'd asked that the teachers be sensitive to any emotional issues the girls might have as they adjusted to his absence. Poor little things. There were so many divorces at this school.

'Did she stay home today, then?' he asked.

'No, she's here,' said Tabby. 'She just didn't want to do netball in case it hurt her tummy more.'

'Fair enough.' Callum patted her on the head.

'She's with Miss Price,' Tabby informed him.

'Who's Miss Price?'

'She's our new teacher. Miss Yates' baby tried to come early and so the doctor said she has to stay in bed for *three months*.' Tabby's wide eyes spoke to the severity of this sentence.

'Jeez, that's awful. Poor Miss Yates,' he said. God love her. That sounded miserable, and scary as hell. He did vaguely recall another email having gone around about a staff change in Chaucer class.

'There's Miss Price!' shouted Tabby, pointing at the steps leading up to the back of the school.

Callum looked up, and everything he knew to be true, both about himself and about what he wanted from life, changed in an instant.

~

She was stunning. *Stunning.* No, not stunning—she was an angel. It was as though he'd floated up and was looking down at himself as she walked towards him. Instantly, his sweat glands switched on inside his hoodie, despite the grim November weather. His mouth went dry, and past, present and future converged in a way he'd never experienced outside of taking ecstasy in Ibiza. His vision was closing in and he took some deep breaths. Jesus. Get a grip! She walked down the steps, hand-in-hand with Ilaria, who looked sheepishly thrilled to be getting some alone-time with this celestial being.

'This is Miss Price!' announced Tabby, like a talk-show host.

He quashed an irrational desire to shove Ilaria out of the way and extended his hand, but not before wiping his clammy palm down the side of his jogging bottoms. Nice, Callum. Very fucking smooth.

He flashed her what he hoped was his best grin, the grin for which he received universally positive feedback from the female race, and shook her hand. 'Welcome, Miss Price,' he said. 'I'm Mr Pearce—I run the PE department here.'

She gave him what could only be described as a vague, pleasant look. Nothing. She felt nothing, he could tell. Her hand was cool in his.

'Thanks, Mr Pearce,' she said. He was aware he was drinking in as much of her as possible, as quickly as he could, but he wasn't sure he'd be able to remember any of it later. Her skin was golden, with a smattering of tiny freckles across her nose and cheeks. She had huge, hazel eyes with ridiculous eyelashes, and a tiny button nose. Her lips were hypnotic—soft, pillowy and rosy pink. Her mouth was so delicious he was worried he'd lose control of all his senses and just lean in to kiss her in front of the girls.

She had long, caramel coloured hair, and it swirled around her in untidy waves, down to her waist. She was wearing a strange, mustard cardigan and an indecently short corduroy pinafore that exposed long, long legs covered in woolly grey tights.

She was everything he'd never known he was looking for. He saw her in a rocking chair, bathed in sunlight, feeding a baby—their baby—and the image felt like a knowing. She was home. He was home.

'Mr *Pearce*!' Tabby was tugging him. 'Where should I put the bibs?'

He stared at her. Tabby. Astrid. Oh, fuck. Suddenly Astrid, as well as every other person in his life who was not this angel before him, felt tiny and indistinct.

He shook himself. 'In the blue duffel bag. Thanks, Tabs. Nice one.' He high-fived her, and returned to look at the angel, but she was busying herself with the girls while holding onto Ilaria's hand. Ilaria gazed adoringly up at her. He should probably take control of the situation. He did the special teacher clap, and the girls repeated it back, standing to attention.

'Right, Chaucer class!' he roared. 'Well played today. I saw lots of great dribbling and, most importantly, some lovely teamwork. Well done. Now, come and line up here for Miss Price.'

She smiled at him gratefully, and he responded with a grin he suspected was less lust-worthy and more pathetic. The girls crowded around her like a flock of ducklings. They, too, were already under her spell.

'A line, I said!' he shouted, and he watched as she strolled gracefully up the steps with her pupils in tow.

As soon as she was out of sight, he pulled out his phone

and scrolled through his emails, looking for the one Miss Clark had sent.

Jenna. Her name was Jenna.

25

NATALIA

He was gone. Thank fuck. They hadn't agreed it as a permanent arrangement; Lorenzo was adamant it was an interim measure. But to get him out of there, and to soften the blow for the girls, she agreed to humour him. For now.

Valentina was being vile, and Ilaria was devastated. Of course, Valentina's vileness masked devastation too. Her daddy had moved out, and Natalia remained as whipping-boy, a role that had died out centuries ago in its official capacity but lived on in all households that had a pissed-off child and an available parent. She told herself she could take it; that enduring Valentina's wrongful wrath was far preferable to her daughters discovering their father was a misogynistic pig and a sexual predator.

Still, it was a lot to bear alone. The pain of his infidelity coupled with the trauma he'd caused those women and the agony of his having ripped their family apart was hard enough to endure. She'd had lofty ambitions of cosy girls' nights at home, tucked up on the sofa with her daughters while they ate popcorn and watched *Clueless*. Instead, darling little Ilaria was suffering from a string of imagined maladies and had cried every morning this week at drop-off, while Valentina's vitriolic outbursts escalated. This morning she'd called Natalia a bitch, backtracking only when she saw her mother's eyes fill with tears. The viciousness of that word from her daughter's sweet little nine-year-old mouth felt intensely personal, even though she knew Valentina was just taking out her own misery in her 'safe place'. Sometimes, it was a real brute being her kids' safe place.

That was why she'd asked Bex and Elsie over after their regular Wednesday hockey fixture. Ilaria could do with some semblance of normality, and she herself could use a bit of moral support. Valentina liked Elsie and would hopefully play nicely with the younger girls.

She'd prepared a vat of amatriciana sauce earlier in the day and it now simmered fragrantly on the Rangemaster while she boiled some pasta—gluten-free for Bex, regular for her and the girls. It hadn't escaped her notice that her cooking repertoire was still mainly Italian—that would have to change. Bex was pottering around the kitchen, humming to herself as she fetched wine glasses and uncorked a Brunello Natalia had pulled from the wine cellar. The girls sat at the island, homework books untouched, chatting away. She was right to have invited them over. She'd hoped their home might have a cosy female energy with Lorenzo gone, but instead it felt flat and incomplete. *This* was a cosy female energy.

Ilaria and Elsie seemed unable to talk about anything other than their new teacher, Miss Price.

'She's soooo pretty, Mummy,' Ilaria informed her. 'I want to look like her when I grow up.'

'Is she?' Natalia raised a questioning eyebrow at Bex.

'She is depressingly, divinely young and beautiful,' Bex

confirmed, 'and seems incredibly sweet with the girls. She's come from St Cuthbert's in South Ken.'

'Mummy, look at this.' Ilaria opened her book. 'Look, Mummy! Yesterday I got nine out of ten in my spellings and she gave me a unicorn sticker *and* a mermaid sticker *and* she wrote 'Well done' in pearly pink pen!' There was a blissful smile on her face.

'Well, she sounds wonderful, darling,' Natalia said fondly, draining the pasta over the sink. Though she felt awful for poor Miss Yates, she'd been worried about the change of teacher halfway through the term. It was just another upheaval for Ilaria. Thank God this new woman seemed to have bewitched them all. 'Did she teach you anything useful today?'

'We had to write a persuasive letter, using rhetorical questions and veiled threats,' said Ilaria.

Jesus. Perhaps she should sit in on a few Year 3 English lessons before crafting her next email to her husband.

'I want to meet her!' Valentina said. 'When is she doing playground duty?'

'Tomorrow!' Ilaria bounced up and down on her stool. 'She's doing it tomorrow; she told us! And I'll tell her you're my sister and she'll love you.'

Valentina beamed, an honest-to-God, happy-little-girl beam, and Natalia's heart constricted.

When the kids had finished eating, she shooed them off to the TV room. Homework could wait. She and Bex took their bowls and glasses and wandered down to the dining end of the kitchen, where she'd laid a couple of place settings at the large wooden table. She dimmed the lights so the mess in the kitchen receded a little.

'I love this house,' Bex said, looking around. 'You've made it so homely and snug. On an evening like this, there's nowhere nicer. And'—she dug into her penne amatriciana enthusiastically—'you're an amazing cook. Lorenzo is a stupid, stupid guy to put all this at risk.'

'He hasn't put it at risk; he's put every last nail in his own coffin,' Natalia said. 'There's no way I can stay married to him. I'm disgusted just looking at him. I just hope we can keep this place—God, it makes me want to puke thinking about having to uproot the girls.'

'Are you worried there won't be enough to go around financially?' asked Bex. 'God, this wine's amazing.'

She felt bad even bringing up money issues in front of Bex. 'A little. He'll lose his job, and I don't know how easy it'll be to find a new one—no one will want to touch him with a barge-pole. I need to get some expert advice—I'm seeing Astrid's divorce lawyer next week.'

'If it comes to it, the courts will give you the house,' Bex said. 'Given what's gone down at his work, I'm sure you have a cast-iron case for wanting out of the marriage.'

'I hope you're right.' Natalia was putting away her Brunello at a good speed. 'It's just whether we can even afford the house. Does Carl still contribute to Elsie's upbringing?'

'Yup. He's amazing.' Carl was Elsie's biological father, a close gay friend of Bex who'd agreed to be a sperm donor and had been adamant he wanted to play a role in Elsie's life. He sounded perfect; he was a paediatric surgeon who, besides contributing financially, had a close relationship with Elsie and saw her at least once a month, more often when his gruelling work schedule allowed. He and Bex even had a contract to cover it all.

'Honestly, it sounds like you picked the right way to bring a child into this world,' Natalia said. 'None of this philandering husband nonsense.'

'I don't know. It's lonely, doing it on my own. Sorry—that wasn't very tactful.'

'It's ok.' She poured some more wine into their glasses. 'I'm under no illusions. Are you seeing anyone at the moment?'

'Nope,' Bex said. 'I'm not sure how I'm supposed to have time to date between teaching and parenting.' She looked down at her hands. 'But I'm tired of being on my own. I miss sex! And I just want someone to put their arm around me on the sofa and spoon me in bed at night. I know that sounds pathetic. I just want some physical contact, you know? And ideally, someone to love me. It doesn't feel like too much to ask.'

Natalia's gaze ran over her friend, her beautiful, intelligent friend who spent her days coaxing children to fall in love with sports. Bex had had a promising career in British athletics at one point, before a chronic battle with fibromyalgia had dashed those hopes. The girls were lucky to learn from her. Natalia could see, from the focus and grace and self-sufficiency she exuded, Bex's star quality. She had a quiet resilience that Natalia, whose tendency to flap was exhausting even to herself, envied.

Bex's face was tired and drawn this evening. The sculptural curves of her body looked even more finely honed than usual under her fitted sweater; she was losing weight. Natalia reached over and squeezed her hand.

'It's not too much to ask,' she said hesitantly. 'You

deserve to be loved, sweetie. You're a beautiful person and you deserve to be loved.'

She sat there, holding her friend's hand, and her thumb moved over Bex's smooth skin. And as it did, she allowed herself to acknowledge a tiny bud of an emotion that had been quietly blooming for weeks. She had no name for it; it was too complex. But it was streaked with affection, and admiration, and longing—a yearning for possibilities she hadn't known existed. And desire, but not any kind of desire for which she had a reference point. Finally, there was terror. Terror that felt either as sickening or as exhilarating as jumping off a cliff into a bottomless sea; she had no way of knowing which.

She pulled her hand away and busied herself with stacking their plates.

26

ASTRID

Callum was ghosting her. She'd had a string of dirty, witty WhatsApps from him on Sunday, and then nothing.

Their reunion had been glorious. Tabby hadn't returned from Oman until late Saturday, so he'd spent Friday night at hers in London. He was gradually inserting himself into her life, and it felt strangely right to have this young guy, with his infectious energy and levity, by her side. To say that it had been gratifying to have him in her marital bed was an understatement. This was the bed whose pillows she'd cried pools of tears into when Mark had abandoned them. This was the bed whose left-hand side had lain cold for years.

This weekend she and Callum had rampaged over it, desperate for each other, and she'd had the rare pleasure of waking up with him, his warmth seeping into her bones and his body pressed against hers. Having him in her bed, being with him in her home, had seemed to legitimise what they had, bringing him further into her world. She'd even started working through the mental machinations around whether this could ever work as an official relationship, despite the obvious hurdles of age and money, of his role as Tabby's teacher and of their very different stages in life.

He'd left on Saturday afternoon, apparently reluctantly, but had gone silent on Monday. He hadn't even confirmed their standing Wednesday date at the Connaught, despite a couple of messages from her on Monday and Tuesday. It was time to take matters into her own hands. She went along to the hockey fixture. It had become part of their routine; she'd leave work early on Wednesdays and come to the fixtures, before meeting up with him a few hours later in a hotel room. He'd told her it turned him on massively to see her there, playing the role of glamorous, ice-queen tycoon, knowing that in a few brief hours he'd get to rip off her expensive clothes and watch her burn for him.

If he wanted ice-queen, she'd give him ice-queen. She turned up at the hockey pitches in a white version of the grey outfit she'd worn in New York: ivory silk pussy-bow blouse, winter-white wool skirt and vertiginous heels, a sumptuous white double-faced cashmere coat slung over her shoulders, and her biggest, darkest sunglasses. She stood chatting to Natalia about the progress of the content they were creating for Constellation, while watching him from behind the safety of her shades. He'd swapped the shorts for jogging bottoms, but they couldn't disguise the beauty of his body as he ran across the pitch.

'Holy shit,' she heard one mother from the visiting team murmur to another. 'That teacher is ridiculously hot.'

She wanted that body bearing down on her in a few hours and wrapped around her in the bath afterwards. It wasn't fair—he couldn't ignite every nerve-ending she had after her years of carefully preserved asexuality and then leave her hanging. What the hell was going on with him? One of the things she enjoyed about their arrangement was that there was no game-playing: not outside of the bedroom, in any case. He was always engaged and enthusiastic; he was open about wanting to see her, and they'd fallen into a rhythm pretty quickly. Now she had no bloody clue what game he was playing.

She and Tabby were in a black cab heading home when a WhatsApp message from him flashed up. God, he was predictable. He'd fallen for the outfit, exactly as she'd intended. The message read:

See you at 7 as usual? Don't change your outfit. I want to be the one to take every single thing you're wearing off.

It was infuriating and hot in equal measure. His presumptuousness after nearly three full days of silence galled her, but she knew she'd squirm in an agony of anticipation for every minute of the next two-and-a-half hours.

She didn't exactly change her clothes. She took everything off and put them all back on again over a boned lace corset fitted with suspenders. No knickers. If he was in any danger of growing bored by her, or at least complacent, that should keep his attention. Her lingerie habit was costing her a fortune at the moment. If someone had told her two months ago she'd be heading to a hotel for sex with a younger guy, trussed up in La Perla and brazening it out without knickers, she would have laughed in their face. But however ominous his behaviour had been this week, she was utterly confident in the effect her underwear choices would have on him.

She arrived at the Connaught fully intending to question him on his silence as soon as she saw him. But when she let herself into the room he was already there, wearing just his jeans, pacing. He strode straight over to her, and grabbing her face, kissed her like a desperate man, tugging off her coat and feverishly trying to unzip her skirt, while pulling at her blouse too. Her desire instantly ignited to meet his, and she fumbled with his belt as she kissed him back.

She pushed him away. 'I have a surprise for you,' she whispered.

She loosened the pussy bow on her blouse and pulled it over her head to expose her corset. Unzipping her skirt, she let it slide to the ground and stepped out of it, watching for his reaction. All that remained were her corset, stockings and heels.

His face contorted with need. 'Oh fuck,' he groaned. 'Oh, God, baby.' He started kissing her again, yanking off his jeans and boxers as he did so. He lifted her and she wrapped her legs around him. Shoving her up against the door, he pushed inside her and her arms tightened around his neck.

'Fuck,' he panted, 'you're wet.' She groaned and matched his rhythm as he started to slam into her; she was lost in the deep, deep well of sensation as he moved inside her. Then he swore incoherently and stiffened as he came.

'Oh, Jesus,' he said. 'Shit, sorry baby—I couldn't last.' He bent his head and rubbed his face between her breasts.

'Don't apologise,' she murmured. He'd never come that quickly before; it would appear her surprise had met with a favourable reaction.

'That's what happens,' he said, stroking her bare backside, 'when you show up wearing this and no panties. Did you have this situation going on at the hockey match?'

'Yes,' she lied, delighted she'd been able to make him fall apart. After three days of sitting helplessly by the phone, it was pretty damn empowering.

'Jesus, baby; I don't stand a chance around you,' he said.

She was still wrapped around him, her heels on, supported by the door and one of his arms. He eased himself out of her and put her down, gazing down at her corset. His hands moved gently upwards, and he pinched her nipples through the lace. The fire went straight to her groin.

'Callum,' she moaned.

'It's ok, baby,' he said. 'It's your turn now—let's get you out of this thing.'

SOMETIME LATER, they lay on top of the covers, entwined as they caught their breath.

Astrid stretched luxuriously and ran her hand down the bulk of his thigh. 'Do you fancy some room-service? Or a bath?'

'Nah,' he said. 'Thanks though. I need to get back. I'll just have a quick shower.' He kissed the top of her head. She watched, stunned, as he swung himself off the bed and sauntered, alone, into the bathroom, closing the door behind him.

27

ASTRID

His premature departure undid all the benefits of the orgasm. She'd never seen him so agitated and full of need as when she'd arrived last night, but as soon as he'd come inside her for the second time, a shutter had fallen, quick as a guillotine, and obliterated any connection they'd just had.

He hadn't been able to get out of that room fast enough. He'd hugged and kissed her and thanked her for an incredible time, but he'd seemed incapable of making eye contact, and he'd made no mention of when they'd meet up again. She'd wallowed in a decadent but solitary bath, wondering what the hell had just gone down. Soaping herself up, she'd tried to rinse off a lingering feeling of grubbiness. The sex had been more intense than ever, but she couldn't shake the feeling that it had been transactional.

The next day, she was unnecessarily short with Tabby, who'd chosen that morning to have an epic meltdown over the fact that the gusset of her tights was uncomfortable. While she could sympathise—there was a reason she only wore hold-ups or stockings—she didn't have the capacity for Tabby's arbitrary sensory issues today.

She eventually got her off to school, just in time for registration, after a lengthy, bare-legged standoff. The memory of her daughter's small, tear-stained face would now sit with her for the rest of the day, while she could be sure Tabby would have brushed the matter off before the first lesson was over. She was cranky with her wholesale team during their weekly meeting and was relieved when it was time to grab her bag and head to Notting Hill.

She had a late lunch meeting with Honour Chapman. It had been in the diary for a few weeks and was at Farmacy, the hip, plant-based restaurant in Westbourne Grove. Honour could be a little neurotic, but she was a good friend and her recent messages to Astrid suggested she'd been going through a tough time recently with Jackson.

The restaurant was bustling when she got there, full of girlishly radiant Notting Hill women whose boho vibes belied the cost of their maxi-dresses and the intensity of their beauty regimes. Honour was already waiting for her in a quiet corner, looking far more Chelsea than Westbourne Grove in a snug-fitting camel polo-neck, tailored trousers that Astrid recognised as Givenchy, and heels. As always, she was the best-looking woman in the room. Autumn suited her colouring; her green tiger eyes sparkled and her chestnut hair gleamed in the sunlight streaming through the restaurant's tall windows. Tabby always said Auntie Honour looked like a mermaid. She had a point.

They took care of business, namely a brainstorm on the next campaign Astrid would shoot using Honour Chapman Cosmetics on the models. Then, once their earth bowls and matcha tonics had arrived, Astrid leant forward.

'Are you doing ok, sweets? You mentioned on WhatsApp that you've had a rough few weeks?'

'Ugh.' Honour ran a hand over her flawless face. She turned her head to both sides, checking they couldn't be overheard, and whispered, 'It's Jackson. I think we're out of the woods, but I'm not sure.'

'What's going on? Another indiscretion?'

'You can say that again. He was pretty well behaved over the summer; we had a lovely time in Umbria as a family. But as soon as we got the kids back to school, he started screwing Rollo's *teacher*, for fuck's sake!'

Astrid stiffened. This was far too close to home. She'd toyed with confiding in Honour about her torment over Callum, but this was one woman who would not appreciate that story.

'Oh God,' she said instead. 'What on earth possessed him to do that? You give him enough free rein as it is.'

'Look.' Honour toyed with her earth bowl. 'I don't mind him playing away. I know you think it's fucked up, but honestly, the guy's libido is the size of Britain and I can't be the one to deal with that for him the whole time—I have way too much on my plate. So he can screw who he likes, as long as he comes home to us.'

It was, in Astrid's opinion, seriously fucked-up, but she guessed most couples operating at that level of fame were a little dysfunctional. Also, Jackson could be a handful, and Honour was juggling a makeup empire with two kids, an intense fitness regime and all the promotional crap that went with being one half of a major celebrity couple.

'So what happened with the teacher?' she asked.

'He started acting strangely, literally overnight,' Honour said. 'He was mooning around the place; he stopped nagging me for sex, and he even started spending entire nights at his flat. He wasn't being present with the kids—it felt like he was slipping away from us. It was the first time I've ever really been afraid of losing him.

'So I called him out on it one morning; he was texting on his phone as soon as he woke up, and he had this goofy smile on his face. I had to drag it out of him, but eventually he came clean, told me he was seeing—*seeing*, not fucking—Rollo's bloody teacher!'

'Oh, God,' Astrid said again, her hand across her mouth.

Honour continued. 'I. Went. Nuclear. I mean—how fucking *selfish* is that? Did he, at any point, consider what that would do to Rollo? Or me? We've always had an agreement—keep boundaries with these women; don't screw anyone we know as a family, use NDAs. I mean, if the press ever got a whiff of this stuff, our whole brand would go up in smoke.

'Not to mention, he was obviously smitten. I mean, it was pathetic. Whenever he said her name he'd grin like a big, stupid kid. It was the most surreal thing, sitting up in bed, listening to my husband tell me how special this girl was. I thought—fuck, he could leave me for her; this could be the end of absolutely everything we've worked for.'

'Were you actually hurt, or just angry?' She could never figure out how much of Jackson and Honour's relationship was a PR arrangement these days.

'I was devastated.' Honour's green eyes were enormous. 'The other women—I try not to think about what he actually does with them. My therapist says it's a really unhealthy way to run a relationship.'

I could have told you that for free, thought Astrid.

'I do love him,' Honour continued. 'I mean, I adore him! How could I not? He's so gorgeous; he lights up every room he's in. And I've had it in my head for so long now that I can't have him to myself, that he has needs I can't fulfil. But I'm his fucking wife; he still needs to want to come home to me more than he wants anybody else.'

'Did you put a stop to it?'

'Oh, yes. Like, immediately. I called Alex right there and then—he's our lawyer. Can you believe Jackson didn't even get this girl to sign an NDA up-front?! So fucking stupid. Alex came right over and I told Jackson, if you don't want me to take you for everything you've got and full custody of the kids, then you never see this girl again. Cold turkey. Finish it right now.

'I called the school and screamed at the headmaster and told him we'd pull our pledge for their new astroturf and pull Rollo out too, if he didn't get rid of that girl straight away. He sacked her that morning and then Alex went over and paid her off.'

She sat back and exhaled, taking a long sip of her tonic.

Astrid's mind was racing. What a hellish situation all-round. It made what she and Callum were doing seem tame, but it also brought home the risks she'd been courting by getting involved with him.

'You poor thing,' she said, putting her hand on Honour's. 'God, what a nightmare for you. How are things with Jackson now?'

Honour considered. 'Ok. Not great. He's a big boy; he knows he has choices in life; he chose us. But he was pretty subdued for a few days.'

'Do you think you guys will make it?'

'I do. He'll come round. He slept in the spare room for a few nights, but he's back in our room now, and he's being pretty sweet, actually. He's making an effort with me and throwing himself into Rollo's football—he knows he did badly. He admitted he let himself get in too deep; he assures me it won't happen again. So, let's hope that's that.'

'What was the girl like? The teacher?'

'Honour shrugged. 'Young. Beautiful—she had that wholesome, helpless thing going on. I hate her guts, but I imagine it was all Jackson's doing—I know what he's like when he sees something he wants. If I hadn't nipped it in the bud when I did, I hate to think where it could have gone.'

THEY PAID up shortly before Astrid was due at school. She'd do pickup today; there was no point in going back into town at this hour and besides, she might catch a glimpse of Callum.

She touched Honour's arm. 'Fancy strolling up to school with me? Tabby would be so thrilled to see Auntie Honour at the classroom door.'

'Why not?' Honour said. 'I'd love to see Tabs. I'll text my driver to meet me there, instead.'

They walked along a couple of quiet crescents. The school doors had just opened when they arrived. Astrid noticed a few double-takes from the other parents as they clocked Honour. But this was Notting Hill; everyone was far too high-profile and self-important to acknowledge a celebrity openly. Honour was safe.

They made their way up to Chaucer class and waited in a queue of mothers on the staircase. The classroom door opened, and the line drifted forward. As they got to the front, she noticed a ravishing young woman ushering the girls out to their mothers. She must be Miss Price, the new teacher Tabby'd been gushing about. God, she was gorgeous, despite the offensive green sweater-dress she was wearing. Her hair was piled in a huge, messy bun on top of her head, and her face lit up as she bid each little girl goodbye.

Astrid smiled and held out her hand. 'Hi, Miss Price. I'm Astrid Carmichael, Tabby's mum. I've heard lots about you from Tabby.'

Miss Price gave her a radiant smile and went to shake her hand.

Then her gaze shifted, her face crumpled in abject horror, and her hand flew to her mouth.

Astrid's forehead furrowed and, catching a movement in her peripheral vision, she turned to see Honour's hand, and facial expression, mirroring those of Miss Price.

Honour spun around and stumbled down the stairs.

28

JENNA

She now understood what it meant to be frozen to the spot. She certainly couldn't coordinate the machinations of greeting the mothers, matching them to a child and ushering each child out while simultaneously processing what had just happened.

A few seconds ago, she'd been lighting up at the sight of Astrid Carmichael in the flesh. She'd had no idea she was Tabby's mother, though they were very alike. She followed Astrid on Instagram and often sighed over her glamorous lifestyle and beautiful brand. It was exciting to see one of her heroines at the classroom door.

And then, as if someone had pressed pause on her nice, new, safe reality in this sweet school, she spotted Honour Chapman. She was standing next to Mrs Carmichael—what on earth was she doing at Chiltern House? Did she have a kid here? Surely not. As soon as they locked eyes, she felt her body shut down and her head go fuzzy. She clamped a hand over her mouth, ignoring Mrs Carmichael's obvious confusion, and stared at Honour.

Honour seemed to be equally frozen in horror. Her

enormous eyes filled up, and she turned and bolted down the stairs. Mrs Carmichael turned and watched her go and swung back to Jenna. Jenna watched, in apparent slow motion, as understanding dawned on Mrs Carmichael's beautiful face. She leant forward and put her hand on Jenna's arm.

'Are you alright?' she asked. But it wasn't a casual question; she whispered it intently, as if Jenna would understand exactly why she was asking.

She knew. She must be friends with Honour. She knew about Jenna and Jackson. God, that meant she must be friends with Jackson too, or at least be in his social circle. The yawning gulf she'd felt between herself and him seemed to lessen slightly with this knowledge, and Mrs Carmichael's concern was, in a strange way, a relief. It was a comfort that someone else knew; it made her predicament marginally less lonely. There was no isolation like mourning a relationship bound by an NDA.

She felt herself blinking, gasping; she couldn't remember what she'd been doing in the seconds before Honour had appeared.

Mrs Carmichael kept her hand on Jenna's arm, and she said gently, 'Tabby, please, Miss Price,' as if she were talking to a small child.

As soon as Tabby emerged, arms clamping around her mother's hips, Mrs Carmichael nodded at her and said, 'It'll be ok. I'll deal with—' and gestured at the staircase down which Honour had vanished.

Then she was gone, and a mother she didn't recognise asked for her daughter by name, and Jenna found she could smile, shout that name into the classroom and have the child materialise in front of her. She mechanically repeated that step as many more times as it took to clear the room, and as she was doing so she ignored the trembling of her chin and hands.

When the last little girl had gone, she called out to Sofia in an artificially bright, high voice, 'I'll be back in a sec, ok?' and bolted up the stairs to the tiny staff kitchen in the attic. As she'd hoped, it was empty. The staff seemed mainly to congregate in the bigger staffroom downstairs. She bent over and leant her elbows on the counter and her face in her hands. The tears exploded in great, heaving rushes and her entire body shook as she wept into her hands.

It had been impossible to miss the devastation on Honour's face. That was the worst of it. She'd been struck by how distressed the other woman looked, as though she'd been kicked in the stomach. For all her endless obsessing about the way she and Jackson had ended, she'd never considered that Honour might actually be hurt. Angry, affronted, territorial, yes, but not heartbroken. She'd taken Jackson's explanation of their open marriage as an indicator that they weren't really in love anymore, but that wasn't what Jenna had seen on Honour's face.

She'd had her own heart broken by Jackson, but now the additional consequences of their relationship were apparent —she'd become involved in someone else's marriage; she'd turned his wife's world upside down, and now this woman hated her. And right here, four days into her process of rehabilitation, her past had caught up with her.

She grabbed a piece of kitchen roll from beside the kettle and blew her nose into noisily, trying to catch her breath. At that moment the fire door creaked agonisingly open behind her. Shit.

She looked over her shoulder, still holding the kitchen roll to her nose. It was that guy, the PE teacher. Mr—she had no recollection of his name. He froze in the door frame.

'Sorry,' she mumbled from beneath the clump of kitchen roll. She gestured. 'Come in.'

He bounded over to her and put his hands on her upper arms. 'Jenna, isn't it?' he said. 'What's wrong?'

'Nothing'—this before a fresh flood of tears assaulted her—'I'm fine, honestly.'

He stood in front of her, waiting, his hands still on her. 'You might be wishing I'd just fuck off,' he said, 'but you've only been here—what—a few days? And we've already made you cry! We can't have that now, can we?'

He had a lovely voice, a warm, comforting Dublin accent.

She rubbed her hand over her eyes. 'It's nothing to do with the school,' she said.

'Ok,' he said. 'Well, that's good. Can I ask—has someone died? Is your family ok?'

'They're fine,' she said. 'It's not that important.' She blotted her eyes wearily with the same piece of kitchen roll. God, he must think she was a total nutcase.

'I tell you what.' He was looking around the room. 'Let's get you out of here. This is a miserable fucking room to be miserable in. Will you let me buy you a cup of tea? I'll grab your coat and then I'll show you the back way out. Ok? You don't need to see anyone.'

She exhaled, wearily. He was so sweet. And ridiculously handsome. If she wasn't so cut up about Jackson, he'd be just her type.

She nodded at him. 'Ok.'

29

CALLUM

He'd never moved so quickly. He shot into Chaucer's classroom, to the obvious delight of Sofia.

'Where are Jenna's coat and bag?' he asked. 'She's not coming back this evening; she's a bit unwell.'

Grabbing his own jacket and wallet from the staffroom as well as a wad of tissues, he took the steps back up to the attic two at a time. His head was in turmoil. He'd been delighted to find her alone in that crappy little kitchen until his brain caught up a fraction of a second later and informed him she was deeply upset. She looked so beautiful and fragile in that second; he wanted to gather her up in his arms. He couldn't believe he'd had the chance to touch her already, though he felt a bit pervy for taking advantage of her distress. She hadn't seemed to mind, though. To be fair, she hadn't registered him much at all. He had to get her out of that place.

He found her again in the same position. 'Here you go,' he said, holding out her coat so she could slip her arms in. He shrugged it over her shoulders, handed her her bag, and then offered her a tissue from the wad. 'Supplies,' he said, stuffing the rest of them in his jacket pocket.

He led her down one flight of the main staircase and then round to the fire exit where they could descend to the ground floor and escape via a side gate using his swipe-card.

There was a little café around the corner; it didn't have much to recommend it, but that should mean it was nice and empty at this time of day. He longed to put his arm around her. She was silent on the walk; he didn't push her but walked alongside her, his hands in his jacket pockets, his fists clenching.

Inside the café, he ushered her to a table in the corner and fetched them two mugs of builders' tea and a couple of KitKats. It was as quiet as he'd been hoping.

'Right,' he said as he sat down next to her. 'This is grand, isn't it?'

She gave him a weak smile and seemed to look at him properly for the first time. 'This is so kind of you, thank you. I'm really embarrassed.' She twisted her mouth and looked away.

'Sure, you have nothing to be embarrassed about. I'm just glad I found you. It would have been awful if you'd been stuck up there, all alone, in that state.'

Her sweet little nose was rosy-red, her face puffy and streaked with a snail-trail of unwiped tears. Her eyelids were so swollen they looked sore. He wanted to cup her face in his hands and kiss them better. She fished out her tea bag and squeezed it against the side of the mug with the spoon. He did the same, and then ran a thumbnail cleanly down the foil of his KitKat, breaking off a finger.

'So.' He shifted awkwardly in the hard chair. 'Do you want to talk about it at all?'

She gazed at him. 'I actually do. But I can't.'

'Oh, a secret, is it?'

'Kind of. It's a legal thing; I'm not allowed to discuss it.'

Jesus. What kind of legal issue had flared up at the end of the school-day? She was very mysterious.

'You need a priest, then,' he said. 'Someone you can talk to confidentially. Come to think of it, I'm Irish. I'd make a very convincing priest, if you didn't know me.' *And a very unconvincing one, if you did.*

A smile flickered on her face and, encouraged, he went on. 'Ok, close your eyes for a second.'

She closed them.

'Hello, my child. How long has it been since your last confession?'

She giggled. Actually, that was turning him on. He'd better shelve that particular role-play for another time.

'I'm only kidding,' he said hurriedly. 'So, you have a legal problem, is that it?'

'Not really, I have a guy problem, but I can't legally talk about it.'

What the fuck? In a distant place in the back of his mind, something surfaced from Miss Clark's email. *Please welcome Jenna Price, who joins us from St Cuthbert's Preparatory School.*

'What school were you at before Chiltern?'

She looked at him warily. 'St Cuthbert's.'

Holy fuck. One of his housemates, Mac, had a mate, Dave, who taught at St Cuthbert's. Over beers the previous week, Dave had regaled them all with the hottest gossip from over there, which was that Jackson James had been caught shagging one of the teachers before half-term and she'd been instantly fired. Staff had been warned that anyone caught talking about it would be slapped with an NDA.

'You should see her, though,' Dave had said. 'She's smoking.'

The conversation had stuck in his head because they'd all then speculated as to how hot the teacher must have been to have ensnared a Hollywood star like James (they were all reluctant admirers of his), and also because it had been a nasty reminder of the risks he was taking with Astrid. Happily, though, she was neither an A-list celebrity nor married.

He leant in towards Jenna. 'Did you just leave?'

She was looking at him as fearfully as a tormented kitten might regard its abuser. 'Yes,' she said slowly, searching his face.

'*Fuck*.' He ran his hand through his hair and stared at her.

'Are you telling me you know about my situation?'

'I think so. I'm sorry.'

'God.' Her eyes darted around the room in a panic, landing back on him. 'How on earth do you know?' she hissed. 'Does everyone at school know, do you think?'

'No!' He put a hand up in protest. 'God, no, not at all. I have a mate at St Cuthbert's. The word seems to be going around over there, alright, but not here. Nobody has a clue.'

She pulled the tissue he'd given her out of her sleeve and started crying into it, quietly. He tried to compute this recent information. He hadn't thought about anything else but her for four days now; he'd spent the entire time trying to figure out how he could get her attention. He'd never had to pursue an uninterested party before. And here was his explanation. She'd been fucking Jackson James, a fucking movie star, for Christ's sake. Jesus! That was another level. The guy was practically superhuman. Callum would never have admitted it, but he'd saved a photo of James on his phone when he was trying to motivate himself to bench-press heavier weights. His body was a machine.

And to think that machine had been all over this beautiful, fragile... he was filled with an unfamiliar cocktail of rage, revulsion, and voyeurism. She and James would make an insanely hot couple. No wonder she was devastated. He wasn't sure how you moved on from someone like him. And he'd got lawyers involved, from the sound of it, and had her kicked out of school... it was a fucking disgrace, the way a guy like that could throw his weight around and trample innocent people underfoot.

He put his hand on the forearm that rested limply on the table. The wool of her coat was scratchy under his palm. 'I'm assuming the guy you're crying over is Jackson James,' he whispered.

She flinched and nodded.

'That's shit. I'm sorry. The whole thing must have been horrific for you. I can't even imagine.'

'Well.' She gave a humourless laugh. 'Most of it was amazing. But getting dumped and fired within five minutes of each other was horrific, yeah.'

'So, how come you were so upset this afternoon?'

'His wife was at school.' She peered out at him from under the tissue.

'What—Honour Chapman? At our school?'

'Yep. I think she's friends with Mrs Carmichael—Tabby Carmichael's mum? They came along together at pickup. Then we spotted each other, and she just bolted off down the stairs. I was so—I just froze. Her face. It was like she'd seen a ghost; she looked absolutely gutted. And it gave me such a shock, but also it made me feel really shitty, to see how much I'd upset her.'

Jesus. This was all way too close for comfort. Someone up there must have been having a laugh. He hadn't known Astrid was friends with the James family. Of course she was. The awful irony was that in theory he could enquire on Jenna's behalf, get some information, or some closure for her. But he needed to at least try to stay away from Astrid.

He was furious with himself for succumbing last night. He'd known exactly what she was playing at yesterday at the Year 3 match, dressed up like that. She'd looked good enough to eat, and he hadn't been able to help himself. He'd been so tormented—and agitated, and aroused—all week over Jenna, and he'd known Astrid would be exactly the release he needed. And then when she'd shown up in that get-up, with no fucking pants on... Jesus. He'd lost all control.

But as soon as they'd finished, and he was completely sated, he'd had an overwhelming urge to bolt. He'd been thinking with his dick, as usual, and he hadn't been able to escape the feeling that he'd cheated on Jenna. That was ridiculous, for fuck's sake; she was right here beside him and had not an inkling of interest in him. Nevertheless, he wished he'd been able to keep it in his pants for her. If he was honest, Astrid and Jenna occupied spaces in his brain that were far apart enough that he could be besotted by Jenna while emptying his desire and frustration into Astrid.

Now he patted Jenna's arm. 'Don't you go feeling guilty because that gobshite can't behave himself. You're the victim here. Don't give any of them another thought. Chiltern's a great little school. I know you'll be happy with us if you give us a chance.'

30

ASTRID

The next week passed in a colourless pastiche of work and motherhood. She saw Callum again on Saturday evening when Tabby was on a sleepover; against her better judgement, she'd messaged him that morning to invite him over.

It was perfectly nice; he was much sweeter this time, if subdued, and he even stayed the night. But there was a distance there; there was some part of him she couldn't reach, which was hard to get used to after regarding him as an open book. It was as though he was slowly withdrawing from her, and she felt stupid for having entertained any thoughts that their relationship might make it to the next level.

She was clingier than usual with Tabby, especially after a week apart from her over half term. Tabby even slept in her bed a couple of times. It was something she'd tried not to encourage, even after Mark had left; she didn't want them to become unhealthily co-dependent. But this week she savoured her little daughter's unselfconscious chatter on their Saturday morning shopping trip to Harrods and her delicious warmth in Astrid's cavernous bed.

The following week, she was sitting up in said bed in her yoga pants and a cosy sweater, looking over the information her Finance Director had sent her to review for Constellation, and making good work of a delicious Burgundian pinot. It was one of the few reds she enjoyed drinking without food, and its austere sophistication soothed her as she sat back against the headboard and tried not to think about the fact that it was Wednesday, and she should be in the Connaught, devouring Callum, who'd gone quiet again.

She was WhatsApping back and forth with Gray Landau on various matters pertaining to the due diligence process, which had now kicked off in earnest as Constellation's lawyers and accountants delved into her company's affairs. He was far more involved in the process than she'd expected, though Eleanor's team was running the show. Now, as she pinged him a reply to his question about headcount forecasts for the next three years, her phone informed her Grayson Landau was incoming via WhatsApp video.

She hastily forked her hair with her fingers and accepted the call. Thank goodness she hadn't taken her makeup off yet. His face popped up on the screen. He looked well—really well. He'd loosened his tie and unbuttoned his shirt a little; he lounged in a dark leather chair, looking quite the tycoon with a stunning New York skyline slightly visible behind him.

'Hey, you,' he said. 'You're working late. Trying to impress your buyer?'

She smirked. 'My buyer keeps wanting to talk shop and won't let me drink my wine in peace. Cheers.' She brandished her glass.

'That's a great call,' he said, looking at his watch. 'I might keep you company on that front.'

'What time is it over there?'

'It's four-forty-five and our stock-price closed up two percent today, so we live to fight another day. I'd say that's worth a couple of fingers of scotch.'

He carried his phone across the room with him and the image bumped around as he poured himself a drink from a decanter. He settled back in his chair and held up the tumbler. 'Cheers.'

'Look at you,' she said. 'Could you be any more Don Draper, drinking scotch in the afternoon with Madison Avenue behind you? That's quite a view you have there.'

He laughed. 'I'll take that. Draper's a good-looking sonofabitch. It's beautiful, isn't it? A perfect fall day in New York.' He swivelled and flipped the camera view, tilting the phone upwards so she had an uninterrupted view of the skyline.

'Meanwhile, London is predictably cold and bleak,' she said, shivering.

'Are you in bed?' he asked.

She nodded, embarrassed. 'I'm on the bed, not in it.'

'Where's your toy-boy? Is he not keeping you warm?'

She looked down at her glass. 'Something's not right at the moment,' she admitted. 'I'm not sure what's going on. He's blowing very hot and cold.'

He inhaled through his teeth. 'I'm sorry to hear that. I hope you sort things out. But don't let the kid mess you around.' His expression was kind; he looked genuinely concerned for her.

'You going to tell me who he is now?' he continued.

She shrugged. What the hell. 'He's my daughter's PE teacher. I couldn't be more of a cliché unless he was my tennis coach.'

'Oh, shit. Well, if you're going to go for a younger guy, do it in style, I say. Life is short. Get your kicks where you can.'

'Hmm,' she said. 'I suppose so. Anyway, what's up with you?'

'I'm in London next week—wanna meet up? I'm speaking at the Morgan Stanley Luxury Goods conference.'

'Oh, I'm doing that too,' she said. 'I'm on a British Brands panel.'

'There you go,' he said. 'We can hang out at the conference; it'll be fun. I'm sure you'll know a lot more people than me—you can introduce me.'

He was very modest; she suspected most people in the room would be lining up to shake his hand.

'Can I take you for dinner afterwards? Scott's? I can't come to London without getting my Scott's fix.'

'I'd love that.' She realised she would. A grown-up dinner at a sophisticated restaurant with a fully functioning adult sounded exactly what she needed.

'Excellent. Now, Ms Carmichael, hopefully the tedium of my conversation and my headcount requests will send you swiftly off to sleep. I'll let you go. Sweet dreams.'

When she snuggled down into her feathery bed an hour later, clutching her trusty hot water-bottle to her stomach, she felt slightly less bereft.

31

NATALIA

She was enjoying an intensely erotic dream. Morning was beckoning, and she was in that magical portal that led back from oblivion to her conscious self, a portal where the strangest things could happen.

In her dream, she was lying on her side in bed. Someone was curled behind her, skin pressed against skin. Their hand stroked her stomach and moved up to her breasts, deft fingers rolling over her nipples. Then their hand moved downwards again and slipped between her legs, and she parted them willingly, arching her back. But the body behind her was soft, and the hand caressing her was smooth. She realised that the hand, the body, and the lips that were now kissing her neck, all belonged to Bex.

The revelation pulled her to the mouth of the portal and spat her out into wakefulness. Her clock showed 6am—still dark outside and far too early to be awake on a Saturday—but it seemed her body had had sufficient rest to perform some tricks on her. She lay in the dark, heart hammering, pulling her legs up to her chest in a vain attempt to dull the thudding ache that lay between them.

It had been months—years, possibly—since she'd had an erotic dream, and she'd certainly never dreamt about another woman. Well, not since her school days, at any rate. She was shaken by the depth of the desire she'd felt as well as by the person her dream had cast as the object of that desire. She sat up. It had felt so real as to be all-consuming. But dreams were ridiculous; they sifted and sorted through the debris of everyday experience and pieced together the most nonsensical things.

A few days ago, Bex had mentioned to her that she missed sex and wanted someone to spoon with, and there'd been that weird turn she'd had when she'd held Bex's hand. Also, she was feeling—what was that word—heteropessimistic—at the moment, and Bex was the only lesbian she knew. Her brain had clearly extrapolated these nuggets into a scenario and then inserted Natalia herself into the frame. The logic of dreams was not the logic of consciousness; they proved nothing. This was exactly like having a dream about a teacher or a boss—you could find them attractive in the dream and yet feel violated when you woke up.

The problem was, the spirit of the dream followed her into the shower, where she went precisely to try to drown it out, and it followed her to the hob later as she tossed Saturday pancakes for the girls, and it followed her through the immaculate avenues and crescents of Notting Hill as she walked the girls over to Holland Park. It brought with it a frisson of magic, of awakening, that reminded her she was not a soon-to-be-divorced, middle-aged woman, but a sexual being with desires that hadn't yet dried up for good. It cast a glow over the ordinary activities that made up her Saturday, as she attempted to entertain the girls alone.

Somewhat awkwardly, they were meeting Bex and Elsie in Holland Park for a walk and play. She was quickly learning that weekends were a tricky time to be a single parent. When the girls were young, she'd dreaded Lorenzo being away on the weekends; opportunities to socialise were limited when everyone else was indulging in family time. Bex, of course, faced that problem most weekends.

Ilaria and Valentina ran through the park, kicking the piles of flame-coloured leaves so they whirled into life. Bonfire smoke, acrid and evocative of countless Novembers past, curled through the crisp air and made it hazy. She tugged the zip of her enormous, quilted Moncler coat further up her throat, glad to be enveloped in its duvet-like cosiness. She was conscious she'd spent more time than usual this morning on her makeup, foundation transforming her blotchy winter pallor into something more lustrous and uniform. She'd even curled her eyelashes before applying her mascara. The look she'd been aiming for, a natural winter glow, was possibly oxymoronic.

She gave a little start as Bex and Elsie materialised from the formal gardens. A pom-pom-topped beanie framed Bex's face, and her cheeks glowed—although likely with less help from her makeup bag than Natalia'd had. She looked beautiful. It was surreal to be meeting up while her dream still hung over her, colouring everything she saw and did. She felt at an unfair advantage to have that perspective when Bex was oblivious. Now, Bex gave her an affectionate hug, and they strolled over to the vast adventure playground, which had been built that summer and was still a novelty for the girls.

They found a wooden bench and she was once again glad of her coat's bulk under her backside. She took the lid off her portable coffee mug—it was always hazardous, trying to sip scalding liquid from those tiny holes in the top—and the steam spiralled upwards as the cold air hit the surface. She snuck a sidelong glance at Bex, who sat serenely, spine ballerina-straight, hands folded in her lap, a soft smile on her face as she watched the girls scurry like hamsters over the climbing frame. Her ability to be utterly still and present was as mesmerising and unfathomable as ever. In Natalia's life right now, there was separation and divorce and sexual misconduct and #MeToo and guilt and fear and heartbreak and worry and exhaustion. And beside her, this woman, who had battled chronic pain and ill-health and financial struggles and dashed dreams and single parenthood, sat like a seraph, seemingly lit from within. She longed to lie down on the bench and put her head in Bex's lap and feel the toxicity drain out of her. But for now, just being beside her was enough.

'Bex,' she blurted out. 'When did you know you were gay?'

Bex's mouth curved open in amusement. 'Where on earth did that come from?'

'Sorry,' she said, flustered. 'I'm not sure—I think it was just watching the girls; it made me wonder when this kind of knowledge kicks in.' It wasn't true, but it would do as a cover-up. Her real answer was: *it came from my wondering if I could possibly be gay after forty-four years of existing as a straight woman, or whether, for the first time, I've seen the light inside someone and that person's sex is utterly and laughably irrelevant.*

'I figured it out properly when I was thirteen or fourteen,' Bex said. 'Puberty, I guess. I wasn't one of those kids who always knew. I liked hanging out with boys, but when all my friends started kissing them I knew I didn't want to. There was one girl at school, Adeline. She was so beautiful and golden, like an angel. I adored her so much—I think I loved her the whole way through school.'

'Was it sexual—did you know what it was?' she asked.

'It wasn't at first, or least I didn't let myself think that way. I just wanted to be near her. It was definitely sexual later; God I had so many dreams about that girl.'

Natalia stiffened and felt her face burn.

'I think being involved with athletics helped,' Bex continued. 'Everyone was so in tune with their bodies and open about their physicality, and as we went through our teens, a few of the girls came out. I was out with my athletics team years before I told my family.'

'How were they about it?' Natalia could not imagine coming out as a teenager to her conservative British family.

'They were cool—I don't think they were hugely surprised. But they were supportive. I never gave them any trouble in any other way; I was super focused on school and training. And then I got sick, and that took up most of our focus for a good while.'

They sat in silence, Natalia pondering the curveball fibromyalgia had thrown her friend. Bex was in good health and mostly pain-free these days. She was the healthiest person Natalia knew, avoiding most of the crap that other people ate and bringing in homemade daals and bone-broths and kimchi to school for her lunch.

Around them, the squeals of contented children filled the air, and their girls trundled each other up and down on the zip-wire. She lifted her face and allowed the familiar playground sights and sounds to ground her. Everything that was happening in her life at present was threatening to destabilise her from the predictable path she'd trodden to date: university; City career; hot, successful husband; two daughters; stay-at-home mum.

'At least you had the courage to just be yourself,' she told Bex. 'You actually thought about what you wanted, and went for it. You know, I'm not sure I ever even thought about it. I just did what was expected of me.' She laid her head on Bex's shoulder. There was that citrus scent again. Maybe if she stayed like this long enough, she'd absorb her friend's courage and calm. Bex put an arm tightly around her and she exhaled.

32

ASTRID

The Morgan Stanley Luxury Goods conference was thankfully being held in the West End instead of at their offices in Canary Wharf. It was a one-day event, with keynote speeches, panel discussions and breakout sessions being held over the course of a full day. Astrid's panel was in the morning, and she and Natalia turned up for registration straight after the school run. Natalia had been helping her to pull together insights on her panel's topic—The Importance of Authenticity for British Brands. She'd been surprised at how much she'd enjoyed having Natalia as a sounding-board. She knew the industry dynamics inside-out, despite her long hiatus from working in it. They'd agreed that, for the time being, Natalia would do one day's consulting for them per week.

Ushered through to the main conference area's foyer, they awaited their coffees from the barista while sipping fiery ginger and turmeric shots. The space was milling with the great and good of the luxury industry; Astrid spotted CEOs of British, European and US brands scrolling on their phones, drinking espresso and catching up with each other.

A hand touched her elbow.

'Astrid.'

Turning, she found Gray, and her face broke into a smile. He looked handsome and distinguished in a charcoal suit and a tie instantly recognisable as Hermes.

Having kissed her and introduced himself to Natalia, he said, 'So, are you ready for your panel? It's a good line-up of brands.'

'I am.' This was her tribe, her comfort-zone. She knew where she was with these people and she could hold her own. The rules of engagement were clear, unlike when you screwed thirty-year-old gods who blew burning hot and icy cold for no obvious reason.

He made small-talk with them until they were called in for the first session. After he'd wished Astrid luck and taken his leave, Natalia exhaled.

'God, he's attractive,' she sighed. 'It's so unfair that men age so well.'

'He's definitely got something,' Astrid said.

'Yeah, it's called looks, power, money and sex-appeal. And he couldn't take his eyes off you, you lucky cow.'

'Really?' She'd definitely noticed a vibe from him in their interactions, but she hadn't realised it was obvious enough for a third party to pick up on.

Natalia rolled her eyes. 'Hell, yes. I suspect Mr Landau wants you even more than he wants your company.'

THE BRITISH BRANDS panel went off well and made for an energetic discussion between disparate industries. Once it was over, she was able to relax and enjoy the rest of what was shaping up to be an informative day. After catching up with the managements of Mulberry and Goodwood over lunch, she settled down for Gray's presentation. He'd been tasked with the somewhat turgid mandate of providing an outlook for the US, European and Asian luxury goods markets for 2020. This would be the first time she'd seen him in action, speaking publicly.

He'd taken off his jacket, and she noticed how well his slim-cut shirt fit his lean, broad-shouldered frame. When the audience had quietened down, he smiled at them.

'I hope you all ate as much as I did at lunch,' he quipped. 'No doubt half of you will enjoy a nice siesta during this presentation. Thanks, Morgan Stanley, for giving me the graveyard slot. Speaks volumes about what you think of our stock.'

And he was off. Hands in pockets, he sauntered around the large stage in a leisurely manner. It was more like watching a perfectly executed TED talk than a market update; he spoke without notes, and his witty, energetic delivery made light work of his data-heavy slides. She felt her mouth curving into a smile and a tug in her belly. He couldn't have been more different from Callum—and was almost twenty years older—but the force of his personality was undeniably attractive. His complete assurance in his status, and in the validity of what he was saying up there, had a powerful pull. The rest of the audience sensed it too; they laughed more during what should have been a dry outlook presentation than they had all day. She felt a quiet sense of gratification that this evening she'd have him to herself; she'd be the sole focus of this magnetic man who had a roomful of industry captains in his thrall.

~

Later that evening, a sommelier poured her a glass of Krug, its effervescent nectar dancing in the flute. Around her, the iconic seafood restaurant, Scott's, pulsed with a well-groomed, Thursday-night clientele. Art Deco mirrors, shaped like fans, lined the room, and their dappled glass muted the diners' reflections. The delectable scent of lobster filled the air, and opposite her sat Gray, tie and jacket discarded, shirt open at the neck, sitting back in his chair and regarding her with what looked like appreciation.

He raised his flute. 'To a perfectly pitched performance today.'

'I can say the same for you,' she said. 'I'm honoured to be here with the man of the hour.' It had been hard to get away from the post-conference drinks; he'd been cornered and waylaid by industry executives, bankers and fund managers for most of the networking session.

He gave her a slow smile that brought heat to her face.

'Before I relax into Lobster Thermidor heaven,' he said, 'I need to lay my cards on the table. I'm going to buy your company, Astrid. That doesn't change, no matter what you say next—the deal's safe, as long as we don't find any skeletons in your closet. But I also want, very much, to be with you.'

Her stomach flip-flopped at the intent in his eyes and in his voice.

He continued, 'I know we'll be working together and we live on opposite sides of the Atlantic. I know you're dating a guy who probably has sub-ten percent body fat. It's not an ideal situation, but you're worth it. That night in Manhattan when you walked into that restaurant—well, you just turned my whole universe upside down, and I haven't been able to stop thinking about you since. My favourite days are the days I get to FaceTime you, and when we're chatting I wish I could just crawl through my damn phone and be with you. I'm absolutely blown away by you. I told you we'd make a superb partnership; I meant it.

'I'm not asking you to go all-in, but I would like to know if I'm in with a chance, and if I am, I'll move heaven and earth to make it work with you.'

33

CALLUM

Callum was at home in his room, surfing Netflix ineffectually on his laptop and eating an enormous bowl of tuna pasta. Mac had rustled it up for them both after they'd returned from a gruelling weights session at the gym. Mac was his accountability partner; they were committed to getting each other's arses down to the gym three times a week. It was paying dividends; he was gaining muscle all over his body. He'd be like Jackson fucking James soon. The thought of James made him feel nauseous.

His phone rang—it was Astrid.

'Hey baby,' he said, his mouth full of pasta. 'What are you up to?' This could be a booty-call. He stretched. He'd be up for that.

'I'm in a cab on my way home from dinner,' she said. 'I've been at a conference all day.'

Her melodic voice with that cut-glass accent always turned him on. He pulled up an image of her at work in some fancy dress and heels, preferably with that corset thing on underneath it, and felt himself getting hard. She was a piece of work. Just when he'd thought he had her worked out, she'd gone and pulled that pantie-less stunt last week. Then she'd been putty in his hands when he'd stayed over at the weekend, and he'd felt like he was drowning in her. His heart belonged to Jenna, but the rest of his body was still too firmly invested in Astrid.

'I dare you to have phone sex with me in the cab,' he said, putting down his bowl of pasta. 'Are you wearing a skirt? I bet I can make you come before you get home.'

She snorted, not unattractively. 'I bet you could too, but no bloody way. I wanted to talk to you, actually. I want to know what's up with you at the moment.'

He stiffened. 'What do you mean?' he blustered.

'Oh, come on. Ghosting me last week; running for the hills as soon as you got a chance at the Connaught—which was incredibly insulting, by the way—and you've been much quieter than usual this week on WhatsApp. Something's up. I want to know what it is.'

She sounded curious, not scary. She'd already been pretty cool considering the way he'd treated her recently. He took a breath.

'Em—ok. This is going to sound so lame. I met someone last week. I literally saw her, and I fell in love—nothing like that's ever happened to me before. She has no fucking interest in me, but I can't stop thinking about her, and then I feel guilty about being with you. I know that's ridiculous, but I feel like I'm cheating on both of you.'

There was a silence. 'I see,' she said. 'So—you think you're in love?'

'Unrequited love, yeah. That's never happened to me before. It feels shite, doesn't it?'

She gave a dry laugh. 'It does,' she said. 'So, who have you fallen in love with?'

'Oh.' He shifted on his bed. 'Someone at school, actually.'

He heard a sharp intake of breath. 'Shit. Not Tabby's new teacher? Miss Price?'

'Jesus,' he said. 'How the hell did you work that one out?' Women were seriously fucking weird. 'Jenna, her name is.'

'It's not rocket science,' said Astrid. 'She's stunning, and she's just started at school. It was a lucky guess.'

'She's stunning, alright,' he said, poking at his pasta gloomily with his fork. But she has no fucking interest.'

'Callum,' Astrid said. 'She's—that's complicated.'

'I know,' he said. 'I know what her gig is. She didn't tell me,' he added hastily. 'I worked it out; the story's been doing the rounds. But I saw her the other day after she saw Honour. She was devastated. She told me you weren't surprised, though.'

'Let's just say I have additional colour on that situation,' Astrid said. 'Anyway, Callum, look—I think you and I should call it a day. Your head's not in this and I'm not some seventeen-year-old who's going to sit by the phone hoping you'll want sex badly enough to call me.'

He sat bolt upright. 'No way—don't say that. I don't think of you in that way at all. We have an amazing time together, baby—Jesus, we're absolute magic together. It's not normal, what we have.'

'You're telling me,' she said, her voice softer. 'It's been spectacular, and you've brought me back to life; really, you have. But it was never going to amount to anything, was it? There always had to be a point where we ran out of steam.'

'Baby, you don't need to do this,' he begged. Jesus, he'd be in some sort of celibate limbo if she pulled out of their arrangement. He'd been arrogant and thoughtless this week because his head was so full of Jenna that he didn't have the capacity to worry about anyone else's feelings. But his hook-ups with Astrid had grown in meaning and had come to represent glittering snatches of a life he rarely had access to, where women bought their own Aston Martins and ran companies and thought nothing of getting a room at a top hotel for a few hours and spent more on underwear than he could imagine.

If she called this off, he wasn't sure how he could bear Wednesday afternoon fixtures, seeing her in ice-queen mode, knowing her beautiful body and everything she represented would no longer be available to him a few hours later.

'I do need to do this,' Astrid said. 'I thought there must have been someone else; your behaviour changed so quickly. I'm sure she'll get over Jackson in time and then she'd be stupid not to go for you. I have far too much self-respect to be with you when I know you're pining for her.'

'Hey,' he said. 'When I'm with you, believe me, I'm with you. Do I ever seem like I'm even remotely distracted when I've got you naked in front of me?'

'No,' she admitted. 'But I meant more generally. I don't want to be your fallback plan. Anyway, I've met someone too.'

'What?' He was gobsmacked. 'When were you going to tell me?'

'I'm telling you now. Just like you're telling me now, even though I've had to drag it out of you.'

'Who is he?' He was astonished by the force of the pain he felt. He'd been so complacent about her emotional attachment to him. When he'd met her, she'd been so prickly and unsure of herself, and now she was a wanton goddess who knew exactly what she wanted from him and was utterly confident that he wanted her. It was sexy as hell, and he liked to think it was all his doing.

'He's a business associate,' she said matter-of-factly. 'I've just come from dinner with him. He told me tonight he's interested, but I had an inkling before. Anyway, I haven't quite worked out my feelings yet, but I'd like to see where things go with him. We have a lot more potential for a future together than you and I have. So, honestly. This thing between us has been the most fun I've ever had in my life, and I have you to thank. But it's time to call time on it; let's be adults and agree on that.'

No Jenna. No Astrid. Fuck. He rolled over on his bed while the pasta congealed beside him.

34

JENNA

Teaching little girls was just as much fun as teaching little boys. They were more complex: their playground spats involved less scrapping and more name-calling, they bore grudges for longer and seemed intuitively to understand the power of passive-aggression, and they were curiously adept at finding each other's sources of insecurity. But mostly they were sweet little things, with wide smiles dominated by their inappropriately large new front teeth. They'd made her feel at home, and they'd given her back her purpose.

Each morning as they came in, they wound their still-tiny arms around her waist and told her they loved her and brought in all their favourite pens and colouring pencils and furry Smiggle notebooks to show her. Without fail, they commented on what she wore with the observational skills of a fashion editor, and they complimented her more zany hairbands and scrunchies. She found herself putting on extra accessories in the morning, smiling to herself as she imagined their delighted reactions.

She'd been at Chiltern House nearly a month now, and

the pain of losing Jackson and her old job had become bearable. There was, however, a flatness about her life, especially when she first got to school in the mornings and had to remind herself that in this new classroom, Jackson wouldn't walk in in his running gear and whisk her off to some clandestine corner to feel her up. A few of the dads were particularly attentive to her, but she shuddered and ignored them as best she could.

It was lunchtime, and she was keen to get some air and pick up a sandwich from Pret on Notting Hill Gate. As she walked away from the school, she spotted Callum just ahead of her. They'd spent a bit of time together over the last couple of weeks; the odd coffee in the staffroom when their free periods coincided, and a walk to Pret together. He'd been so sweet that horrible day when she'd seen Honour, and she hadn't forgotten his kindness. She found herself going up to that top-floor staff kitchen from time to time, hoping to bump into him. As her time with Jackson morphed slowly into a distant land of fantasy, she allowed herself to quietly enjoy Callum's good looks.

Now he ambled ahead of her, his head bent and his hands in his pockets, pulling the fabric on his jogging bottoms taut. He had an extremely nice bum; it was difficult not to notice it. She quickened her pace and fell into line beside him.

'Hey,' she said, nudging his shoulder.

He looked at her and his entire face lit up. 'Hiya,' he said. 'Going to Pret?'

'Yeah,' she laughed. 'I'm a creature of habit.'

'I have an idea. There's an amazing café hidden away off Portobello. If we hurry, we can have a quick bite there. D'you fancy it? My treat.'

The entrance to Farm Girl café was through the quaint little pale-blue doorway of what looked like a church facade. Beyond the door lay a charming, white-washed courtyard that accordingly led into the restaurant. It was her idea of heaven: retro turquoise tiles lined the walls and the open coffee bar was painted the same colour. The room bustled with elegant local women and the odd push-chair, but there was a little table in the corner that felt like it had their names on it.

After they'd ordered their poached eggs and smashed avocado on sourdough—a significant upgrade from Jenna's usual Pret sandwich—she sat back. He was watching her, but she couldn't tell what he was thinking behind those big brown eyes.

'Are you ok?' she said. 'You looked the picture of misery when I saw you on the street.'

He gave her a small smile. 'I should be asking you how you are—how's the broken heart mending?'

'It's ok.' She squirmed; it was so weird that he knew about Jackson. 'I'm just trying to focus on the girls, who are great. I don't know—the more time that passes, the more I feel like it was a dream. A heavenly one, but not something that could happen in real life.'

'Well, it'll be a great story to tell the grandkids one day,' he said. 'Do you want to know a secret? I wouldn't tell anyone else about this—I'm a lot more discreet than I look—but I think it might make you feel better about your situation. Or you'll sympathise, at any rate.'

'What is it?' she asked. A waitress brought glasses of tap water, and she took a sip of hers.

'I was seeing a parent from school.' He was looking at

her tentatively, as if trying to gauge how she'd react. 'She dumped me last week.'

'Wow!' This was major gossip, but she was surprised by the pang of envy that poked her in the gut. If pushed, she would have guessed he was single. 'I had no idea—I'm sorry to hear that.'

'Yeah.' He looked down at his cutlery and she was struck by how long his eyelashes were. 'It's fine, but I've been feeling a bit sorry for myself.'

'So, a parent, eh? Are you allowed to tell me who?'

He shifted in his seat, still avoiding her eyes.

'Only if you want to,' she said hastily. 'I would never mention it to anyone. It's not like you don't have a ton of dirt on me.'

'It was one of your mums, actually,' he said. 'Astrid. Tabby's mum.'

She felt weird—nauseous, almost. Astrid Carmichael was amazing; Jenna had a huge girl-crush on her and loved seeing her at drop-off, on her way to run her glorious fashion empire, always dressed as if she was off to Buckingham Palace. She was also ridiculously beautiful and well-groomed—glossy skin, immaculate makeup, and not a hair out of place. She'd been charming to Jenna each time they crossed paths at school, despite the fact that Jenna'd slept with her friend's husband, and yet she wore an air of impenetrability that Jenna found both fascinating and intimidating.

And Callum had cracked her; he'd been sleeping with Astrid Carmichael. She couldn't imagine them together, except that they were both indecently attractive. She gazed at him with newfound respect. Mrs Carmichael really was a coup. But no wonder he looked flat; he must be devastated.

'Say something,' he joked. 'You're freaking me out here.'

'Sorry.' She shook herself. 'I just wasn't expecting it to be her. She's so beautiful—I think she's amazing.'

'She is amazing,' he said firmly. 'She's an incredible woman. But it's run its course.'

'Why did she break it off, do you think? Did her husband find out?'

'Oh Jesus, no. She's divorced. But she thinks she's met someone, and she also quite rightly got sick of my behaviour and called me out on it.'

Their eggs and avocado arrived, and they both followed the plates appreciatively with their eyes as the waitress put them down.

Callum sliced through his poached egg so the rich, golden yolk seeped silkily over the avocado.

'Why would you not behave well with someone like her?' she asked him.

'Oh, well that's a minefield,' he said. 'Because we were never going to end up together, were we, no matter how exciting and novel it was. We didn't really fit into each other's lives. If you took away the sex, we didn't have anything in common.'

She had a sudden, unwelcome image of Callum pulling Mrs Carmichael into his arms and kissing her passionately. She grimaced and took a mouthful of delicious avocado and sourdough.

'That's the thing about the parents at schools like this,' she said when she'd swallowed. 'They are honestly like creatures from a different planet. I mean, they're all so unbelievably rich and successful and they live these lives that you can only dream about, but really, there's nothing normal about them.'

'Well, you had the most extreme version of that, dating

Jackson James,' he said. 'I bet you'd have some stories to tell, if they hadn't gagged you.'

She coloured. 'You can say that again. But Mrs Carmichael must lead a pretty glamorous life too.'

'She does,' he said, 'and she's very generous. It was great fun, driving around in her Aston Martin and going to all her fucking palatial homes, but she's knackered a lot of the time, keeping all those balls in the air. I don't think I envy her.'

'And so you said she's met someone else?' she prompted.

'It seems so. I don't know anything about him, but I imagine he's rich as fuck and runs ten companies. I'm not sure what she saw in me apart from my biceps.'

She suspected he was being disingenuous; it was pretty obvious what any woman, no matter how old or wealthy, would see in Callum.

'Hmm,' she said. She pursed her lips. 'I have no idea either; it's a total mystery.'

She smirked as she bent her head to take another mouthful.

'Thanks a lot,' he said. Then his face darkened. 'There was another reason I didn't treat her very well, the last couple of weeks.'

'What was that?'

'I met someone else,' he said. 'I told her that; I told her the reason I'd been neglecting her was because my head was full of somebody else.' He gave her a look that she thought suggested the someone else might be her, but she couldn't be perfectly sure. Then he took a long drink of his water and fixed a smile on his face.

'So,' he said. 'Are you going to the party at the Savoy?'

She was grateful for the change of subject. 'Someone was talking about it in the staffroom the other day. When is it?'

'It is'—he tapped his phone—'two weeks today, in fact.'

'And what's the format?'

'It's supposed to be a fundraiser, but the school fees are so high that they can't outright ask the parents for yet more money, so they pick another charity to support instead. This year it's Great Ormond Street. Basically, the parents pay an extortionate amount for their tickets, and the teachers go for free. The PTA started it up a few years ago; it's kind of a way for the parents to thank the teachers. Oh, and it's black tie.'

'Is it fun?' she asked. 'It is like a sit-down dinner?'

He grinned. 'It used to be sit-down but it was fucking awful. We all dreaded having to make small-talk with the parents for five courses. So they ditched that idea a couple of years ago and now it's just shit-loads of booze and dancing, and lots of grub doing the rounds in little bowls and on trays. It's really good *craic* actually; we all just ignore the parents and get arseholed. And the Savoy is gorgeous at Christmas—it gets me in the festive mood. You should come; it'd be a good way to meet more of the staff.'

'Will Mrs Carmichael be there?' She wiggled her eyebrows at him.

'Probably,' he said. 'I have to face her sometime. So you see; you have to come and give me moral support. Imagine if you had to go and face Jackson alone.'

She rolled her eyes. 'That's emotional blackmail. But point taken. Count me in.'

'Excellent.' He looked at his watch. 'Shit. We'd better get back to school.'

He signalled for the bill. When it arrived, he offered the waiter his credit card. 'This one's on me.'

'Oh, no,' she said. 'Honestly, you bought me tea last time. Let's split it.'

He smiled at her shyly. 'I'd like to treat you. Please let me.'

She thought of Jackson, and the money he'd lavished on her on that first date with a penthouse suite, Dom Perignon and designer swimwear. It must have cost thousands and thousands of pounds. Then she looked at the man in front of her, smiling and willing her to let him treat her to eggs on toast. His dark hair had fallen into his beautiful eyes, and he had a small smudge of avocado on his polo-shirt.

Her heart expanded inside its cage. 'Thank you,' she said.

PART IV

DECEMBER

35

EVERYONE

Jenna's hair was as straight as Katie was going to get it with the GHDs. She'd spent ages on her makeup, studiously following the smoky-eye tutorial that she'd found on YouTube and already trialled twice this week. Now she slipped on the black silk Stella McCartney dress she'd worn on her first date with Jackson. Mimi had kindly lent it to her again. It was posh enough to wear to the Savoy, in front of all those parents, and it had certainly elicited a positive response from Jackson. She tried to force the memory of being with him on that penthouse terrace from her mind.

'You look gorgeous, babe,' Katie said from the door-frame. 'Will I be meeting this guy tomorrow morning?'

She made a face. 'Dunno. He's been so sweet, but I'm still not a hundred percent sure how he feels. If I can't get him tonight, tarted up like this, then I haven't got a hope in hell of pulling him at school.'

Her precious White Company bed-linen was clean on the bed. She wasn't being presumptuous; she was simply covering her bases. Since their lunch a couple of weeks ago, he'd been much the same with her—friendly, thoughtful (he'd fetched her a sandwich from Pret one lunchtime when it was chucking it down with rain) and very entertaining. But he hadn't made a move on her, or asked her out, or treated her to any more of those intense looks. It was driving her downright crazy.

Hugging Katie, she put on her coat and headed out. As she tottered down to Fulham Broadway in her strappy heels, she checked Instagram. The first post was from Jackson; Instagram clearly knew she'd spent far too much time on his feed. It was a photo of him with Rollo. They were both grinning, and Rollo was wrapped around him like a koala bear. She zoomed in. Jackson looked heartbreakingly gorgeous. Scrolling down, she read the comment.

I'm severely dyslexic, it read. *It's a huge part of who I am. Rollo has just been diagnosed as dyslexic too. A very special person once told me I should talk more about my dyslexia, and they were right. If you have special educational needs, please know you can still achieve all the success in the world. From now on, I'll be talking about my experiences a lot more, because I'm thrilled to announce I've become an ambassador for the British Dyslexia Association. I'm dyslexic, and proud of it, and I wouldn't change a thing. JJ x*

Her heart was full. Jackson thought she was special, and her words had meant something to him. And now millions of neuro-diverse kids would have a wonderful role model. Thank God they'd had Rollo assessed; she'd suspected that outcome all along.

So, something good had come out of their brief time together. Perhaps she was supposed to have crossed cosmic paths with him, so the universe could unfurl the tendrils of magic they'd woven together, in the most unexpected ways.

She typed *qualifications needed to become a SENCO* into her phone.

THE LIGHTS of the Park Lane hotels streamed past the black cab. Inside, Natalia sat bolt upright, the only posture available to her in this dress. She'd gone all-out Monica Bellucci in a heavily corseted Dolce and Gabbana number made from red and gold jacquard, and she'd even splashed out on one of their eye-waveringly expensive bejewelled headbands to match. Heavy, winged eyeliner completed her vampish look.

She was in love with the dress, though slightly worried her boobs would spill out at some point. It was more money than she should have spent, but it would only go into the divorce lawyers' pockets if she'd left it in the bank. For all his faults, Lorenzo was generous, and he'd rather she saved face at such a big school event than skimping on her clothing budget and setting people talking.

Things had moved quickly in the last month. Loeb had fired him and, as she understood it, he wasn't having any luck talking to any of the bulge-bracket banks about a role. With his record, and in this climate, they'd be unlikely to want any association with him. She wouldn't be surprised if he ended up striking out on his own and setting up a hedge fund or a boutique brokerage. But that would take time, and it wouldn't provide the reassurance of a steady salary to clear those massive monthly bills.

She'd filed the divorce petition through Astrid's, now her, lawyer, and Lorenzo's lawyer had already filed an acknowledgement. It was all bizarrely easy. Lorenzo's cocky protestations that their separation was temporary had dried up after he'd been fired and hung out to dry by the City. It was as if he'd needed the external censure to fully comprehend the severity of his misconduct.

They'd tersely hammered out the main terms of the divorce, without lawyers, in their kitchen over coffee one morning. It had been surreal to sit there with her estranged husband and agree on custody arrangements. The upshot was that he wouldn't fight her for the house or the girls; he'd have them every other weekend. She was relieved and grateful for the efficiency with which her marriage was winding up, though a part of her was sceptical as to Lorenzo's motives. Presumably, being out of the family home and relieved of most childcare duties would allow him to find a luxurious flat and live the bachelor life he'd seemed to want to live for some time. She suspected it wouldn't be long before he'd found himself a Lara or Juliana to keep him warm at night.

Meanwhile, she was essentially parenting solo. During the past few lonely weeks, she'd found herself thinking about Bex incessantly. It was normal—she'd been abandoned by her husband, and Bex was one of the few people she knew and trusted. It was understandable that while she was vulnerable and disoriented and panicked, she would cling to someone who made her feel secure and purposeful and calm. All she knew was that when Bex and Elsie were in the house, she went from spiralling into desolation to feeling perfectly cocooned.

She'd also had a couple of repeat performances of her dream about Bex—the contexts changed, but she'd woken up twice thrashing at the duvet cover with frustration. She'd even had to take matters into her own hands and make herself come, just so she could get on with her day. She hadn't indulged in that particular form of self-care since before she'd met Lorenzo; she'd forgotten how efficiently gratifying it was. Perhaps it'd be the only form of action she'd get now she'd kicked her husband out.

Nevertheless, she couldn't shake the sensation that something had been building with Bex—even if it was only inside her own head—and that this evening would give her some kind of resolution. It could be a night that changed her life, it could be a total damp squib, or it could be a humiliating mess that cost her her greatest friendship. She just had to trust.

ASTRID PUSHED her way through The Savoy's iconic rotating doors. The lobby, with its glossy monochrome floors and polished wood, sang with festive spirit. An impressive Lego installation dominated the space—Tabby would love it; she must bring her here for a hot chocolate before Christmas. Gray was staying here; she'd arranged to meet him in the lobby before they wound through the bowels of the hotel together to the Lancaster Ballroom. The short flight of marble stairs leading down to the Thames Foyer had been transformed into an enchanted bower with an arc of seasonal greenery festooned with fairy lights. From beyond it drifted the melodic strains of carols sung a cappella.

She unbuttoned her coat in the welcome warmth and smoothed down her dress. She'd had her team remake one of her favourite styles—a floor-length, strapless sheath with a daring slit up one thigh—in platinum lamé. Her pale gold hair was in an artfully loose chignon and she'd let the dress do all the talking, adding just a pair of diamond studs.

She checked her phone nervously. Gray had insisted on coming over to accompany her to the event. He knew she'd finished things with Callum—although he didn't know the details—and that both he and Mark would be there tonight.

'I can't let you walk into that shark tank alone,' he'd said. 'Besides, I love holiday shopping in London.'

She still hadn't given him a straight answer to his declaration at Scott's. At the time, she'd told him she needed a few weeks to sort her head out. While the tug of attraction was definitely there, it would have felt odd jumping straight into another relationship, however limited her fling with Callum had been. But it spoke volumes that Gray's words had induced her to walk out of that restaurant and end things with Callum immediately. Gray had restored her confidence that a healthier relationship with a fully functional adult was within her grasp.

Since that evening they'd FaceTimed almost nightly, and Gray's kind, handsome face and dorky humour were a balm after her intense days at work. He'd become a kind of staple in her life, and she hoped seeing him in the flesh tonight would give her certainty in her own mind as to how she wanted to take things forward with him.

There he was. He strolled through the bustling lobby, tall and debonair in his dinner jacket. The Savoy suited him. With his hair parted at the side and slicked back, he had a timeless air. She suspected he would have been quite at home here sixty or seventy years earlier, crooning at the piano and drinking martinis in the American Bar.

He saw her and gave a low whistle, his hands resting on her shoulders as he kissed her on both cheeks. She caught the scent of something clean and herbal that was probably shaving cream, and had to stop herself from leaning into him.

'Wow,' he said. 'You look like an icon of the silver screen.'

He held her at arm's length and looked at her appreciatively. 'It's seriously good to see you.'

'You too, Gray.' She meant it. A warm wave of relief washed over her, that his physical presence gave her such sheer joy, and that he was here. She was well aware that on paper he was a great catch. That had actually been off-putting—she'd wanted to make sure what she felt for him was real and not some machination of her mind based on his eligibility. But to have him in front of her, grinning at her like a schoolboy, felt like coming home, having not realised how far she'd strayed.

'Let's go face the Ghosts of Christmas Past, shall we?' he said, and he offered her his arm.

NATALIA HATED COMING to these events alone. She felt self-conscious and apologetic and like a third wheel among the rest of the parents. She would try to find Bex and hang out with her and the teachers. She suspected Bex, who thought most of the parents were pompous arseholes, would stick with her colleagues tonight.

The first people she saw after procuring a glass of champagne were Astrid and that lovely guy, Gray. Astrid had confided in her at work that a relationship with him might be on the cards, and Natalia had urged her to jump right in—the man was heaven. She knew Astrid was no longer seeing the mysterious younger guy who'd put such a smile on her face the night of the class drinks, and she'd love to see her friend settled with someone worthy of her. She seemed to have no idea how spellbinding she was, and she'd let Mark's treatment of her obliterate her self-confidence over the past couple of years. Natalia couldn't see Gray running off with a twenty-five-year-old.

She greeted them both.

'Natalia! You look sensational!' exclaimed Astrid. Her mouth was an O. 'You're a Dolce queen—absolutely stunning.'

'Thank you,' she said shyly. She did feel the best she'd felt in a long time, as though the corsetry and eyeliner and head-dress were armour that allowed her to hide away her inner housewife and let her temptress out to play. The power of the outfit to transform her was incredible, but seeing that power reflected in Astrid's reaction gave her a kick. It was time to find Bex.

She'd had an excited WhatsApp from Bex to say she was already here. She wove through the crowd. There she was, chatting to Valentina's teacher, Mr Munro, and a few others. She saw her from behind first, her toned, flawless back on display in what looked like a backless black jumpsuit. The sight of so much bare flesh acted as a trigger, surfacing the dreams she'd had about her. She swallowed and approached the group.

'Hey sweetie!' Bex swung round and did a comedic double take. 'Holy shit! You look smoking!' She hugged her enthusiastically and Natalia found herself responding, wrapping her free arm around Bex's bare back. Her palm found its resting place on her satiny skin and she laid her chin on Bex's shoulder, inhaling her familiar citrus scent. Everything was heightened; it felt as though she stayed like that for hours when in reality it was seconds. No one else in the group would have thought anything was odd about her hugging her dear friend. This was the magic of being present—the briefest pleasure became meaningful and weighty and imprinted on your memory, just by paying attention.

WHERE THE HELL WAS JENNA? Callum paced by the impressive ice bar erected at one end of the Lancaster Ballroom and requested a vodka and coke. She'd told him she'd be there early, and it was now—he looked at his watch—seven forty-five. He'd been monitoring the main entrance to the ballroom, but there was still no sign of her. He'd held off and behaved himself and sat on his hands for the last couple of weeks. He hadn't wanted to scare her off, to threaten their fledgling friendship, but the more time he spent gazing at her sweet little face, watching her with the kids or talking to her about her passion for special educational needs, the harder he fell.

Perhaps the initial jolt he'd felt when he'd first seen her by the netball courts wasn't love, perhaps it was chemical wizardry by his brain, but he was in love now. He couldn't think of a better gift to the kids he wanted to have one day than to give them Jenna as a mother. His initial fantasy of her feeding their baby had gathered colour and texture over the past few weeks; now it was a full montage of motherhood where she sang and cooed over the baby and kissed its tiny toes and lay on a sun-dappled rug with it in the park. Seriously, his housemates would cart him off to the fucking loony bin if they could see inside his head.

He thanked the bartender and turned. Shit. It was Astrid, looking smoking in a silvery dress that didn't look like it accommodated underwear. She'd let Tabby's nanny do the post-fixture pickups recently, so he hadn't seen her for weeks, and last time he had, he'd kissed every inch of her. She was on the arm of some tall guy who looked like he lived in places like this. Her smiling face tilted up to his, and she nestled into him. So this was the new guy. They looked cosy, and far more glamorous than most of the parents here so far.

She turned her head and saw him, and a series of emotions crossed her face; awkwardness, he thought, and amusement, and some level of desire.

'Astrid.' He nodded to her and then stepped forward tentatively and kissed her. 'You're looking well.' The scent of her perfume wound its way around not just his nose but, somehow, the rest of his body too. It was a portal to all his memories of her.

'So are you.' She seemed flustered by the kiss. 'Callum, meet Grayson Landau. Gray, this is Callum Pearce—Tabby's, um, PE teacher.'

Grayson leant forward to shake his hand, and a look passed between him and Astrid. She'd obviously told him.

'Great to meet you, Callum,' he said heartily. He hadn't expected him to be American. 'Why don't I get us a drink, Astrid, and you guys can catch up.'

With a wink, he slipped into the throng.

Callum smiled and looked her slowly up and down.

'You look hot.'

'Callum.' She looked about her in a panic.

'Relax. No one's listening; they're all too mesmerised by the sound of their own voices.'

'Made any progress with Miss Price?'

'A little, but nowhere near enough. Tonight, baby, tonight. Hey, what's your douchebag ex doing here? I saw him with his hot little fiancée.'

She grimaced. 'Unfortunately, he's on the board of governors. I haven't seen him yet.'

'That'll be fun for you—you'll be playing whack-a-mole tonight with all your exes. I was tempted to compliment him on the robustness of his old bed.'

'Oh my God.' She giggled. 'I would pay serious money to see that.'

'It'd wipe that smug smile off his face. So Grayson is the new guy?'

'Yep.'

'Is he one of the don't-want-to-see-him-naked crowd?'

'What?' She stared.

'The first time we had sex,' he explained, 'you said the only people you'd dated since you got divorced were older types that looked good in a suit but you'd never want to see them naked.'

She seemed shocked at the recollection. 'That's so funny. I did say that, didn't I? No, thank you for your concern, but it's definitely not like that with Gray.'

'Well, I'm glad. Remember, if he can't come up with the goods, there's always the shower. Callum's Handy Household Hints and all that.'

She was shaking with laughter now, head bent, hand clamped over her mouth, looking up at him through her eyelashes.

'You are a piece of work,' she said. 'Thanks for the memories. Go find your girl, Callum.'

'That guy's a lucky man, baby. Make sure he knows it.'

He winked at her and turned to look for Jenna.

JENNA CHECKED her coat and scanned the crowd for Callum. The ballroom was already heaving; she'd got delayed on the bloody District Line. But she was here now, and it was spectacular. She felt like she'd wandered into Versailles. The room was all creamy blue and white and gold plasterwork, and candles and white flowers adorned all the poser tables dotted around. A band played some jazz version of White Christmas, and the parents milling around looked glamorous and expensive, as if all the mums had had their hair professionally done and were wearing brand-new dresses.

She waded through the crowd, pulling her hair over one shoulder and twisting it in her hand. It seemed even longer when she straightened it. She spotted a couple of Chaucer class mums and encountered a small group of teachers already dancing. They hugged her and tried to pull her into their midst, but she was far too sober to dance yet. She hoped there'd be some proper music to dance to later.

Accepting a flute of champagne from a passing waiter, she took a large gulp and felt the bubbles fizz at the back of her throat. Then she saw him. He looked beautiful in his dinner jacket, his hair combed sleekly off his face. He was talking to Mrs Carmichael. No one else around them was paying them any attention, but if they had, they surely would have observed that these two couldn't possibly be talking about hockey fixtures.

They were swimming in chemistry. Mrs Carmichael looked like an A-list celebrity in her silvery-goldy dress. They both did. Their bodies mirrored each other; they both had their hips thrust forward, and Mrs Carmichael was at one point bent over in laughter. Callum was grinning at her, and Jenna could see the look in his eyes. He looked like he wanted to devour her. She wanted him to look at her like that; he'd been so kind and sweet the last couple of weeks, but that wouldn't cut it. She didn't want kind and sweet; she wanted him to consume her, to blot out everything else but him.

She was being a voyeur, but she couldn't help it. It was equally sickening and spellbinding to watch these two gorgeous people doing their mating dance and to glimpse what they'd had together, what Callum was capable of when he was unleashed.

And then it was over. She watched him whisper something to Mrs Carmichael and then turn in Jenna's direction. She wriggled and tried to avert her gaze while keeping enough of an eye on him to ensure he spotted her.

Their eyes met, and he increased his pace, shoving his way past the few people between them to get to her. He was smiling a smile of what looked like pain and wonder. He reached her and crushed her into a hug, holding his glass away from her while his other hand pressed against her back. She exhaled with relief and relaxed into him. He wasn't wearing aftershave; she inhaled shower gel and the smell of him, a smell she was slowly getting to know through the few brief, matey hugs they'd had.

He uncurled himself from her. 'You look beautiful. You should definitely wear that dress to school. How are you doing this evening? I've been looking for you.'

'Tube issues,' she murmured. 'Sorry. I saw you chatting to Mrs Carmichael, though. You two were having fun.'

'Yeah.' He ran his free hand through his hair. 'She broke up with me by phone so the last time I actually saw her, I was in bed with her. That was weird. But she's good *craic*.'

Ugh. Thanks to the performance she'd just seen, it was too easy to imagine them wrapped around each other in bed. 'You looked amazing together. Are you still upset about it?'

'God, no.' He stared at her. 'We were just having a laugh together. We had a great time; it's over; she's here with her new boyfriend. It's all good.'

'She looks incredible tonight.' She wasn't sure why she was persisting with this perverse line of conversation.

'She does,' he said. 'But she's not the most beautiful woman in the room tonight, Jenna. You are, and no amount of diamonds or face-lifts on the mothers can change that. Now, let's go and get some grub—I'm starving.'

Astrid had been equally dying to see Callum and dreading it, but after their sparring match she felt nothing but pleasure. He was as easy to banter with outside of a relationship as within one. It was a relief to be back on firm footing with him after the way he'd made her feel the last couple of weeks they'd been together. In this dynamic she could hold her own, aware that they were still awash with chemistry even if they'd both moved on emotionally, and that was enough. He'd looked indecently hot dressed up in that tux, but he wasn't what she wanted: he couldn't make her happy in the long run. She would start showing her face at hockey fixtures again.

She was surprised by the pang she felt when he'd suggested she wouldn't want to take Gray's clothes off—it had been a pang of loyalty and outrage on Gray's behalf, but also a jolt of understanding that her feelings for him were far more carnal than she'd realised. Those beautiful, bespoke shirts he wore showcased his rower's body, and she was intrigued to see more.

He came back a couple of minutes later with two flutes of champagne.

'So that's the competition?' He raised an eyebrow. 'Holy shit, the guy's wasted in education. He should be on billboards modelling Patek Philippes.'

She laughed. 'He doesn't always scrub up that well. But yeah, he's a good-looking guy, and cocky with it. At the end of the day, he's a kid. What you see is exactly what you get.

'I owe him a lot, though. When I met him, I'd been single for two years and I was going through the motions—every ounce of energy went on work and Tabs. And he reminded me how to have fun again.'

'So, model-grade looks, and your saviour. That's one hell of an act to follow.' He gave her a wistful smile. 'How did you guys finish it?'

'I actually called him as soon as I left Scott's that night and told him we should move on.' She watched for his reaction.

His smile blossomed into something more hopeful. 'You did? Why didn't you tell me?'

'I needed to buy myself some thinking time before I gave you a definitive answer. What you said to me meant so much, and I wanted to give it the consideration it deserved.'

'And has the consideration yielded any definitive answers?' He moved so he was standing in front of her.

She looked up into his dear face and nodded, putting a palm on his chest, between the lapels of his dinner jacket. 'Yes.'

'Oh, my darling.' He stepped forward and, curling his hand around the space where her neck met her shoulder, gently pulled her towards him. She bent her head to the side and nuzzled into his hand like a cat. Her head fitted snugly under his chin, even in her heels, and he kissed her hair.

She wanted to stay like that, quiet and still with him in the centre of this laughing, shouting, drinking mass of people. She shut her eyes, swaying to the jazz music that the band was playing at the other end of the room, as his hand slid down over her shoulder blades and the slippery fabric of her dress before tightening around her waist. There was something in the firm determination with which he held her that told her she could lay down her mask, and spill out of herself, and he wouldn't budge. The reassuring rhythm of his heart pulsed through her palm.

She shifted and raised her face to his. He bent and gave her a single kiss, but it wasn't a chaste, taut-lipped peck. His lips were soft and his mouth slightly open, and she had to curb an adolescent desire to find his tongue with hers.

He closed his eyes and frowned and then grinned. 'Oh boy,' he said. 'You've just made me a very, very happy man. I can't wait to kiss you properly. But not here. Let's get you some food and a top-up. Ok?' He grazed her cheek with his knuckles.

She nodded contentedly and slipped her hand back through his arm, hugging him to her. She was in that wonderful limbo of anticipation she remembered from her twenties, right before something happened with a guy she liked. They squeezed through the crowd to accost some waiters with trays of bowl-food, and she nodded and smiled and waved to parents and teachers she recognised, all the while wondering how few people aside from Gray she could get away with talking to tonight.

Oh, shit. There was Mark. He always looked good in black tie, and he was holding court, Juliana by his side in a scarlet Versace number that left little to the imagination and looked sensational on her.

'Incoming, ex-husband,' she murmured to Gray.

Mark caught her eye and dismissed whomever he was boring with a hand on their arm. He kissed Astrid awkwardly.

'Mark, meet Grayson Landau,' she said. 'Gray, this is my

ex-husband Mark Carmichael, and his fiancée Juliana.' She had no idea of Juliana's surname.

Mark did a double take and pumped Gray's hand. 'Constellation, right?' he said. 'I know you by reputation. We've been in and out of your stock the last few months.'

'Great to meet you, Mark, Juliana,' said Gray genially, sliding an arm around Astrid's shoulder.

Mark looked from Gray to Astrid. 'Is there something going on with you guys and Constellation I should be aware of?'

'Nothing's going on with the company,' said Astrid firmly. Mark was dodgy, but surely not even he would be stupid enough to try to trade Constellation around a takeover of his ex-wife's company before it because public knowledge. 'I'm dating Gray, though,' she added.

Gray's hand tightened around her shoulder.

'Oh, wow.' Mark's eyes narrowed, and he cocked his head. 'Congratulations.'

'How's your weekend with Tabs going?' Astrid said to change the subject.

'Fantastic. We did the Science Museum this morning and then lunch at The Good Earth. I had to work this afternoon, so Juliana took her to see the Harrods Christmas windows.'

'It was a lot of fun.' Juliana held out her hand. A red glitter tattoo in the shape of a heart adorned the back of it. 'They were doing these in the toy department. Tabby insisted I get one to match my dress. She got a purple and turquoise flower.'

'It's fabulous,' Astrid assured her. It could only be a good thing that Tabby and Juliana were hitting it off, she told herself.

As they took their leave, Gray hugged her to him. 'So, we're dating, are we?'

'Oh, yes,' Astrid said.

'Sounds good to me. Now, how about you try to introduce me to some people you haven't been romantically involved with? I feel like we've nailed the Ghosts of Christmas Past.'

THE EVENING FLOWED on through bowl-food, and chit-chat with the parents, and joking and eventually dancing with the teachers. Callum didn't leave Jenna's side, but tried absolutely nothing on with her. The band had given way to a DJ, but Jess Glynn and David Guetta weren't conducive to romance, and instead she found herself and Callum on the dance floor in a little gaggle of teachers including Bex Oliver and Mike Munro, a Year 5 teacher. Callum was a wonderful dancer; he had impeccable rhythm and was sexy as hell dancing to Dua Lipa. He'd abandoned his jacket and undone a couple of buttons on his shirt, and his bowtie hung loose around his neck. His hair and face were damp with sweat.

She wanted to drag him out of there and wrap her legs around his waist, but she didn't want to spoil his fun. He was now having some kind of dance-off with Mike, and she'd lost count of the number of mothers who'd cast lascivious looks in his direction. She couldn't blame them.

'I'm going to the loo,' she shouted in his ear, and slipped away. The ladies' cloakrooms by the ballroom were huge and plush, with a large ante-room dotted with mirrors and low, chintzy stools. She hesitated. Mrs Carmichael was sitting at one of the stools, looking luminous, applying her scarlet lipstick with a tiny brush. She gave Jenna a tentative smile through the mirror and then turned on her stool.

Pleasantries exchanged, Jenna took a deep breath.

'Um. Mrs Carmichael.'

'Call me Astrid. We're not at school.'

'Astrid.' She edged forward and lowered her voice, unsure who was in the stalls in the room beyond. 'I wanted to thank you for being so nice about—you know. I felt so mortified. I don't know what you must have thought of me.'

'Have a seat.' Astrid gestured to the stool beside her and Jenna sat.

'You don't need to apologise to me. It's none of my business. And the whole thing must have been very traumatic for you.'

'Yeah, it was—I don't think I realised how much I was playing with fire till it all went wrong.'

'People like them operate in a different world from the rest of us,' Astrid said. 'They're friends of mine, but still—the way they conduct their lives is pretty alien to me. I think you're lucky to be out of it, to be honest.'

'I'm sure you're right.' Jenna looked down at the clutch bag on her lap. 'But I just couldn't help it. I was so completely blown away by Jackson.'

'Of course you were. I can only imagine he pulled out all the stops for you; it must have been overwhelming.' She paused. 'I shouldn't say this, because Honour is a friend of mine. But I know what it's like to be left hanging with no explanation. My ex-husband pulled that stunt on me and I felt like a total fool. Jackson really fell for you, you know. He and Honour are much better now, but I thought it might help you to know it wasn't just in your imagination. He wasn't playing you; he was in deep too. That's why it all got shut down so quickly.'

Jenna closed her eyes against the quick sting of tears. She allowed herself to be back, for a moment, in that bed in Hans Place, Jackson wrapped around her, whispering to each other. Astrid had given her the gift of validating everything she'd felt, with a few words she hadn't been obliged to utter. It was extraordinarily generous in the circumstances.

'This means more to me than you'll ever know,' she said. 'It's been killing me, to think I was so into him and he was able to walk away without a backwards glance.'

'That was definitely not what happened,' Astrid said firmly. 'But I still think you're well rid of him. That level of fame isn't healthy for anyone.' She paused. 'Can I ask you something? Do you think you're going to make a go of it with Callum?'

That took her by surprise. She wasn't sure what Astrid knew about her and Callum—lord knew, there wasn't anything to tell. But if he'd mentioned something about her to Astrid, then she must be in with a chance.

'I want to,' she said cautiously. 'I like him so much. Would you mind if I did?' She steeled herself for the answer.

'God, no!' Astrid exclaimed. She held up her hands. 'We're done. It was a lot of fun, but it was never going to be a long-term thing for us.'

'Really?' Jenna said. 'I saw you guys together earlier—you were both on fire.'

Astrid laughed. 'He's very entertaining, and extremely cheeky. But I promise you, we've both moved on. In case you haven't worked it out, he's crazy about you. That was one of the reasons I broke it off—he met you and he completely vanished. I knew when I was beaten.'

A glow spread through Jenna's whole body. This woman was an oracle, equipped to tell her how all the important men in her life felt about her. 'You really think he feels like that about me?' she asked.

'Oh, yes,' Astrid said. 'He's smitten. Go and find him. He's all yours.'

Jenna got up to go, then reached down and hugged her. 'Thank you,' she said. 'You're an angel. I know where Tabby gets it from now.'

Astrid smiled a surprised smile as Jenna stood back up. 'One more thing.' She raised an eyebrow. 'If you get it on with Callum—let's just say, you're in for a treat.'

NATALIA HAD SPENT the entire evening dancing, chatting, eating and drinking with Bex and a few other teachers. The whole time, she felt as though she was giving a performance where nothing came naturally and she had to prompt herself at every step: smile; dance; laugh; slow down on the champagne; say something funny. And the whole time, there was Bex, dominating her consciousness at every turn. It was as if she'd switched lenses and the woman she'd grown close to over the past three years was someone completely different. Where had that easy friendship gone, and why could she no longer remember how it felt to look at Bex, or talk to her, or touch her, and feel nothing at all? Now she could hardly even gaze at her directly, as if Natalia's retinas would burn just from dwelling on her. She was miserable and antsy and frustrated, and she couldn't maintain this facade any longer.

She leant over and put her mouth next to Bex's ear, trying to ignore the heart-shaped birthmark on her slim neck.

'I'm going to head home,' she said above the music. 'I'm not in the mood for this.'

'Nats! No!' shouted Bex, grabbing her arm. 'You can't! That dress doesn't want to go home—it's in the mood to party.' She suspected Bex had drunk even more than she had.

She shrugged off Bex's hand. 'Honestly. I'm just going to put a dampener on things if I stay. I'll see you during the week. Have fun.'

'What about if we go get some air?' Bex asked. We can grab our coats and go back out the Riverside Entrance—take a few minutes in the little park there? It might wake you up a bit.'

'Ok,' she agreed grudgingly. Anything was better than being in this mass of cheery, festive people.

Coats fetched, they headed out the back door of the Savoy into the deserted strip of park that separated it from the river. The filigree trees were all dressed up in charming fairy lights. Natalia crossed her arms over her chest and hunched into them. It was bloody freezing.

'I know why you're upset, sweetie,' Bex said, tucking her arm into Natalia's as they walked. 'This is a really shitty time of year to be going through a divorce. You need to give yourself a break and take things slowly.'

'That's not why I'm upset.' Blood was pumping through her temples and in her ears at a velocity that made her feel she might lose consciousness. The freezing ground beneath the thin soles of her sandals made walking agony, and she stopped and scrunched her toes up.

'Then what on earth's going on?'

Bex was looking at her with concern and infinite tenderness. There was nothing she could say without the excruciating horror of laying herself bare, so she did the only other thing available to her. She jumped.

She turned her head, her arm still linked with Bex's. She cupped Bex's beautiful, anxious face with her other hand and she did what she'd wanted to do for weeks now. She kissed her soft, pillowy lips and relief and desire streamed out of her so violently that they must surely have appeared to passers-by as vivid ribbons, looping and twisting about her in the freezing wind.

JENNA PRACTICALLY SASHAYED BACK through the ballroom. It was extraordinary, the transformative power that generous words from another woman could have.

Callum was still throwing shapes on the dance floor. She giggled. She wanted to uncover the mischievous side of him that he showed Astrid. Perhaps he was nervous around her, and that was why he was always so sweet and solicitous. She marched up to him. 'Come with me?' she whispered in his ear. His eyes widened.

'Where are we going?' he asked, as they wound their way off the dance floor and out of the ballroom. He was behind her, his hands warm on her waist. The fabric of her dress slithered under them.

In the ballroom's lobby, she pointed to the shallow stairs leading upwards. 'Let's explore the hotel. Apparently the Christmas decorations are gorgeous.'

After some trial and error, they emerged out of a jumble of corridors into what seemed to be a small, deserted shopping arcade in the main body of the hotel, its boutiques closed up for the night. In the middle of the space stood a hollowed-out tree-trunk from which sprouted lots of fresh foliage as well as a tree-house. The trunk was dressed for Christmas, fairy lights sprang from the branches, and a child-sized fairy door adorned the front of the trunk. The whole concoction was nestled on a carpet of moss and giant toadstools.

'Oh my goodness!' Jenna exclaimed. 'I've never seen anything so sweet! The girls would love this—I must take some photos to show them.'

She handed Callum her bag and clicked away on her phone. When she turned back to him, his face was miserable.

'You're an angel,' he said, reaching out to stroke her arm. 'I can't pretend anymore, Jenna. I'm a fucking mess. Tell me, am I in with a chance at all?'

In answer, she hooked her arms around his neck and kissed him. His body responded immediately; he wrapped one arm around her and grabbed at her hair with the other. Their teeth clashed, his tongue wound around hers, and she could feel the damp heat of his body the whole way down her front.

'God.' He pulled away gently and studied her. 'I take it that's a yes?'

She kissed him. 'It's a yes, please.'

'I have thought about doing that to you pretty much every waking moment since you walked onto that fucking netball court,' he said. 'You knocked the air out of my lungs; I don't know how I even got my shit together enough to finish the lesson.'

'I'm sorry.' She laughed. 'I was oblivious.'

'I'd say you were. There was not a fucking glimmer of interest from you. It made sense once I knew about your man—Jackson. I didn't think I had a hope in hell.'

'I was still so shell-shocked that first week at Chiltern,'

she admitted. 'I pretty much sleep-walked through it. But then I started to really like you and I didn't know if I'd imagined it all. I only got friendly vibes from you. It drove me crazy.'

'The friendship route was a fairly shite experience for me, no matter how much I enjoyed your company,' he said. He ran his lips down her neck and his hand down her backside. She shivered. 'But it was my only hope; I didn't want to scare you off while you were getting over that gobshite.'

He lifted his head from her neck and ran his hands down the side of her face. 'Oh, Jenna, Jenna, Jenna. I'll never get tired of saying your name. How are you feeling about Jackson, anyway? Do you have some space in your heart for me?'

'Don't worry about him,' she said firmly. 'That door is closed. The only thing I've thought about for the past couple of weeks was whether I'd get to kiss you tonight.'

'For your information, Miss Price,' he said, slipping a thin strap off her shoulder and kissing it, 'we're going to do a damn sight more than that.'

GRAY WAS CHATTING to one of the dads when Astrid got back from the ladies' room—a Swiss guy who was a luxury goods sector banker at Goldman. It figured that they knew each other. It amused her how much networking and deal-making took place at school events like this. He extricated himself graciously when he saw her.

'Sorry,' she said. 'I was being an agony aunt in the loos.'

Wham's *Last Christmas* started playing, and he swept her onto the dance floor. He was an excellent dancer, as befitted the Fred Astaire vibe he was working tonight, and he twirled her around until she was laughing and pleading to catch her breath. Then the DJ put on Otis Redding's *White Christmas* and he hooked an arm around her back and drew her towards him. She put her head on his chest and felt the most bizarre sensation of complete safety. She hadn't felt like that for years.

'I'd like to get you to myself,' he said in her ear. 'D'you want to come up to my suite? It has a drawing room. We can be very British and have tea and toast in front of the fire.'

~

KISSING BEX HAD BEEN an act of intuition and blind faith. She had no plan for what she would do next.

What happened next was that Bex clung to the back of Natalia's neck and kissed her back so lovingly that she felt tears melt down her cheeks. Every nerve-ending in her body was awake and the warmth of Bex's mouth was a panacea against the frigid night. She could have stayed lost in her, but Bex pulled away and ran her thumb over Natalia's cheek. Her face wore an expression Natalia had never seen on it before—hope, and a dawning realisation, and a kind of rapture. Once again, she was seeing the woman she thought she knew so well with fresh eyes.

'How on earth is this happening?' she marvelled. 'Are you for real?'

'Yes.' Natalia wasn't sure where to look. 'It's real; I just hadn't planned on acting on it.'

'Go on, sweetie,' she said gently.

'I just started to feel—differently about you. A few weeks ago. But, honestly, it's been so confusing. I wasn't sure what to do about it; I felt so presumptuous, assuming you'd be interested in me just because you're gay and I thought—oh my God, how on earth should I bring this up with you, because if I make a move and you pass on me then it'll be mortifying and I'll ruin everything. But it's been eating me up—I can't think about anything else but you.'

Bex wrapped her arms around her and held her tightly, and the anxiety seeped out of her.

'Listen to me, Nats,' she said, and her voice was muffled against Natalia's hair. 'I would never, ever have tried something on with you, because as long as I've known you you've been married and I assumed you were only interested in men. But you kissing me is the best thing that's ever happened to me in my whole life, so no, I am not about to pass on you. I am here for you in any way you'll let me be, whatever that looks like to you. Ok?'

Everything was converging in Natalia's brain. It was less than three weeks to Christmas and Lorenzo, who'd weighed her down for longer than she'd realised, had gone. Now Bex stood here in front of her and offered her friendship and loyalty and what sounded like love of a kind she couldn't have imagined a few months ago. It would take time for her to, in Bex's words, work out what that looked like, but the outlines of her dream were clear to her.

'Ok.' She nodded. 'This is all pretty weird and confusing for me—'

'I know, sweetie.'

'—but all I know is that I want to be with you; I want as much of you as I can have, day and night.' She looked awkwardly at her as she said this and shrugged. 'I'm not happy unless I'm with you. Our house only feels like a home when you and Elsie are in it; otherwise it's just this cold shell that we're all tiptoeing about in.'

Bex drew her to her again and kissed her, and Natalia allowed herself to stop thinking and just feel. Her hands were in Bex's hair and she pulled away and moved her lips to Bex's neck, kissing the little heart-shaped birthmark that had beguiled her these past few weeks. As she kissed her, the fear fell away, and all she felt was need. She gently unbuttoned Bex's coat and slipped her hands inside, reverently caressing the satiny skin of her back.

'Is there any way you can come home with me?' she asked, her heart hammering against her corsetry.

Bex groaned. 'I can't. Please don't tempt me. I need to relieve the sitter by midnight.'

'Shit.' This was going to be logistically painful. She thought. 'Come and spend the weekend with us. Please. Why don't you and Elsie come for breakfast; we'll do fun things with the girls during the day, and then you can both stay for a sleepover. I just want to be with you.'

'How would we manage it... with the girls?'

'They can all sleep in Valentina's room in the attic. That puts two floors between us. And my bedroom door has a lock on it.' She looked at Bex shyly. 'If we make a proper go of this, we can have a grown-up conversation with them, but for now let's dress it up as an all-girls' sleepover.'

All she knew was that she wanted to lie next to this woman and wake up next to her and fill her days with her, and the weekend would give her a brief, thrilling glimpse into how that would be. Everything else they would figure out.

They walked hand-in-hand back to the hotel.

THE SUITE WAS beautiful and looked out over the sparkling river to the London Eye in all its illuminated glory on the South Bank. Gray had called ahead to request room service and a fire to be lit while they danced a little more and said their goodbyes. When they walked into the room, a fire danced cheerily in the grate and a silver tea service had been laid out on the coffee table. Christmas choral music played softly through the sound system.

'Oh, yes,' sighed Astrid, sitting down heavily on the plump sofa and reaching down to slip off her shoes.

Gray eyed her with amusement, pulling off his jacket and throwing it onto an armchair. His dress-shirt skimmed his body in the same enticing way his work shirts did, and she felt a tug of desire. He took off his cufflinks and tossed them on the table, rolling up his shirt sleeves.

'That dress doesn't look like it's much fun to curl up and stuff your face in. There are robes in the bathroom, if you prefer.'

He was right. It was digging in at the waist, and her stomach hurt from holding it in. That was the problem with choosing sexy lingerie over Spanx.

'That sounds lovely,' she said gratefully. 'Unzip me?'

She turned around, conscious of his proximity behind her and of the brush of his fingertips where her skin met the zip. He exhaled as he lowered it.

'There.'

Once in her robe, she lifted the silver dome on the coffee table to find toast and crumpets. She buttered some for each of them while Gray busied himself with the ritual of pouring fragrant tea from the abominably heavy silver teapots, through a strainer, into their delicate china cups.

'I love the Savoy blend,' he said. 'I take some back with me every time I visit.'

'When do you leave?' she asked.

'Sunday night.'

Her heart sank, and she met his eyes.

'Yep,' he said. 'It sucks. Well... that was the itinerary before you said yes to—giving this a go. I wasn't sure what state I'd be in after seeing you. I can extend it for sure.'

His arm was along the back of the sofa, and she took his hand and squeezed it.

'So,' she said. 'How would we even make this work?' She took a sip of her tea, already feeling sick for all the future occasions she would miss him and all the time she'd spend reliving moments like this.

'I guess,' he said, 'I come over here as much as humanly possible. And you come over when you can—with Tabby, of course. I don't want to take you away from her; the time goes by too quickly when they're that age. I told you at Scott's I'd move heaven and earth to make this work, and I will. It'll be tough, but I know for sure I want you in my life on any basis I can get. You're the priority, Astrid. Not Constellation —you.'

She wasn't sure what she'd done to deserve the generosity of this man who sat across from her and offered her his heart and his whole self before he'd even kissed her properly. After such a display of commitment from him, she had to show him how fervently she matched his feelings. She put down her teacup and rose, sitting down on his lap. Then she cupped his face in her hands and kissed him, and all the emotion he aroused in her poured itself into her kiss. He moaned as her tongue moved in his mouth and he wrapped his arms around her so tightly that she felt perfectly insulated from the outside world.

He was delicious; she couldn't get enough of the taste of his mouth and his scent in her nostrils—the shaving-foam smell she'd caught earlier mingled with him. She pulled his bowtie loose and, with one hand, attempted to push the little screw-in studs of his shirt through their button-holes.

She got a couple undone and slid her hand inside his shirt and over his hairy, muscular chest.

'My God, darling, what are you doing to me?' he groaned. Her robe was falling open, and he ran a hand up her thigh and massaged it. 'Do you wanna go to bed?' he asked, watching her face.

'Definitely,' she said.

HE DIDN'T HAVE the body of a thirty-year-old athlete; he had the body of a forty-eight-year-old man who kept himself in great shape, and it was all she could imagine ever wanting again. After he'd undressed, he pulled the tie on her robe and opened it, sliding his hands around her waist and kissing her deeply.

'I've imagined this a lot of times,' he admitted between kisses, looking down at her body in its strapless bra and thong, 'but nothing I could conjure up came close to the reality of you. Look at you. You are breathtaking.'

They had all the time in the world to get to know each other that night. It was so different from how it had been with Callum. Alongside the intensity of their desire, there was also an easy intimacy, a sensation that they were in this relationship as equals. She'd never had that equilibrium with Callum, no matter how charged their sessions had been.

Afterwards, they ordered a fresh round of tea and toast and sat in their robes, in front of the fire, adding colour to the broad brush-strokes they already knew of each other's lives. And as she drifted off to sleep in the early hours, burrowing her face into his chest, it was as though the gods had pulled back a veil and shown her her future.

~

A TOP-HATTED doorman hailed Callum and Jenna a black cab from the front of The Savoy. There was no way he was taking this heavenly creature on the fucking District Line and waiting as it chugged its way around to Fulham Broadway. He held her the whole way back and marvelled at how her eyes sparkled in the reflected lights of the river as it sped past.

Back at her place, she put her finger to her lips as she slid the key into the lock. 'Katie's asleep,' she told him, 'so we need to be quiet.'

'I doubt I can be quiet when I'm in bed with you,' he said, 'and I have absolutely no intention of letting you be quiet. So let's hope Katie's a deep sleeper. Now, can I please have a shower? I'm a sweaty bastard after my dance floor bromance with Mike.'

He came out of her tiny bathroom, a towel around his waist, raking his hands through his damp hair. He couldn't believe he was here with his love and that, after weeks of unfamiliar anguish on his part, he was going to be naked with her in a matter of moments. Well, he was naked already, but he'd be slipping that slinky little dress off her beautiful body. He'd got hard in the shower just thinking about it and had had to hurriedly turn it to cold to put a dampener on things.

Now, as he walked into her little room, which was as neat and feminine as in his fantasies of her, he experienced a novel pang of anxiety. He'd managed not to blurt it out to her yet, but this was the woman he planned to spend the rest of his life with. He had no intention of ever screwing anyone else. He hoped what he had to offer would be enough for her, both in bed and out of it. He wasn't going to try any funny business tonight; no talking dirty or any of his usual tricks. He just wanted to spend the night worshipping her.

She'd lit some candles and put on soft music; the gestures made his heart ache. She was sitting on the bed, playing with her phone. When he came in, she put it down and stood up, smoothing down her dress. She seemed nervous, but as she walked over to him her face crumpled.

'Are you ok?' he asked.

'I can't bear it,' she said. 'Look at you.' She ran her hands over his chest and kissed him, softly at first and then harder, more urgently.

He held her head between his hands and groaned. 'God, sweetheart. Let's get you out of this thing.' He reached over and, taking the hem of her dress, pulled it up over her head. She raised her arms and the silky fabric slipped over them and released her shiny sheet of hair in a swoosh. He dropped it on the floor and she stood in front of him, in just her pants.

Jesus. He swallowed and ran his finger around her nipples and the underside of her breasts. She made a noise low in her throat. Her skin was pale and flawless, except for a perfect scattering of moles. She was the most exquisite thing he'd ever seen. She tugged his towel off and pulled him towards her. His nerves were gone; the soft skin of her breasts and stomach brushed his abdomen as they rose and fell with her breath, and her back was like velvet under his hands. He could think of nothing else but the scent and texture of her skin and the fact that he wanted to taste and touch every inch of her.

He walked his feet forward to the bed, and she mirrored him in reverse, clinging to him. He lowered her down. There was a bloody enormous bear on the bed. He picked it up and hurled it across the room.

'Sorry, mate,' he said. 'There isn't room for the three of us in here.'

WHEN HE CAME INSIDE HER, something between a shout and a sob escaped his lips and she clamped a hand over his mouth, laughing between the shudders as her orgasm ebbed away. He had no glib comments to make; he was beyond words. He felt a profound sense of peace, and reverence, and homecoming. Carefully, he tugged her long hair out from where it was caught between her back and his arm, and stroked it, watching her face. Her eyelashes fluttered above her vast hazel eyes as she caught her breath.

'Was that ok?' he asked tentatively.

She smiled and stretched into him. 'Are you kidding? That was unbelievable. What are you doing to me, Callum Pearce?'

He kissed her. 'I'd like to think I'm casting a spell on you, but the truth is you're the one who's bewitched me.'

'Don't leave,' she said, nestling into the crook of his arm. 'Stay the weekend.'

'I can assure you,' said Callum, 'I have no fucking intention of ever going anywhere.'

EPILOGUE

June 2020—3 months into lockdown

Tabby's hair, now white-blonde, fans out on the pillow and her mouth is open. She clutches her favourite toy, Sheepie, to her chest, her hand flexed and fingers outstretched, as if she's about to interrupt someone. She's slept like this since she was a baby. Astrid bends to kiss her impossibly soft cheeks and smells sunshine lingering on her skin. Beside Tabby, in a fluffy little dog-bed on the floor, snores her pug puppy, Maud.

She tears herself away from her sleeping daughter and walks lightly down Marstrand's wide, shallow staircase and through the house to the French doors of the garden room. Gray is still by the pool, his back to her and his legs dangling in the water. She can't see his legs from here, but she can see the gentle ripples that radiate outwards from where he sits. To one side is an ice bucket, and his long fingers straddle the fine stem of a wine glass as it rests on the slabs bordering the pool. It's a few days from midsummer, and still daylight.

He's been in the UK since March. He was visiting her and working out of his London office in early March when President Trump announced he would close the borders to European visitors.

'I can get back,' he told her, 'but this is going to be bad. I mean, it could last months. If I go back, I don't know when I'll see you again. Or I can stay here and be with you and Tabby. What do you want me to do?'

A deep, crushing misery descended over her. He belonged in the US to run his publicly listed company and see his daughters.

'You need to go back for Constellation,' she said, stroking his soft sweater.

'I really don't,' he said. 'Soon we're all going to be in lock-down. I won't be missing anything. I can run it from here.'

'But what about the girls? This is scary stuff; they'll need their dad.'

'God dammit, Astrid,' he said. 'Quit thinking about everyone else and quit trying to invent problems. My daughters are grown-ups; they'll be fine and they'll be with their mom if the schools shut. I'm asking you what you want. Do you want me to go, or do you want me to stay? Think about yourself for a change.'

'I want you to stay,' she whispered. Getting through this without him would be unimaginable. 'I'm scared. And I can't bear months and months of not being with you.'

'Thank God,' he said. He wrapped his arms around her and she leant into his chest. 'I love you, darling, and I don't want to be anywhere except here, with you and Tabby, while this plays out.'

Tabby's school closed a few days later, and they holed up in Holland Villas Road together with Teresa, Astrid's live-in housekeeper. She was aware that their form of lock-down was laughably luxurious, with an enormous house, the neighbourhood's independent food shops a short walk away, a well-stocked wine-cellar and a beautiful garden.

They settled into a routine over those first few weeks. She found it hard to quash her anxiety around what was happening in the world, but the longer they stayed at home, in their bubble, the more the outside world faded away. She gave thanks every minute of the day that Gray had stayed. They set up camp together at the large kitchen table, working on her brand, which was now a fully fledged Constellation holding, and managing the horrifying downturn in revenues as well as the bureaucratic and emotional nightmare of furloughing staff.

Despite the enormous pressures on Gray as the CEO of a luxury goods group, he was beside her for every decision and every judgement call she had to make. He also had an incredible ability to make everything fun. He brought a lightness to their lockdown home that she was certain she wouldn't have been able to provide for Tabby by herself. He was able to put his work aside in the evening and cook up a storm, whirling Astrid and Tabby around the kitchen in time to his latest Spotify playlist.

The weather helped. The spectacular spring nature had granted them made lockdown, in their privileged position, a pleasure. The garden doors by the kitchen table were constantly open, they ate all their meals in the garden, and evenings were spent outside as they continued their assault on Astrid's wine cellar. Tabby's puppy Maud, procured for her by Mark in a rare instance of adding value, scuttled comedically in and out of the house, peeing non-discriminately on any surfaces she could find. Tabby's meltdowns, while still fairly regular, were now more easily derailed by a cuddle with Maud.

Tabby was on an intensive schedule of Zoom classes with her St Cuthbert's teachers, five days a week. Jenna led most of the sessions, and Astrid had to admit her patience and vivacious nature were a godsend when it came to keeping her small pupils calm and engaged. It was no mean feat, motivating young kids online for several hours a day. Astrid took her hat off to her.

Callum made regular appearances too. Jenna had clearly worked out the importance of getting the girls' blood flowing sufficiently and so Callum took over the Zoom call for a few minutes between each lesson, getting them to do jumping jacks and toe-taps. Astrid suspected she wasn't the only mother who found his brief performances gratifying. He looked well; he and Jenna both grew very tanned as lockdown continued.

Tabby was a mine of information on her teachers. 'Mr Pearce is Miss Price's boyfriend!' she announced early in lockdown. 'And they're flatmates, because Miss Price's flatmate has gone to stay with her boyfriend.'

Another day, she was inconsolable. 'Miss Price is leaving at the end of the year,' she wailed. 'She's going to learn how to be a dyslexia teacher.' Astrid comforted her. 'It's ok, darling. You would have had another teacher next year, anyway.' She grabbed Maud and put her on Tabby's lap. This was one for the pug.

Now, she walks softly up behind Gray and bends over him, wrapping her arms around his neck. He grasps her hands and leans his head back into her, and she rubs her nose along the collar of his t-shirt, inhaling him. They decamped to Marstrand a week ago, after months of wondering when they would get to enjoy it, and it's like a permanent holiday despite the routine of work and school.

Gray and Tabby have hardly been out of the pool all evening. When they're in, Maud scurries around the edge, looking both terrified and mesmerised by their antics and the sunlight on the water. Astrid is overwhelmed by how great Gray is with Tabby, patient in a way she simply is not. He'll play with her for hours, and when Astrid feels she's sinking in one of Tabby's tantrums or black moods, Gray has the perspective that comes from being ten years further on in his journey as a parent of daughters. He is consistent and lighthearted and able to remain the grown-up in any altercation with her, something Astrid finds far harder to do.

She sits beside him and lowers her legs into the warm water. The sky is luminescent over to the west. She rests her head on his chest as he pulls her in with his arm and hands her his glass to share; she's not sure where she left hers. The strawberry-spiked nectar is chilled and delicious. Despite the turmoil raging around them, here she is blissfully, outrageously replete. She's in the arms of a man whose generosity and compassion break her heart, and in an hour or two she'll be wrapped around him in bed, skin on skin, drowning in him. She feels permanently drunk on love.

'I had a Zoom with Natalia today,' she says sleepily. 'To go through some ideas for the Giving Back initiative.'

'How is she? Still loved-up?'

She laughs. 'So loved up it's ridiculous. She and Bex are delirious together. It's like Happy Families over in that household. It's funny how many relationships COVID has escalated, isn't it? How many of us, like Nats and Bex, and you and me, now get to be together twenty-four-seven instead of the usual snatched dates?'

He's quiet for a second. He kisses her head and holds her more tightly. 'The last three months, for all their fucked-upness, have been the greatest gift for me. To have been able to be with you properly... the more time I spend with you, the more I love you.' He pauses. 'I had an interesting call from Kering today.'

She lifts her head and looks at him. 'Oh yeah?'

'Yep. They're still fighting a lot of fires, but they're trying to get on the front foot. They have some fascinating stuff in development. There's a role for me, if I want it, working with Pinault and his team on some strategic and sustainability initiatives.'

She's staring at him now. 'London-based?'

He nods. 'I'd probably have to spend a good amount of time in Paris too, once things open up, but that's no hardship.'

'But, wouldn't it be a step backwards for you?'

'Not really. Kering's such a juggernaut, and it's a C-Suite role. It'd be fun. Anyways, it was the location that sold it to me.' He takes her hand. 'What do you think?'

She can't believe he'd do this for her, that he'd give up his CEO-ship to be with her. The size of his sacrifice, and the ease with which he's considering it, takes her breath away. She remembers when he asked her if he should stay in London for lockdown. He's already decided, she realises. He needs to have her blessing, to know this is what she wants for them too.

All her ever-present anxiety about what will happen when life goes back to normal and he's called back to the States falls away. She kisses him, mouths open, pressing her body as close to his as she can. 'I think you should stay with me forever,' she says.

His nose is touching hers.

'In that case,' he says, 'I think we should get married.'

THE END

~

To access an exclusive epilogue from Jenna's perspective, please sign up to my monthly newsletter at

http://saramadderson.com/BONUS

AFTERWORD

All of the characters in this book are fictional, and any remblance to any persons, living or dead, is purely coincidental.

There is one exception. Tabby is loosely based on my daughter Tilly, at her instance at being immortalised.

You don't want to try getting a pair of tights on Tilly (but aside from that, she's perfection).

ALSO BY SARA MADDERSON

Food For Thought

~

"The Daily Post has got hold of some pap shots of me. They're fairly... damning."

What do you do when the person you love threatens everything you've worked for?

Evelyn Macleod has spent a decade helping her husband, charismatic TV chef Seb Macleod, to become a household name. Now they're riding high and enjoying the spoils of their success.

When a tabloid forces Seb to come out as gay, Evelyn and her young son flee to a friend's luxury resort in rural Kent.

Sorrel Farm is the perfect place to hide out, decompress from her disciplined London lifestyle, and comfort-eat. The enforced break also throws into question everything that Evelyn has worked so hard for. Should she continue to chase the glittering heights of wealth and power in London? Or should she choose balance—and the chance to find love—in the beautiful English countryside?

Food for Thought is available on Amazon:

mybook.to/Food_for_Thought

ABOUT THE AUTHOR

Sara Madderson is an author, entrepreneur, wife and mother. She was born in Ireland and moved to the UK with her family when she was ten years old. She lives in London with her husband Chris, their two children, Paddy and Tilly, and their cocker spaniel Charlie.

Before turning to writing, Sara worked in finance for a decade and then ran her own fashion brand, Madderson London, for eight years. She earned her MPhil in Early Modern History from the University of Birmingham.

Parents and Teachers is Sara's second novel. She has previously published *Food for Thought,* as well as a non-fiction book focused on personal development, *Metamorphosis.*

Printed in Great Britain
by Amazon

77155071R00177